A DARK
INHERITANCE

A DARK INHERITANCE

H. F. ASKWITH

PENGUIN BOOKS

PENGUIN BOOKS

UK | USA | Canada | Ireland | Australia
India | New Zealand | South Africa

Penguin Books is part of the Penguin Random House group of companies
whose addresses can be found at global.penguinrandomhouse.com.

www.penguin.co.uk
www.puffin.co.uk
www.ladybird.co.uk

First published 2023

002

Set in 10.5/15.5pt Sabon LT Std
Typeset by Jouve (UK), Milton Keynes
Printed and bound in Great Britain by Clays Ltd, Elcograf S.p.A.

The authorized representative in the EEA is Penguin Random House Ireland,
Morrison Chambers, 32 Nassau Street, Dublin D02 YH68

A CIP catalogue record for this book is available from the British Library

ISBN: 978–0–241–40499–7

All correspondence to:
Penguin Books
Penguin Random House Children's
One Embassy Gardens, 8 Viaduct Gardens, London SW11 7BW

Penguin Random House is committed to a
sustainable future for our business, our readers
and our planet. This book is made from Forest
Stewardship Council® certified paper.

For Grandad Bruce

A NOTE FROM THE AUTHOR

This book contains dark thematic content, along with depictions of intense anxiety, which, if you're experiencing something similar, might be emotionally demanding to engage with.

But there is another theme throughout: the golden thread of hope.

Anxiety is a natural emotion that we all experience from time to time, particularly when we're coping with a time of change or a stressful event. But if anxiety is impacting your ability to enjoy your life or do the things you want to, then help is available. If you can, speak to a loved one or trusted adult, and consider making an appointment with your GP. There is a range of practical information online, through reputable sources like the NHS website, from the charity Mind or from the Mental Health Foundation.

I wrote this book because when I first experienced that kind of anxiety, I didn't know what was happening to me, and it would have been helpful to know that it happened to other people too – and that it was possible for hope and happiness to live alongside the fear.

There is no one way for anxiety to look or feel, and this book is a work of fiction.

12 NOVEMBER 1920

THIRTY DAYS LEFT

1

The day that Mother told me about the telegram, I had thirty days left to live.

As I peered out of my bedroom window that morning, I spotted her stumbling over the unevenness of our sprawling land, a waif-like figure dressed all in grey. Despite the modern style of dresses becoming ever shorter, Mother preferred to glide through the house in long, sweeping creations, and her beaded hemline was trailing in the mud outside.

Mother's erratic gait unnerved me – something was wrong. I turned from the window and threw myself into trousers, a button-down shirt and a pair of brogues that were the first to hand. With as much speed as I could muster, I galloped out of my bedroom on to the landing. Here on the top floor, the rooms formed a ring: Father's study, which had not been opened since he left; my little brother Nick's bedroom, which he kept neat and uncluttered, his teddy bears arranged in a tidy row; and the empty bedrooms, the ones we didn't talk about.

When Father first came into money, he'd bought this prime real estate on Long Island and designed the towering mansion himself. Each floor of Pitch House was smaller than the one below, like a wedding cake. The first floor was the largest of the three, built around a central circular unit that looked like the base of a theatre in the round. The eastern wing formed a squat single-storey block with a sloping roof that met the bottom of the second storey of the central piece. It held the servants' quarters and the kitchen, and led on to a square of cobblestones reminiscent of English country houses. The western wing flew off as a long corridor two storeys high, with large Gothic windows; its top floor was purpose-built to house my father's strange and unusual objects of interest – his 'Collection', as he'd called it. Outside, our land rolled for miles, circled by pitch pines like a dark halo. Finally, at the north-eastern corner there was the memorial garden – which was, I realized, where Mother was heading.

I rattled down the flights of stairs, startling our housekeeper, Miss Price, who was polishing the telephone in the entrance hall. She knocked the receiver off its stand with a dreadful clatter. I must have really made her jump – Miss Price had worked for our family since before I was born, and she didn't become chief of staff by being prone to accidents.

'Mister Felix, there was a telegram . . .' she began, her voice strained.

Telegrams had never brought us good news. I gave Miss Price a quick wave of acknowledgement and hurried on. It was rude, but it was clear my mother needed me urgently.

I hastened to follow Mother's weaving path outside. The awful chill in the air took my breath away.

As I entered the memorial garden, the grief I'd come to know well ached once again. Some families hide their tragedy. Ours commissioned the finest engraved marble stones.

You see, once upon a time, I had four brothers. Three of them had been laid to rest. I mourned them, and at the same time I mourned my own future – because I knew, deep in my soul, that I would be next. The stones were a perpetual reminder that I used to be one of five that roamed these halls. Each with fine chestnut hair and a stocky build. A matching set.

I found Mother standing by George's stone, one hand resting on the smooth marble. Her other hand gripped an envelope, ragged where it had been ripped open like a slit throat. Whatever the insides contained, they had clearly unsettled Mother. She didn't turn to look at me as I approached.

'I miss them so much,' she said.

No explanation was needed. My stomach rolled at the acknowledgement of them. I missed them too. My grief had a strange timeless quality about it – no matter that it had been *years* now, remembering them could make the loss feel so raw and intense all over again.

Mother turned, and our eyes met. I got an uneasy feeling, as though she were seeing a shadow of my brothers flickering behind my eyes. It was as if she were looking at me, but seeing them, or an echo of them.

I placed my hand on Mother's shoulder. She had a bird-like quality about her: tight skin, frail arms, always trembling. *Had* she always trembled, or had that come with the loss, with the war, and the small white pills she'd been given to help her sleep?

'Felix ... your father is coming home,' she said, interrupting my thoughts.

There was a sudden roaring in my ears.

'I'm sorry, what did you say?'

I was certain I must have heard her wrong. There was no way that Father could be coming home. He'd been gone for so long. *Too* long. It had been years; he was badly injured in the war; he was languishing in a sanatorium in England ...

'It's true. Your father ... they're sending him home at last.'

I'll never forget the way she looked in that moment – one perfect sunshine-blonde curl lacquered to the middle of her forehead, her lipstick slightly smeared, and her eyelashes clumped together. More make-up doesn't always mean more beautiful. Her lips were still moving, and I was aware that the shapes her mouth was making and the noises that were coming out were supposed to mean something, but the words themselves refused to take form. How could it be true, after what we'd been through?

In the time before our tragedy, my parents used to host incredible parties that I could hear into the early hours of the morning. My older brothers used to stay up, playing cards, and sometimes I'd join in. But on occasion the music from the gramophone was so loud that nobody heard baby Nick crying in his nursery, and I was the only one who knew how to soothe him, lifting him up on to my shoulder. Mother and Father would spend those nights dancing wildly, laughing raucously and, at the most liquor-soaked parties, arguing intensely. That was how it was between them – every emotion, positive or negative, deeply felt.

But then George died. Followed by the twins, Scott and Luke. I'd gone from being part of a team of brothers to there only being me and little Nick left. And, all the while, war had begun to rage in Europe – a far-off, distant thing at first, and then a terrifying atrocity.

Father became angry at anything he deemed frivolous, whereas Mother, wracked with grief, only seemed to want the music louder, the drinks faster, the arguments more extreme. It was an explosion waiting to happen.

'How can we live like this? It's all so inconsequential!' I heard him bellow at Mother one night when they thought I'd gone to bed.

'I don't know how to live without them,' Mother sobbed in return.

It wasn't long after that he'd packed a bag and gone to volunteer for the war effort, training to transport wounded men from the front, although he'd never had a jot of military experience. Shock rippled out through our social circles – everybody thought it was a heroic choice, but they couldn't understand why he would make it when he didn't need to. Nick was only three – too little to retain any memories of Father. I learned that even the people who are supposed to care most for you can leave, and do.

And Mother? From that day on, Mother lived as if she were already widowed.

But Father didn't die.

Then we celebrated Armistice Day, and still he didn't come home.

Next came the telegram. I can still picture it, draped over Mother's arm as she lay, stupefied, an empty bottle nestled in the crook of her arm like a baby.

A serious injury to the face . . .

We'd never been told what that meant. He had been shipped from France to a sanatorium in England with a specialist doctor. That was all we knew. The message had been unsettling in its vagueness.

Back in the memorial garden, Mother lifted the envelope containing her latest life-changing missive. It flapped in the wind. 'I know him coming home will be a shock. But I have to tell you . . . I had the letter from his doctor a little while,' she admitted.

I immediately struggled to contain my sense of betrayal. We told each other everything, didn't we? How could she keep something like this from me?

'How long?'

Guilt flickered across her face. 'A week or so. And then this morning I got this – confirmation that the ship is docking tomorrow. I have to collect him from the port in the morning.'

'*Tomorrow?*'

'I should have told you sooner, I know, but I've been so worried about you.'

Mother needed me to respond, but I was like an actor who had forgotten his lines. I looked around, and it was like seeing everything through a layer of frosted glass. Every breath was hard to catch, as though something were stuck in my throat and blocking my windpipe. I couldn't focus my eyes any more. This was compounded by a painful sensitivity in my chest, as if somebody had reached in and gripped my heart and was squeezing, squeezing.

I'm dying, I thought. *I'm dying of shock*. And then that was all I could think.

I'm dying, I'm dying, I'm dying.

Because I thought I knew what it was to be frightened, but now I was sure my heart was going to stop, and then Mother's voice started to go all shrill and desperate, and I knew that she needed me, but I still couldn't catch my breath, and then time went fluid and odd, and I staggered towards her, as though I'd lost all control of my limbs, and I was so certain that I was dying, and my heart ran away with itself, and I'd never felt so clumsy before, and I tripped over the edge of George's memorial stone, and my feet went out from underneath me, and everything rolled upward as I fell and went black when my head hit the marble.

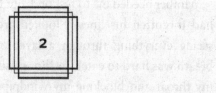

2

Our family had long been defined by what we'd lost. Tragedy lingered in the graveyard on our land, it lurked in the family portrait that showed a family of seven, and – more sensationally than either of these – it was written in all the tabloid articles about us. They hedged around the unlikelihood of three tragic accidents striking the same family, managing to just swerve direct accusations that Father didn't want his sons to reach the age of inheritance.

My father's story fascinated the press – he had grown up in the poorest part of Brooklyn, been sent out to work at thirteen in the same factory where he saw his own father die in a terrible fire, choking on black smoke as he made sure his son got out first. As a boy, his meagre salary was swallowed up trying to help his mother keep a roof over their heads. And then ... he moved on to working on the railways and went hungry to put a week's earnings into making a clever investment in steel that paid off. Eventually, he was able to open his own factory, and his investments continued to yield returns.

He was affluent when he married Mother, but not extravagantly rich. It was a marriage of love, not financial gain – she had an old aristocratic name and had lived a life filled with the trappings of privilege. But when her parents passed away, it was revealed that they'd been hiding some significant debts, and all that remained of their once-great fortune was a crumbling house.

None of us knew exactly which smart move turned Father into a multimillionaire, but when it happened it happened fast.

George was toddling, and the twins were just babies. It took two years to build Pitch House, and I was born there.

At first, Father was Alfred Ashe, *rags-to-riches steel magnate*. Then he became Alfred Ashe, *tragic patriarch*.

Five sons, three of them dead. Three horrible, grisly accidents, each on their eighteenth birthday.

George was first. When I was twelve years old, I watched him die. I was wearing my favourite yellow shirt that Mother would later tell Miss Price to burn in the fireplace; by the end of the day, it was soaked with blood.

The heat of the sun had been thick. It had been a struggle to keep my hair from sticking to my forehead, a layer of sweat forming faster than I could wipe it away.

I was round the back of the house by the servants' quarters. The door was open, leading on to the square of cobblestones ringed off by a large iron fence topped with slender spearheads. I was following George, who had already told me to go away and stop pestering him, but I was bored.

George was clambering up the side of the servants' quarters, where the view over our land was spectacular, shoving his feet into the grooves of the brick and hoisting himself up by clutching on to the top of the window frame. He moved like a spider with swift and darting limbs that froze for a moment to plan their next placement. I was in awe of him. He was irritated by me. He always seemed so bold, so fearless . . . And the harder my parents tried to rein him in, the more George struggled for freedom.

Besides it being his birthday, the day had been important in another way. A lawyer had come to the house with a large bundle of papers. My eldest brother was going to be 'heavily encouraged' to begin working at Father's factory, with a view to learning from the bottom up. Father said it was important that George understood the hard labour that his employees went through, like Father had done, otherwise they'd never respect him. George said he'd rather die.

As George hoisted himself up on to the angled roof, I felt giddy with vicarious joy. He was making a stand, carving out the life he wanted for himself. I longed to be like him. He lifted his foot, got purchase on the slate tile as I called out to him.

'George!'

My shout caught him by surprise. His head flicked over his shoulder in my direction, and his raised foot lost its grip on the slate. He scrambled, wildly attempting to find solid footing. When he stabilized, he smirked at me and pulled himself up to standing. 'Unshakable!' he declared.

It emboldened him, the slip and the recovery. He took a couple of steps across, lightly, like a dancer. There was the screech of the slate tile losing its grip, and his leg shot out a with it. The tile skittered to the ground and smashed, and when George fell that is what I was watching, imagining

Father's anger at the pieces of shattered slate coming to rest in the grooves between the cobbles.

When I looked up, I saw how George had fallen. It was perfectly, impossibly unlucky. Landing backwards on the fence, looking up to the sky. He was pierced through his neck and through his shoulder, and the rest of his body hung limp from the two spearheads that held him in place, feet hovering a foot above the ground. George gasped a little, and twitched, and then went very still. I tried to get him down. I was still trying to get him down when the servants came running from the kitchen, and Father's screams tore through the yard.

The memory has become as ingrained in the deep part of my brain as my two times table or the lullaby Mother sang to me as a baby. It is often the first thing I see in my mind's eye when I wake of a morning, even now.

And there is one more thing about the way that George died. Something else I turn over and over in my mind when I have the strength to think of it. After he took his final breath, a wisp of midnight vapour unwound from between his lips. It sparked, as though it held stars inside. It weaved through the air and then dispersed into nothing.

I never told anyone about that part.

Everyone said it was a tragic accident. Real bad luck. But then the twins died the following year, and it didn't seem like it was just luck any more.

*

Scott's greatest treasure was his horses. He spent day after day out on the land, tending to them. Never mind that Father employed a groom: Scott insisted on learning everything he could and wasn't afraid of getting his hands dirty, even mucking out the stables and shoeing the horses. On the morning of the birthday he shared with Luke, he went out for a ride – just like he always did.

Only that morning his horse flung him and his poor head was crushed beneath the hoof he'd shod so carefully.

I was in the drawing room with Luke when Mother sent our butler, Mr Reed, a stiff rake of a man, to tell us. Luke let out a strangled noise. Turned out they'd been arguing. The last words he'd said to Scott were sharp and cruel. He sped away from the house in his roadster and was pierced through the chest by the steering-wheel column when he crashed it minutes later.

They died an hour apart, a perfect mirror of the day they were born – Scott first, Luke second. There was no eighteenth birthday party.

Father scrapped the car and shot the horse. As if it made any difference at all.

After that, I drew some conclusions: this was more than a terrible, awful coincidence. Something was killing the boys in our family. The creeping fear of it grew over time, like mould – a dark thought here, a sleepless night there – until it took over my life so completely that I found myself unable to function. The mounting dread had won when it made the idea of attending school become untenable and terrifying. It won again when it convinced me I was worthless and caused me to push the ones I loved the most away. Like Lois … Until, finally, fearfulness became as much a part of me as my short build and my hazel eyes.

Fear became a curse on my life.

But it was worse than that – *more* than that. I knew – without knowing how – that whatever was happening went beyond paranoia.

My brothers and I were truly cursed. Cursed to die before we could inherit the fortune our father had strived to build.

And if there really was a curse that killed the young men of our family on their eighteenth birthday, then I would be its next victim.

3

When I regained consciousness, I had been placed in the sunroom, a parlour at the back of the house with large glass panes looking out on to the riotous colour of a wildflower garden. Two large mirrors hung at angles reflected the garden view and encouraged the light to flutter around like a caged bird.

Mother crouched in front of me, flapping like a moth. In her panic, her dress had been hitched up about her knees, the gunmetal satin puddling. She brought her face very close to mine, studying my eyes like a particularly eager lepidopterist inspecting a butterfly that might vanish.

'Felix darling, are you all right?'

My throat was dry, and my head was thumping, and there was thick crusted blood around my nose and on the side of my head. The intricate beading of the chaise longue dug into me. I pulled myself to a sitting position, and my stomach swirled. Just past Mother, my tutor, Geoffrey, stood, coming into focus like a photograph. As if he could read my mind, he reached for a glass of water and held it to my lips. I gulped greedily, as though I'd been lost in a desert. My pallid face was reflected back in the shiny buttons of his waistcoat.

'Do you think we need to call the doctor?' Mother murmured. 'He hit his head.'

They both stared at me.

'How do you feel?' Geoffrey asked, worrying at the arm of his gold spectacles and the place where it rubbed behind his ear.

I raised my hand to my head. There was a blunt ache pulsing through my temple. I pinched the bridge of my nose, and the pressure seemed to release the pain, or at least distract from it. 'I think I just need to rest.'

'What happened, darling?' Mother asked.

The worst, most intense fear I've ever known.

I floundered around for a way to explain. 'I don't know. I thought my heart was just going to stop.'

Mother glanced sideways at Geoffrey. 'Do you think there's something wrong with his heart?'

'No, I don't think it's his heart.' He cleared his throat. 'Felix, I think it might be time to give the talking cure a try,' he said very gently.

'No.' That was my default response whenever the topic of the talking cure was raised.

Geoffrey had been encouraging me to visit a psychotherapist ever since he started tutoring me. Mother had pulled me out of school after the 'funny turn' I'd had in the summer, and she'd asked Geoffrey to keep up with my lessons at home. He was Mother's confidant, her closest friend since childhood.

Geoffrey Garton was 'old money' and a scholar who had retired from his glittering academic career at forty when he came into his inheritance. He was an excellent tutor, patient and methodical. He maintained his family's mansion in the Hamptons, but he'd taken up an unassuming lakeside house just a short walk from Pitch House. If you asked him, he would have said the real estate was too good to miss, but I knew – well, everyone knew – it was to be close to Mother.

He was also genuinely concerned about me. Geoffrey had researched as much as he could about being gripped by a crushing fear with no immediate threat. It was, he assured me, a medical condition, and he'd been adamant that the 'talking cure' was the solution. It was a new treatment for a condition few understood.

I could see the potential it had to help. Talking might help me to unravel the mess of threads in my mind that tangled me up in anxious knots. But I'd also heard this sort of thing called hysteria, a woman's malady. Or, worse, I'd heard it called madness.

Do you really want documented evidence of your instability? Sure, it starts with talking, but what if it cascades into other treatments . . . ?

My mind threw up images of a fizzing electrical cap designed to fry my brain. Geoffrey wasn't the only one conducting research.

Besides. What was the point in trying to 'cure' me if I was doomed to die anyway?

'I've sourced a specialist in New York,' Geoffrey continued. 'Without help, I'm concerned that you're only going to get worse.'

Lois would have told me to start the talking cure. She thought psychotherapy was a new and fascinating science. But what did it matter what she thought of anything any more?

I was surprised to see Mother was nodding along. 'It might be for the best,' she said, picking at her nail bed and unable to look me in the eye as she said it. She had previously been reluctant too. She was paranoid about how it would appear, what people would say.

But then she'd never seen my fear in action as severely as this before now.

'I understand it's a huge shock, your father coming home like this, Felix. I'm sorry it's unsettled you so much.'

'He's really coming home?' I still couldn't quite believe it.

Mother nodded and picked up the envelope from the side table. 'It's signed by Doctor Leery, who has been treating him at the sanatorium in England. They've done all they can, and it's time for him to be reunited with us.'

It seemed impossible to create an image of what life would be like with my father. It wouldn't just slip back to the way it was before. We'd changed too much. Mother had become so fragile, seeking solace in a bottle; Nick was unrecognizable from the chubby little toddler that had been left behind; and I'd been reduced to a bundle of nerves.

Father had been gone a very long time.

How had *he* changed in the time he'd been away? I'd heard of soldiers returning from the war struck with a new propensity for violence and a raging temper, others still who were catatonic and tormented by their inner worlds. What version of Father would be coming home?

And that was without even considering his physical injuries . . .

'Did the doctor say anything about what he's like now?'

Mother cleared her throat and read from the letter. '*It is important for you to know that Alfred's injuries are life-changing, and you should be prepared to find him different from how you remember him.*'

'What does that mean?' I asked, quivering and panicky.

Mother shook her head and gave a defeated shrug. Geoffrey placed a steadying hand on her shoulder as she began to sob.

I tried to remember Father's face the way it had been, and found that time had blurred the image. The most recent photograph I had of him was in a copy of the gossip rag *Disclosed*, which had often liked to follow him and Mother – the new-money multimillionaire and the failed tennis star. They were always good for a story, and they sold magazines. They'd been arguing outside a restaurant and were photographed by a journalist. In the picture, Father had his arms up around his head in exasperation, anger splashed across his face. That was not the memory I wanted to hold on to.

'I really think it would be best if you had the opportunity to talk this through with a professional,' Geoffrey said. 'Doctor Albass has a fantastic reputation.'

It seemed a particular cruelty that the one thing that might help me required me to open myself up to an awful vulnerability. I would have to be brave to allow someone a glimpse inside my mind.

My thoughts had become a dreadful form of torture, and it was exhausting. I tried to keep them all locked away in the deepest, darkest hiding place inside me . . . But I had reached my capacity, like a cupboard filled to bursting. It might be futile – but it might also be a relief to let it all spill out, to release the badness out of me like the yellow viscosity of a lanced boil.

'Okay,' I said. 'I'll talk to her.'

Mother looked up as fast as a whip crack. She and Geoffrey exchanged a glance I couldn't read.

'Thank you, Felix. I'll book you an appointment,' Geoffrey said. 'And maybe . . . maybe we should pause your lessons for a while.'

I realized he was trembling. Had Mother kept Father's return a secret from him too? He must have known that there would be no place for him in a home that held my father, even though, in Mother's darkest times, it was with Geoffrey that she'd seemed bright again.

I felt heavy with the knowledge that Father was on a ship, waiting to disembark and be dropped into our lives again like an explosive device. I had tried to keep things together the best I could in his absence. Looking at the fragility of us all, perhaps I didn't do a good enough job. I did try, though.

The one thing I always could do well was look after Nick. Whereas Mother frustrated him and became frazzled herself, I'd become an expert on my little brother and communicating in the way he needed. It took patience, but I'd learned that, where Nick was concerned, it was no use leaving room for interpretation or assumption.

Pitch House was a large place, teeming with busy household staff. Nick always managed to find nooks to hide in and projects to keep him occupied, which, in his more unsettled moments, might be rearranging an entire shelf of the library by the first word of the first sentence, or unpicking the hem of a curtain stitch by stitch.

As I left the sunroom to begin searching for my little brother, I practically bumped into Lydia, one of the maids, who immediately pretended to look busy sweeping. I knew she had been listening at the door – that's how she was. I felt sick at what she might have overheard. Lydia had been caught talking to a reporter at the gate once. She'd said she hadn't known who he was, but I had my doubts about that. The following week she was wearing a new pair of shoes. Any other maid would have been fired on the spot, but Lydia's grandmother had been Mother's nanny, and as such there was a loyalty that had kept her in our employ – though I wasn't sure Mother would be as forgiving again.

I started my search in a methodical way, testing the door handle that led down underground to the wine cellar and the armoury. When I found it locked, as it should be, I ducked my head in the music room. It lay empty, the piano inside cutting a lonely figure in the centre of the room, surrounded by chairs where an audience of ghosts waited for a performance that would never come. None of us had ever learned to play. Father had once told me that a music room was a necessary feature of a mansion, but, sadly for him, none of us had a musical note in our body.

I eventually found Nick curled up like a cat in a great armchair in the reading room, poring over the diaries of a botanist recounting an expedition to Haiti. Unlike most of Nick's short-lived passions, this one had yet to burn out. I truly hoped one day he'd get to go on the adventures he craved. We really ought to have been thinking about getting him into a school – at seven years old it was long overdue. And yet we'd had so much else to think about, to worry about, that Mother had resisted sending him to the boarding school the rest of us went to, perpetually saving the decision for another time, a better time . . . that hadn't yet arrived.

'Nick,' I said, and he looked up from his book. His eyes went all round, like someone had lassoed the moon and its reflection from the sea and poured both into his face. 'I've got something to tell you. Our father is coming home tomorrow.'

'Okay,' he said, returning his gaze to an illustration of a delicate stem with a vivid orange bloom at the top.

His blunt reaction didn't surprise me. Even if he wouldn't look me in the eye, I could tell that his mind was still turning over the new information, clicking away on it like clockwork.

I hovered. I wanted to be on hand for the moment when it sank in, and he needed me.

'I know what you're going to say next,' Nick said.

'You do?' I couldn't help but feel the smile crawl over my lips.

'You're going to tell me that everything will be okay, but I don't believe you.' Nick turned the page.

My smile fell away.

'Okay. Well, do you have any questions? About Father, I mean?'

Nick's hand lay on the book, but he wasn't looking at the pages any longer. He was staring into some middle distance. Thinking.

'Do you think Father remembers me?' he asked.

'Of course,' I said gently. 'He's missed you.'

Nick's forehead creased into a knitted furrow that hurt my heart. I'd tried to keep him from pain, from worry. My little brother was like a ball of wool that's been unwound and wrapped back together too tightly – I didn't know where to start trying to unravel him. When he got distressed, he got more anxious to keep things in perfect order. He began to chew at the corner of his mouth, and the skin started to look sore.

'Hey,' I said, knocking his chin. 'Don't do that – you'll hurt yourself.'

Nick flinched.

'Hey.' I got down on my knees, trying to look him right in the eye. He wouldn't meet my gaze at all, staring someplace over my shoulder instead. 'I know you don't want to hear this, but it really is going to be okay.'

Nick needed me to be calm, authoritative, brave; I wished those qualities came more naturally to me, but I could attempt to wear them for my little brother.

He shivered a little, as though somebody had walked over his grave.

'I mean it,' I said. 'It's not going to change things.'

'It's going to change everything,' Nick said quietly, and all I could do was squeeze his shoulder because I wasn't convincing myself with my spiel, let alone him.

13 NOVEMBER 1920

TWENTY-NINE DAYS LEFT

4

The following morning, Nick refused to get out of bed. In the end, that felt the safest place to leave him, tucked beneath his quilt with a book. Our chauffeur, Harold, brought around the black Model T Ford while I waited for Mother. When she appeared, she was dressed in a more understated way than I had expected.

I was used to glittering jewels and heavy make-up being her armour to face the world. Instead, she looked familiar; she looked like home. She had swept her hair back and pinned it in place with an elegant clip. A navy pleated coat with big gold buttons and a belt tied around her waist fought away the chill, but her ankles were bare, peeping out from a dress that grazed the top of her navy heels. I recognized them as a pair my father surprised her with one Christmas. She was so delighted with them, it almost made up for the explosive argument they'd had the evening before.

The veneer slipped the second we got into the vehicle. Prohibition be damned, Mother plucked out a brushed-silver flask from her coat. Gin, from the floral scent on her breath. Her knee jittered up and down, and I wondered if I'd be holding her hair back by the end of the day again.

On the drive to the port, we sat in silence, ruminating separately.

Father had become such an abstract concept to me, not a real flesh-and-bones person who was about to rejoin our lives. The thing to understand is that we didn't lose him all at once: we lost him piece by piece. A bit on the day he left in his uniform, a bit when we received the telegram about his injury, a bit when we were told he'd been admitted to a sanatorium, a bit on the anniversary of his confinement there . . . This was the man who had raised me, and yet I felt like I'd lost any sense of who he was. It was Father who had ignited my love of collecting, it was Father who taught me the satisfaction of a good puzzle and the art of cryptography, and it was Father who had been the architect of my life until he left. And yet I could not conjure any idea of how he would slot back into our family.

When Harold opened the car door for us, Mother thanked him, then linked her arm through mine, and we pushed through bustling crowds to take our place at the railings. A heavy fog was rolling over the sea in the distance.

'I don't know how to feel,' Mother said.

I had nothing to offer her by way of reassurance, but there was comfort in knowing that we were both the same in that moment: a little lost.

The ship was smaller than I'd expected. A team of burly workers dressed in a uniform of white shirt and dungarees secured the gangway down to the quayside where we were waiting. They reminded me of a troupe of dancers, each one tracing their steps, interweaving with ropes and tying knots.

As the passengers began making their way from the ship down the gangway, an anxious roiling started up in my belly. There was a great hubbub of reunions and delight all around me, but I didn't feel part of the moment that everybody else was experiencing. Instead, there was just a deep dread that dragged at my insides.

When the crowds had cleared, the gangway was hauled over to a different door lower down on the boat for those in steerage. I was struck with a sudden horror, imagining Father cramped up with the other passengers for a week, sleeping in bunk beds, no privacy and the stench of unwashed bodies. Even so, I reflected, steerage must have seemed the height of luxury after what he'd experienced in the trenches.

A new stream of passengers came down the gangway. I strained on tiptoes, as if that would make any difference to being able to see him sooner.

'Who are you waiting for?' asked a man with a thick Boston accent.

'My husband,' Mother replied, her voice shaking just a little. Unless you knew her, you wouldn't have noticed it.

I turned and appraised the questioner – he didn't look much older than me. I took in his inquisitive eyes, the smartly starched collar of his shirt . . . and the notebook in his hand, pencil hovering.

'War veteran? I heard this liner was bringing back some of those who were being treated at a sanatorium in England.'

Mother nodded, smiling politely. I frowned. He was leading us into a trap. He wasn't asking us questions because he was interested or because he cared. No, he'd got a sniff of a story.

'Hey, aren't you Gracie Ashe?' he asked my mother, as if on cue.

She flushed pink instantly, the shame of her old failures immediately creeping back.

Given Mother's wealthy family, everyone had expected that she'd dutifully get married and achieve little else with her life. But she'd been a tennis prodigy, and at nineteen had been playing at the highest level. She might have had a stellar sporting career, but at twenty she crashed out of the Women's National Championships as a semi-finalist, having been a favourite to win. And by the age of twenty-one she was married and pregnant, the dream over. After she'd had George and the twins, there were a couple of years where she attempted a comeback. The press were vicious in their reporting of her – no longer a sparkling ingénue tennis star, she was always presented within the context of her failure.

'That's me,' she said with a resigned tone.

'Robert Flatt, *Disclosed* magazine.' He gave her a wide, charming grin that no doubt got a lot of his interviewees to lower their guard. 'You must have been waiting for this day a long time.'

'A long time,' Mother repeated.

I couldn't believe she was giving him the time of day. She was normally astute – so scandal-aware and keen to avoid gossip spreading about the family. But her nerves seemed to have got the better of her today, which was making her more vulnerable to this fellow's probing questions.

The last thing I wanted was for us to become a featured story. When the twins died, *Disclosed* published a detailed op-ed describing the deaths of my brothers in gory detail. The fact that all three of them died on their eighteenth birthday was used to insinuate Father had murdered them to retain a tight grip on his business and his fortune. The accusation was ridiculous, of course, but Father raged at the injustice. For a short while, he was adamant about getting lawyers involved, but a lifetime of being in the public eye had taught Mother that the best response was no response at all, and she convinced him to leave it be.

A few weeks later, another piece was published in a magazine for paranormal fanatics, which suggested our mansion was possessed by malignant spirits. We were visited by a spiritualist who had read that article and showed up with bundles of herbs, offering to 'heal the house'. Luckily, the household staff and I were able to get rid of her before my father saw, and I think he remained none the wiser.

Despite my silence and my mother's short replies, Flatt was persistent. 'I heard they were kept in that sanatorium for two years and weren't allowed to write home.' His pencil quivered.

'Don't you think your timing is a little inappropriate?' I asked, finding my voice.

Flatt looked at me. 'You must be Felix,' he said. 'There's

just the two of you boys at home now, right? Well, if there's ever a more *appropriate* time to talk, this is the number for my office.' He rummaged through his pockets for a business card and pressed it into my hand.

I couldn't believe the audacity. Before I had a chance to tell Flatt where to go, he was accosted by another man, this one holding a large press camera close to his chest, the expensive piece of kit bulky in his arms with its wide eye and large reflective plate with a fixed bulb.

'I've got a great shot of them!'

'What do you mean you got a shot?' I snapped.

I shoved the business card into my pocket, thinking I had half a mind to call Flatt's boss and make a complaint about his conduct. Flatt pointed to the gangway. A troop of four men were stumbling along it together. From the look of them, they represented a host of injuries, and it had been some time since any of them had seen a hot bath.

I didn't recognize my father at first. He was wearing a thick crimson scarf, up high around the lower half of his face, but there was something familiar in the way he walked, the way he carried himself, and of course he towered over the others. You always could spot him head and shoulders above a crowd. My stomach clenched up as tight as a fist.

Father approached us, ever so slowly, and Mother reached her arm out to him. She met his eyes above the top of the scarf. There were no two ways about it, he looked haunted. The creased crow's feet were new, doubtless etched by the unthinkable sights he'd witnessed.

'Alfred,' Mother murmured. He touched her cheek softly. Then he turned to me, and there seemed to be genuine shock in his eyes. He patted me on the shoulder, and I froze. Father removed his hand.

'Let's take you home,' Mother said gently, with the same soothing tone she'd use to help Nick get back to sleep after a nightmare. She looped her arm through Father's to steady him, but reached her other hand out behind her, grasping for mine. When I slid my hand in hers, she pulled me close on her other side, so we made a strange three-headed creature ambling through the port.

All the speeches I'd mentally rehearsed dissolved inside me.

When we silently returned to Harold and the car, I hopped in the front seat and witnessed the alarm on Harold's face before he rearranged it into a veil of neutrality. Mother guided Father into the back, where she sat and held his hand tight while he clutched a little knapsack. In the absence of anything better to say, I didn't utter a single word for the entirety of the drive. Mother seemed equally lost, and every so often would simply point out buildings that had sprung up or changed in the time that Father had been gone.

Father didn't speak. I began to wonder if he even could. I sneaked a glance at him in the rear-view mirror, the only way I could stare without being seen to. The top half of his face was exhausted and haggard, and the rest was hidden from sight. Gone was the handsome man who had stolen my mother's heart all those years ago.

And when he breathed, a strange thing happened. In the pause between each breath, there was something I could hear if I concentrated – a clicking sound, rhythmic and steady. It deeply unsettled me. It sounded just like the ticking of a clock.

5

By the time the car crunched up the gravel of the drive, I was thoroughly unnerved. The strangeness of the situation was exacerbated by that odd ticking sound, and I wondered if I was the only one who could hear it. Miss Price and Mr Reed were waiting to greet us formally at the door. It was the sort of welcome they might have performed if Father had merely been away on business for a few days, and yet it seemed hollow and cheerless.

Once Father was out of the car, and with Miss Price's help, Mother guided him up to one of the guest bedrooms instead of to their own. When she came back down the stairs, she was wringing her hands.

'What are we going to do with him?'

I hesitated, nervous and uncertain. 'I think the best thing we can do is let him settle in,' I said. 'We just need to behave as if everything were normal and give him a chance.'

The persistent creak of a floorboard sounded above my head. Father must have been pacing to and fro.

Mother wretchedly wrapped her arms around herself, as if she were trying to keep her insides from falling out. 'I'm sorry, Felix,' she said. 'I don't know how to do this.'

My stomach churned, and I forced a swallow to release a little bit of the tightness in my throat. I pressed my hands to my eyes, overcome by a desperate tiredness. I tried so hard to stay strong, stay presentable, keep the emotions squashed . . . But all I wanted to do was crawl into my bed and pretend that none of it was happening.

I told Mother that I needed to rest, and as I climbed the stairs I ran my hand along the mahogany bannister, feeling every notch of its intricate pattern of roses that Father had had carved especially for Mother. The ridges and hollows of the wood were almost enough to keep me grounded in the physical world. Almost.

Then, as I turned the corner at the top of the stairs, I was brought sharply back to reality by the sight of Father standing in the entrance to the Collection. My heart puttered away inside me, and the breath I was taking stalled.

The Collection.

When I was younger, I used to think of the Collection as simply a strange foible of Father's.

'When you've had nothing, and you've grown up believing that you are nothing, the acquisition of items can be strangely addictive,' he told me once.

Father had a notion of what people with money do – and the Collection was one way that he asserted his belonging. He'd heard that wealthy gentlemen would pay incredible amounts to lay claim to rare items and display them in specially designed cabinets. They'd gather – at dinners, at auctions – and boast enthusiastically about their spoils. So he'd decided to follow suit.

It was always preternaturally quiet in the corridor to the Collection, as though the walls were under some sort of enchantment to keep disturbances out. Inside, the gallery housed a hundred stories in glass cases; every item was painstakingly catalogued in a heavy leather-bound tome resting on a plinth at the entrance.

A chalice made of rhinoceros horn and bezoar. An antique desk once belonging to an apothecary famous for poisoning his clients. A crocodile embryo floating in a jar of preservative. The body of a 'mermaid' that had been displayed in a travelling circus from England – that is, half a monkey sewn on to the tail of a trout.

Each item had its own twisted tale. The common thread? Each one purported to have magic properties.

'It's creepy,' Mother used to say with a shudder. 'And self-indulgent.'

My brothers had no interest in the Collection whatsoever – Nick was too little, Scott had his horses, Luke loved the cars, and George just wanted to play baseball. But as I grew, so did my morbid fascination with the Collection.

When I had just turned eleven, a box arrived at the house. It was wrapped in plain brown paper.

'I think I know what this is.'

Father had a twinkle in his eye when I took it to him in the library. He lounged back in his favourite easy chair, the book he was reading falling into his lap. The furniture in the library, unlike anywhere else in our home, was chosen for comfort, not aesthetics. The library was his space to rest from the pressures of the steelworks.

'I'm not sure I should tell you about this one, Felix,' he murmured tantalizingly. 'Would you like to open it? It would take a brave boy to peek inside this box.'

I hovered, uncertain. But I wanted to please him. And I certainly wanted to show him I was brave.

'I'll open it.'

The very tips of my fingers were sweating as I slipped them beneath the seal of the paper. Anticipation flooded me, and burning curiosity wouldn't let me take my time to savour the opening. I started ripping the outer skin of the package. Father chuckled. The paper tore easily, falling about my feet – and inside there was nothing more remarkable than a shoebox. But my nose was quickly assaulted by a smell I couldn't place. Whatever was inside had been scented with oils. And there was a deeper smell beneath that. It felt permanent, like a tattoo etched on the inside of my nostrils.

Grinning at my hesitation, my father took the box from me and removed its lid.

A hand nestled inside, surrounded by thick purple velvet. It had turned a slug-like grey through age, and the skin was withered and puckered. The fingers curled up at the ends, and the palm cupped a candle. A scraggly wick twisted up from the thick wax. Despite the thrill of horror the hand gave me, I couldn't stop myself from touching it; it was softer than the shrivelled skin suggested.

'It's called the Hand of Glory.' Father's voice boomed with a storyteller's cadence. 'That hand belonged to a murderer. People used to believe that it could light the way for thieves, casting a glow that only the user could see, and even unlock doors . . . What do you make of that, my boy?'

I was fascinated. It was as though I'd been invited into some secret club that I couldn't bear to be cast out from.

'Is it really magic?'

'I highly doubt it,' Father said, his mouth twisting into a grimace. 'They rarely are. If you ever come across something with real magic inside, you'll know about it.'

He sounded displeased. I dropped my gaze to the ground. Was I failing some sort of test?

'If they're not magic, then what's the point of the Collection?'

He didn't answer me.

There was something he was searching for, but I knew better than to press him – Father could turn taciturn and ornery on a dime. All I knew was that I wanted to start collecting too. Perhaps I could help him find whatever he was looking for. From that day, I entered Father's tutelage, becoming a regular at the auctions he attended in the city, despite being the youngest there by a mile. I also attended the collectors' dinners with him, and brushed shoulders with the other gentlemen who shared this peculiar hobby.

After my brothers died, I wondered if Father would dismiss the Collection as one of the 'frivolities' he so raged against. But, if anything, his collecting became more frantic, desperate even.

But no object could fill the void they left.

Then, in the time that Father was gone, the Collection became my obsession. As fear increasingly crept into my bones, I was struck by a sense of not having enough time, but the Collection was something physical and tangible to hold on to, with which I could imagine making a mark.

The formal curation process became a distraction from my panic, and I started to allow myself to dream that the Collection would become a spectacular and memorable legacy, and I would not fade into insignificance. In the time that Father was gone, I doubled its size.

I kept notebooks filled with detailed instructions, scribbled floor plans, text for exhibit labels telling the tales of the items. The Collection would be proof that I had lived, and at one point I'd hoped to open up the gallery to a public audience, like a museum of oddities, on the eve of my eighteenth birthday. I wanted to see the reaction to my great triumph before my demise the next day.

Now that my father was home, what did that mean for my dream? He already had a legacy. I didn't want to share the Collection with him again. I had put in too much work. It was mine now . . . And he was the one that had left us.

As if sensing my presence, Father turned to face me. He seemed to want to say something. But I couldn't deal with him right now. I bit my tongue and stalked away, my breath coming all heavy and uneven.

My eighteenth birthday was only twenty-nine days away, and I knew that death was lurking, watching over me. The closer my birthday got, the more I was unravelling – becoming distrustful, suspicious, fearful.

I couldn't have known then the truth behind the darkness that lay in wait for me.

But I could sense it.

6

Mother was already waiting for us in the dining room. She looked like a movie star, wearing a white dress with soft cape-style sleeves and a V-neck with a string of pearls at its centre. Deep plum lipstick overexaggerated her Cupid's bow. She was alone, and the crack in my heart ached – I could still bring to mind what the table looked like when our family had been whole. Luke used to sit with his legs tucked beneath him, and it drove Mother wild. George would regale us with his latest triumph on the baseball field. Scott – quiet, thoughtful – always made you feel listened to.

Sometimes I thought that Nick was lucky that he had no real memories of his other brothers. Nothing to miss that way. But when I remembered the completeness of being surrounded by all my family, I felt lucky to have known things that way. Nick had only ever seen us broken.

Nick and I took our seats at the table, but the fourth place next to Mother stayed conspicuously empty. It remained empty long after our cook, Margie, had brought bowls filled with a rich and creamy roasted-pepper soup, and after they had begun to cool.

Where on earth was Father?

Nick played with his spoon. 'I'm hungry,' he whined. 'Can't we start?'

When Mother didn't respond, he sneakily spooned some soup into his mouth. I couldn't understand his appetite – my stomach was like a deep pit of writhing snakes, and I couldn't imagine being able to swallow anything.

'Stop,' Mother said. 'We should wait.' But she sounded unsure.

Nick paused, his spoon hovering in mid-air.

I shot a pointed look at Mother. 'Are you going to get him?'

Her eyes flickered away from mine.

'Why hasn't he come down?' Nick's bottom lip was quivering now. 'Doesn't he want to see us?'

I felt the strongest tug of protectiveness. He had no experience or understanding of what a father should be, how a father should make you feel. It should not be terrified and unsettled, as I felt.

Nick's question hovered in the air. Mother looked at me, pleading.

'Fine,' I said, scraping my chair back.

Before launching myself up the stairs, I quizzed Mr Reed about Father's movements. 'Have any staff been in to see him?'

Mr Reed hesitated. 'I tried,' he said. As butler, Mr Reed had previously served my father well, been the person Father could ask to do anything.

'Your father . . . I don't think he can speak, and his hands

45

appear to shake too much to write. It's very difficult for him to make his wishes known, but it became clear to me that he wanted me to leave.'

I thanked him, then took the stairs at a pace, as if going faster than normal would stop my nerves catching up with me. Outside the guest bedroom, I rapped on the door before I had a chance to overthink.

There was no response, so I knocked again, sharper and louder. There was a brief moment before the door opened when I almost thought that he might look the way he used to, and I could nearly conjure a memory of his smile, sitting at the dinner table, beaming with pride at George's tales of victory. I tried to hold on to the picture, but it slipped out of my grasp like a hooked fish making a bid for freedom.

When the door did open, what met me was not the smile from the memory, but the scarf once again. The sad eyes above it were ringed with dark circles that seemed too heavy for his face to hold.

'It's time for dinner,' I told him.

He touched his chest, and I noticed he had put on one of the pressed shirts Mother had left out for him. It was open, revealing his vest beneath. As he ran his fingers over the buttons, I watched the way they tremored and convulsed. He couldn't fasten the buttons himself. That was why he hadn't joined us – he'd been in his room, struggling to dress himself, but wanting to make the effort that he knew would matter to Mother.

It made me want to cry.

I reached over and fastened up his buttons one by one. When I was done, the shirt hung loose on him. He must have lost thirty pounds at least. In fact, with the bulky layer of his overcoat removed, he was almost skeletal. Now that I was close to him, I could hear that odd ticking sound again.

'Are you ready?' I asked.

I saw him as something fragile, to be handled with kid gloves, like a precious item from the Collection. He was a relic from a previous life, something to be kept safe behind glass.

Mother and Nick seemed to be holding their breath as we entered the dining room. Nick's spoon stopped mid-journey to his mouth, and he gawped, his mouth falling wide open. It must have been like seeing a stranger.

'Father . . . welcome home,' Nick said, his voice a little strained. He wasn't sociable at the best of times and hated meeting new people, so my heart swelled with pride at his effort.

Father pulled out the chair opposite, next to Mother, and took a seat. He didn't say anything.

'I'm Nick,' Nick said, and my heart broke. 'I've been learning about botany. Do you also like unusual plants? I can tell you about some if you like.' His sentences were halting and awkward, with none of the ease he had with Mother and me.

Mother bit her lip nervously and placed a hand on Father's shoulder to encourage him. Father stared blankly ahead, and the only thing that broke the intense silence in the room was that awful, terrifying ticking sound.

'He can't speak,' I said finally. 'Can you ... can you speak?' I asked Father, emboldened by the small flicker of connection we'd had outside his room. He snapped alert, as if pulled out of a dream.

He shook his head. His hand hovered at the scarf and then became a fist. He looked trapped, like a caged animal, and I wondered what thoughts lay beneath the surface. He slammed his fist down on the table, a ripple of rage moving through him, and then he burst up, knocking his chair down as he fled the room. Mother's eyes grew wide, and Nick started to quietly whimper.

The delicate equilibrium I'd tried to maintain for my family was shattering already.

Mr Reed appeared at the door. He cleared his throat, no doubt feeling the tension in the room. 'Mister Felix, a caller on the line for you. I've left the receiver off the hook.'

Leaving Nick and Mother at that moment felt like leaving a shattered glass on the floor. And yet I also felt flooded with relief – it was physically easier to breathe outside of the stifling atmosphere of the dining room.

I lifted the cold metal receiver of the candlestick telephone to my ear.

'Who is it?' I asked, bristling slightly.

'A Miss Bouwmeester on the line,' the operator drawled. *Lois.*

'Connect,' I said, but my voice was reduced to a hoarse gasp. Not that long ago, it had been normal for us to have long telephone conversations that went on late into the evening – talking about her interest in art and the techniques she had been attempting to imitate in her own drawing, or me describing the latest addition to the Collection. It had been so easy.

Lois and I had grown up learning to navigate the same parties, the same social conventions. In most circumstances, she was the person who understood me best. We had something special before I ruined it.

The last time I'd seen her was in the summer – I had just begun to wonder whether what we were actually doing was courting, although neither of us had said as much. One of Lois's schoolfriends had booked out the top floor of a Manhattan hotel called The Lunar for her eighteenth birthday. I picked Lois up from her place on the other side of the bay. She had convinced her brother, Conrad, to cover for her if her father rang that evening to check up on them, to say that Lois was unwell and couldn't come to the telephone. Mr Bouwmeester was a high-profile lawyer and was rarely home, so it wasn't difficult for Lois to negotiate the freedom to do the things she wanted to do. In fact, the surprising turn of events would have been if he called at all.

Lois had worn a blue party dress that matched the colour of her eyes. Her hair was bobbed fashionably along the side of her jaw. As she slid into the passenger seat, the sweet caramel notes of her perfume had filled the car.

Later that evening, we'd sat by the window of the suite, looking at the twinkling skyline. Little flasks of gin and vodka had been doing the rounds among the revellers, but Lois and I were just content in each other's company. While everyone around us lost their heads and their clarity, we had sat talking about the future.

'I started working on my admissions essays for college,' she said, her voice filled with tenacity. 'A woman got a PhD in psychology from Brown a few years ago. I don't see why that shouldn't be me too.'

'I see no reason either,' I said. If anyone was going to achieve the goals they set their mind to, it was Lois.

But I hated to imagine her leaving to go to college. I had already started to feel that it wasn't an option for me. It wasn't that I didn't care about my education or didn't want to go – I had hoped to study to become a lawyer – but it had begun to seem so utterly unachievable for me. How was I supposed to move away from home when I could barely keep a grip on my mind? Let alone think about leaving Mother and Nick . . .

'Have you thought much about it?' she asked.

'What – going to college?'

She nodded.

I flinched. 'I just don't see how I can.'

'Why not?'

'It's not that simple,' I snapped.

'Because of your mother and Nick?'

'And all the terrible things that could happen – to them, to me.'

Lois was the only person besides Mother and Geoffrey that I'd confided in about the way my thoughts had become increasingly irrational.

'It's not surprising that you feel that way, after

everything you've been through. But, Felix . . .' She looked nervous, and then she suggested what was on her mind. 'There's this growing practice called psychotherapy. It might help.'

The suggestion had immediately made me bridle. 'So that's it. You think I'm insane. Is that why you've been spending time with me? To have someone to study for an admissions essay? So you can say you've got hands-on experience?'

Lois looked shocked and deeply hurt. 'Felix, that's an awful thing to say. You know that's not true. Don't be like this.'

But I couldn't stop. My feelings were getting jumbled – jealousy at her freedom, desperation at the thought of her leaving, and underneath everything the judder of fear. 'Well then, I think you need to learn when to shut your mouth.'

'The way you're behaving is really ugly,' Lois said, shaking her head. 'I'm not going to let you speak to me like this.' Grim distaste was splashed all over her face.

I knew I'd gone too far.

Lois paused. She was waiting for me to do better, be better. And I just . . . couldn't.

'This isn't you, Felix,' she said, and she stormed away from me, left the party early, arranged for a friend to take her home.

I think I knew, if I could bring myself to call and say sorry, that she was kind enough to be able to forgive me. But I was too ashamed. She was still the voice I wanted to hear most when I was feeling hopeless, but it was easier to push her away. What did I have to offer her? I was anxious, angry, increasingly reclusive, frightened of everything . . . I would just hold her back, clip her wings, or, worse, impart my fearfulness to her. I had hurt her.

Better to be the one to run than the one left in the dust.

The distance kept us both safe. She deserved to find someone who dreamed as large as she did. Meanwhile, Mother took me out of school, and I became more reclusive by the day. Lois and I hadn't spoken in months. Until now. Now she had finally called.

The line connected. 'Felix.'

The husky catch of Lois's voice felt like a punch in my chest. It sounded as if she were standing right next to me. My mind was flooded with the image of her – her smooth honeyed locks, the round curve of her cheeks, the flick of her nose, the soft pink of her lips.

'Hello,' I replied, after taking a moment to compose myself.

'Hello. Listen, Felix, I have a favour to ask you.'

She sounded so businesslike – there was none of the warmth she usually emanated. I supposed that was fair – I owed her a huge apology. And if she needed a favour, well then, of course I'd try to help if I could.

'What do you need?'

'I've been invited to a college interview in the new year. I was wondering if you could put in a good word with Geoffrey for me. Could you ask if he'd be willing to give me some tutorials to prep?'

Geoffrey still volunteered on the Board of Admissions

for his alma mater. I had no doubt he'd help Lois if I asked, but the timing was dreadful.

'That's incredible about the interview. I wish I could help, but I . . . Things are a bit complicated here,' I said, and the familiar twin spectres of shame and guilt peered over my shoulder.

'Oh. I understand,' she said, sounding deflated.

'I mean . . . of course I'll ask him, but . . .' I paused. Should I tell her? 'Lois, my father's come home. Tutoring has been . . . paused. I don't know when I'll see Geoffrey next.'

'Your father is back?' The shock in her voice was palpable. 'Are you okay?'

'You know me well enough to know that I'll be fine,' I said.

'I know you well enough to know that you bury things as far down as you can, and you'd rather push people away than let them get close enough to help you.'

'Is that something you read for your admissions essay? It sounds like it could be from an introduction to psychology,' I said, deflecting – again – when what I really wanted to do was apologize. She had seen right through me, and even though I desperately wanted to be seen, I just kept pulling on a mask.

'You don't need to be so sharp with me,' Lois said.

'I'm sorry,' I said. 'I'm getting this all wrong.'

'No, no.' She sighed. 'I understand. I should just take the hint that you don't want to speak to me ever again, right?'

When she said that, it split me in two. I wanted to tell her that the reason I'd stopped seeing her, stopped calling her, was because I had been frightened. That I was still frightened.

'You're the closest friend I've ever had,' I said, before I talked myself out of it, stopping just short of pouring out everything I felt for her. 'I know I've been awful, and that I disappeared, but I don't want to be this way.'

Trying to explain filled me with something akin to emotional pins and needles, but it felt very necessary.

'Okay,' she said quietly. 'Well, the way I feel about you hasn't changed, you know. I want to help you.' The warmth of her voice that I knew so well was back.

'Can I see you?' I asked.

'Is this you trying to apologize?' she asked.

'Yes. I'm sorry,' I said. 'Truly sorry.'

She hesitated, and my heart stopped while I waited for her to speak. 'I'm still here for you,' she said. 'But if you ever do a disappearing act on me again, next time I won't be. I know you're scared, but you still have a choice about the way you treat people.'

After she'd disconnected, I stayed by the telephone for a moment, still clutching the receiver to my ear. Hoping that I would have the guts to abandon the defences and fortifications I had built to protect myself and really, truly let her in again.

Before it was too late.

14 NOVEMBER 1920

TWENTY-EIGHT DAYS LEFT

7

I woke the following morning with a heavy heart. Twenty-eight days left. What to do with them? Twenty-eight days. Not enough time to make any of my ambitions come true. My dream of inviting a public audience to the Collection was dying. As I came down the stairs with a notebook full of museum plans tucked under my arm, I saw Father waiting at the bottom. His eyes were searching, desperate, and he was clutching something close to his chest. Even though it wasn't very large, it took both of his trembling hands to offer it to me – a gift.

I took it from him. It was a leather journal embossed with an unnerving symbol – a ghoulish set of skeletal wings protruding from a detailed anatomical heart. It was at once eerily familiar and grotesque, as though it had been in the corner of my vision before now – and yet I could not place it. Surely I would remember if I'd seen it before? It was so unsettling.

Beneath the image was an inscription in elegant calligraphy, stamped into the leather: IMPERIUM MORTIS. The words oozed with an ominous energy, like black tar.

I'd heard that phrase once before. When Father was packing to leave, I overheard an argument between him and Mother. It wasn't like their usual screaming matches. This time, they spoke in low tones, but the anger was palpable.

'I'm telling you – Imperium Mortis are the answer.' Father's words were brittle. 'Leery is the only person who can help me undo it.'

'You just said yourself, you've never even met him! And you're going to leave us? Plunge head first into danger?' Mother snapped in return.

'I have to go,' he'd said. 'For the sake of our sons.'

'I can't listen to any more of this, Alfred. If the things you're telling me are true, then I should hate you for what you've done to this family,' Mother hissed, and then I'd heard the warning clack of her shoes on the parquet floor and bolted before she caught me eavesdropping.

'I didn't know, Gracie!' Father had called after her. 'How could I have known the cost?'

None of it made any sense to me at the time, and it made even less sense as I held the journal in my hands. What was Imperium Mortis? Why had Father left us for it? What was he trying to achieve?

I opened the cover – the first page read *Dr Hugo Leery* in a scratchy hand. It was the doctor that Father had planned to meet with when he left to join the war. He was the one who had treated Father and sent the telegram.

'You took this from the sanatorium?' I asked him.

He nodded. I wanted more. Just a murmur of affirmation would do, but all he could give me was that awful wheeze, catch, crackle and the *tick-tick-tick* sound. His eyes were intensely focused.

I flicked through the book – page after page of the same spiky handwriting, tall, pointed letters whose order refused to reveal recognizable words. It made for a stream of confusion. The journal was written in code.

Before Father left, we had often used cryptograms to communicate about the Collection. It was just a game really. Hidden messages. It seemed that he'd given me another one to play.

Father tapped the book. He lifted his trembling hands, hands that had once been so strong, now unable to button his own shirt or hold a pen steady enough to make his thoughts known. It seemed to frustrate him so terribly, the inability to communicate.

'You want me to solve it.'

He nodded his head, and closed his eyes then, as if he were finally able to find enough peace to rest for just a moment.

'Okay, I promise,' I said. 'I'll solve it.'

Father reached for me and wrapped his arms around me, the journal pressed between us. For a moment, I was comforted. He was still my father, and he *loved* me. With my head resting on his chest, I could hear, clearer than ever, the unsettling ticking sound where his heartbeat should be. My stomach churned. I wasn't imagining it. What had happened to him over there?

I took the journal back to my room. Before I had a chance to thoroughly assess what I was working with, I was interrupted by the arrival of Mother.

'Knock, knock,' she called through the wood.

Even my teeth felt on edge. Father couldn't tell me what Imperium Mortis was, or why I needed to solve this journal – but Mother could.

'Come in.'

She perched on the end of my bed and reached across to tuck my hair behind my ears. I let her do it, although I was desperate to undo her tidying of me.

'I asked Geoffrey about the psychotherapist,' she said. 'Doctor Albass is coming to the house tomorrow to speak with you.'

'Thank you. I promise I'll give it a try,' I said, though really I was sure of no such thing.

The air was heavy between us. I cleared my throat, trying to shift the discomfort and dislodge my unasked question.

'Mother, tell me about Imperium Mortis.'

She froze, a flash of recognition reflected in her eyes. My mouth started to go dry. So she did know who they were.

'Where did you hear that name?' she asked.

I lifted up the journal, showed her the stamp in the leather. 'Father gave me this.' I showed her the encoded pages. 'He wants me to solve it.'

Mother shook her head. 'Oh, Felix . . . I don't know what to say. I hoped this day would never come,' she said. 'I

60

hoped – I *trusted* that your father would be able to mend it, and then you'd never need to hear any of this.'

'Mend what?'

She cleared her throat and began to brush down my quilt, although there were no creases that required her attention. Her dainty mouth twisted out of shape.

'Let me try and start from the beginning. You know that your father had a very different life from yours or mine when he was growing up. But neither of us can really imagine, Felix, what it was like for him. We've never had to worry about money the way his family did. You know he worked in the factory, and then he switched to the railways. He saved every dollar he could.'

'And then he invested it in steel.'

'That he did.'

'And that's how he made his millions.' I'd heard the story a hundred times. 'It's family history.'

Mother winced, as if it were painful to release what came next. 'Yes. But it's not the whole story. Your father believes he's responsible for what happened to your brothers. He told me, after we lost the twins, that he believed it was his fault. It was like a confession. He told me that we'd lost them because he'd meddled with dark magic.'

'Magic?'

Once upon a time, I might have laughed at the suggestion. But I'd seen what had happened to my brothers. I knew what was coming for me next. Now I was apprehensive about knowing more. It felt safer, the not-knowing.

Mother went on. 'I couldn't believe what he was telling me either. Just ... listen. When he had just started Ashe Steel, he was making some good money, but a terrible accident happened at the factory and a man was killed. Your father told me that somehow there was ... magic. In the death.' She paused and took a deep breath. 'Here's what I understand – he was somehow able to catch this magic. He could see it, and he caught it and tucked it inside his wallet, and the magic was trapped inside.'

A memory rose inside me – the sparkling strand released from George's broken body when he died. *Magic in the death*. Was that what I had seen all those years ago?

'After that, the wallet was never empty,' Mother continued. 'Your father filled the accounts; he bought this land; he built this house ...'

Father's wallet. It was a battered, cheaply made thing. He'd always been so protective of it and carried it with him everywhere. We'd always joked that a man of his wealth should have been able to toss it in the trash and purchase a fine leather wallet. I'd always assumed it was sentimental; a symbol of where he'd come from. Now it took on a greater significance.

Somehow the death at Father's factory had allowed him to harness magic. Magic that was responsible for our fortune. The thought made the hairs on the back of my neck rise. I had a sense of it being true, of my body *knowing* that it was true.

'But there was a cost. The Death Magic wanted something in return. A huge inheritance, but no heir. No surviving sons.'

No surviving sons. It was as though Mother had struck a tuning fork inside my chest cavity, and the reverberations hit every nerve ending within me. It was precisely what I'd feared.

I started to cry, the panic rising in the back of my throat. 'I'm going to die, aren't I? Like they did.'

And the way each of them died was so bloody, so painful, so desperate. No peaceful falling to sleep for the victim of a curse.

'Oh, darling, I don't know if I can bring myself to believe it or not.' My mother crawled over to me, wrapped her arms around me. 'I'm sorry. I'm so sorry.' She bit her bottom lip and stared up at the ceiling, trying to blink away the swell of tears.

'Why didn't you tell me?'

'Some things are better off not being known. You've been so anxious, Felix. I didn't want to make things worse. You mustn't tell your brother,' she said.

I wasn't going to tell Nick, but that moment reminded me of the other dark, looming fear inside my heart. That this curse would be coming for him too.

'I won't,' I said. I couldn't bear the idea of him becoming as controlled by fear as I was.

'I've gone over this time and time again in my head, tried to understand, to decide what I believe. Three of my sons died on their eighteenth birthday . . . That's not . . . it's not normal. Believing in a coincidence that large and that horrible takes the same leap of faith as believing it was something magical.'

'I don't think it's a coincidence,' I said quietly. 'I've felt for a long, long time that there was something wrong with this family, that what happened to my brothers would happen to me. Why do you think I am the way I am?'

The creeping dread was part of me.

'Felix . . .' Mother's expression was pained.

We both fell into silence.

'I'm frightened,' I said simply. My fear filled the space between us. A cold feeling settled inside me. 'If it is real, then I'm next.'

'Please, darling – don't be frightened. We can't know if it's true or not. It all just sounds so fantastical, doesn't it . . .?' She trailed off. 'We have no way of knowing whether to believe in it or not.'

And yet . . . I knew. It was a confirmation of what I'd feared for a long time. I had long felt the presence of misfortune nudging at the edge of our lives.

I turned the leather journal over in my hands, rubbed my thumbs across the stamped insignia. Mother watched me closely.

'When your father started collecting, he was hoping to find someone else who had seen the same phenomenon as he had seen. It was without success . . . until he found Imperium Mortis. They seem to be some sort of underground secret faction. Your father wouldn't tell me much, except that he'd met this Doctor Leery. He trusted that Leery had the answer to undoing it all, that he could save you and Nick from the magic, and so Father followed him . . . into the war.'

My father had put his faith in Imperium Mortis and Hugo Leery. The book in my hands was an invitation into a world of secret dealings and magic born from death . . . And maybe, just maybe, it was the key to releasing the grip of darkness, the key to surviving.

I didn't dare allow that moment of hope to take flight from my chest, and instead I cradled it up tight inside.

15 NOVEMBER 1920

TWENTY-SEVEN DAYS LEFT

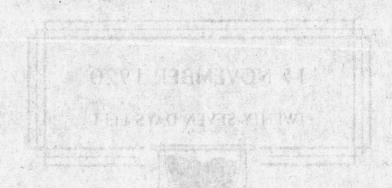

8

Preparing for Dr Albass to arrive, I ran a comb through my hair, appraising myself in the mirror and practising holding a neutral expression. If I had to be seen by a psychotherapist, reveal the inner workings of my mind and ask for help in taming it, then I had to maintain the appearance of someone sensible and considered.

I realized my face was more angular than it used to be. When I was still in school, I was thicker around the chin, rounder in the cheeks, but all of that had melted away. My eyes were wired and overly alert, constantly searching for danger.

A laugh nearly burst out of me. I had worried that the therapist would think I was insane, and that was before I'd begun to obsess about secret societies with gruesome insignia and knowledge of powerful magic that grew out of death.

It wasn't as though I could tell Dr Albass the true origin of my fears, or the way they'd been validated. I needed to keep a lid on it, keep the conversation based in the real and the tangible . . . but letting out even the tiniest bit of steam

69

must surely be better than continuing to boil my brains in a stew of worries.

I met Mother outside the sunroom, where Dr Albass waited inside.

'Here goes nothing,' I said, trying to make light of the tension bunching in my shoulders by shrugging them nonchalantly. Mother gave my arm an encouraging squeeze. I took a deep breath and entered.

Dr Albass filled the space with her gargantuan frame. Her spectacles were slightly skewed, but she had a meticulously neat bun fastening her red hair on top of her head, the scraping back so thorough that it pulled her forehead tight. The way she was dressed was striking too, as she wore a pair of tan high-waisted trousers. She was not what I had been expecting.

'Felix, hello. Please take a seat,' she said, gesturing towards the chaise longue.

'I don't know how this is meant to work,' I said as I made my way over.

'We're just going to talk,' Dr Albass replied. 'I'll ask you some questions, and I want you to answer as honestly as you feel able to. Everything we discuss here will remain confidential.' She settled herself in a chair nearby.

'You won't tell anyone what I say?' There was some comfort in that, at least.

'I won't tell anyone. The only exception would be, say, if I thought you were going to hurt someone, or hurt yourself.'

I considered the possibility that perhaps I wasn't about to be carted off to an asylum, even if I was honest with Dr

Albass about the thoughts I'd been having. I didn't want to hurt anyone, and I didn't want to hurt myself. I was just . . . terrified of awful things happening.

'Do you think you could tell me about what's been happening recently?' Dr Albass asked calmly.

I tried to damp down the thoughts about magic. I couldn't let any of that begin to spill out. I didn't mean to be obstinate, but I just couldn't seem to find a route into talking to her. I just kept thinking about the magic, about the darkness, about all the things that I couldn't say. It was like entering a labyrinth and bumping up against dead end after dead end.

'My father just came home.'

Dr Albass made a gentle sound of affirmation to indicate that she'd heard me; it turned up a little at the end, the inflection prompting me to continue.

'He went away to war. He volunteered and . . . he was injured. Since he left, I've had these thoughts. All the time,' I said, and then my throat clammed up.

'What kind of thoughts?'

'I'm always frightened.'

'Can you tell me some more about the thoughts that frighten you?' she prompted, and her voice was softer somehow with this question.

'They push their way into my brain. It's always the worst-case scenario of what could happen. I try to squash them, but that makes them stronger . . . Sometimes I feel like I'm going to die.'

'Can you describe what that's like, in your body?'

I took a deep breath, but I couldn't stop myself from shaking. 'My heart leaps inside me, as though somebody were squeezing it. It's like a punch in the chest. My fingers go numb, and the breath gets stolen out of me.'

The panic really started to rise in me then, describing it to her. All the familiar sensations started to flood through me.

'Do you think you can help me?' I asked, and it sounded like I was begging.

'I do,' Dr Albass said, and just the tiniest bit of relief sparked within me. 'But it can be a lengthy process. There are some recent studies that have begun to suggest that we experience a real physical reaction in our body when we're affected by something emotionally. Usually, this is a helpful thing because it helps us to flee a dangerous situation or fight a predator. It's called fight or flight. When this response happens at inappropriate moments, it can cause great distress.

'I believe that the solution to these emotional struggles lies somewhere in our past or underneath the surface, and that, by unlocking where this response comes from, we can find relief in the present. If you allow it to work its way through your system and then leave again, you'll notice that you can start to slow down your breathing, slow down your thoughts, and the feeling will begin to pass. This mental rehearsal of the things we're afraid of is our brain's way of trying to protect us.'

Fight or flight. It made sense, and my body felt the truth of it. The fears stimulated my desire to run away or attack. It would be useful if the danger were physical, but, when it was internal, the impulse remained trapped inside my body, tremoring, making me sick.

Perhaps there was a way out of the panic after all. Maybe it was just an illness like any other. If that were the case, then maybe it could be cured.

The hope was almost too much to bear.

Dr Albass and I spoke a little longer, and at the end of the hour she shared one final thought with me. 'You know, Felix, when we are experiencing heightened anxiety, we often overestimate the likelihood of something terrible happening, and we underestimate our ability to cope if the terrible something does come to pass.'

She told me that she would await a call from Mother if we wished to proceed with regular sessions, and I let her out of the front door, feeling a lightness of heart that was unfamiliar.

That's when the shot reverberated out from upstairs, an echoing blast that circled down the staircase.

9

Energy coursed through my body. When I reached the third-floor landing, Nick poked his head out from his bedroom doorway.

'What was that?' His eyes were wary.

'Go downstairs.' My voice was a snarl.

'I heard a bang,' he said, pointing at Father's study. I'd known, instinctively, that the sound had come from there. I held on to the newel post at the top of the bannister to steady myself.

'I said go downstairs!' I shouted. He jumped, and I was struck by a pang of guilt as he catapulted himself down towards Mother, who was standing at the bottom of the steps, ready to scoop him into her arms, her eyes wide and fearful.

The door to Father's study was shut. I approached it with caution. Something irreparable had happened behind that door. I knew it in my very bones. Taking a breath, I turned the ornamental doorknob. The door was locked – from the inside. The latch had been pulled across. I rapped gently with my knuckle, but as I expected there was no response. My dread increased, and my breathing became shallow and quick. I pounded my flat palm against the wood, but of course it was futile.

I wanted to give up, walk away from the door as if there were nothing behind it. I knew what I was going to find, and I wanted to live in the moment where it hadn't happened yet.

But Nick and Mother needed me, as they always did, to take control of the situation and protect them from it.

I ran to my bedroom to grab my pocketknife instead. I jimmied the edge of the blade between the latch and the doorjamb. Just as I thought the blade of the knife was about to snap, the latch gave in, like the release of a breath. I went in.

My father was sitting in his chair, his neck at an awful angle.

The back of his head was gone.

A splatter of gore on the wall kept drawing my eye. The red scarf still covered the bottom half of his face, where all the damage from the war hid.

My stomach tumbled over, and I emptied its contents all over the floor. After a second or two of retching, I looked up again, my head spinning.

I saw that behind my father the mounted shotgun that was usually fastened to the wall had swung away from its frame. The wire that should have held the barrel of the gun firm to the frame had gone loose and slack, but still linked the two so that the gun remained attached to the wall.

It had been an accident.

75

It had been an awful accident so unbelievable I was unable to accept its truth. The number of times I'd been in this study, yet I never knew the gun was even loaded.

A cold numbness spread through my chest in the place where I knew sorrow would take root. I had grown the sensation of loss before, remembered that the seeds of grief could take time to sprout.

Something childish in me wanted to call for Mother, as if she would be a comfort or a help. But I couldn't let her see this. I was seeing this so she and Nick would never have to.

I drew nearer to the figure of my father, and touched his hand, still warm. I half expected him to jump to life. His left hand was clenched into a fist, the tiniest flick of white poking out of his grip and catching my eye. Wait. A piece of paper?

I unfurled his fingers, and it fell to the ground, like a lost feather from a bird. I picked it up; it was sodden with sweat. There was a splatter in the corner.

Printed neatly on one side was my father's name – *Alfred Ashe* – and beneath that it read *15 November 1920, 12 p.m.*

I glanced at the clock ticking away on his desk. It confirmed what I thought the paper was saying – it dictated the exact moment he had died. Midday. I turned the paper over. On the other side of the slip, there was an official stamp in ink. It was the insignia of Imperium Mortis – the wings made from bones and the anatomically correct outline of the heart from the cover of the leather journal.

Father had believed that dark magic was at the centre of the tragedies that had befallen our family, and had trusted Imperium Mortis and Dr Leery to help him find a way to break its hold on us.

Instead, all that we had was his broken body. As if enough blood hadn't been spilled here: Luke pierced through the chest in his car, Scott and his dashed-in head, and George, impaled on the spearheads. And now Father.

I couldn't stay in the room any longer with the stench of blood. I stumbled out, dazed and weak, and took the stairs down.

Nick was tucked beneath Mother's arm. I turned to them, unsure of how to say what had happened. It was clear that Mother knew already. Her eyes filled with tears.

'Nick, go to the library and find something to read. I need to speak to Mother alone.'

He didn't move.

'Oh no, oh no!' Mother cried, and it sounded almost ridiculous the way she wailed. She drew her hands to her lips as if in prayer.

I was numb. Father was dead, but the words meant nothing.

Mother began to shake, her knees buckling. She knelt on the floor, curving her feet underneath her and curling over into a ball. 'Not again, not again, not again,' she whimpered.

Nick started to cry. For the second time, I found myself snapping at him. 'I said go!'

He skittered away down the corridor, glancing over his shoulder at Mother, all curled up. I rubbed her back, feeling the hard pearls of bone that made up her spine through the light satin of her dress.

'We need to call the police,' I told her. She startled beneath my fingers as if a current of electricity had run through her.

'No, I can't bear it.'

'We need to report it immediately,' I said. 'It will look suspicious if we don't.'

'He did this to himself, didn't he?' she whispered.

'No,' I said. I wedged my hand underneath her armpit to help her back up.

'He didn't?'

'It looks all wrong, like a freak accident. The shotgun on the wall broke away from its frame and discharged.'

Mother shook her head. 'That's not possible.'

She was right. It shouldn't be possible. It seemed so implausible. And yet ... the evidence was what it was. I decided not to tell her about the slip of paper – she already had enough fear and distrust of the name Imperium Mortis. That piece of information could wait.

'We have to call the police,' I said. 'Any detective worth their salt is going to query what's happened up there, and it's the only way to avoid drawing suspicion upon ourselves. We don't want them thinking we murdered him. The timing is already suspicious enough.'

I called the station and told them the bare minimum – an accidental, fatal gunshot wound. I sat Mother down in the drawing room and asked Mr Reed to bring her a cup of herbal tea. We waited. Her soft hand reached for my face, the scent of her lavender hand cream cloying after the iron smell of Father's blood. The two mingled in my senses, winding together like ivy. I would never again be able to smell lavender and be soothed – instead, from that moment on, it would always remind me of the day my father died.

10

It was less than an hour till I heard the rapping on our door that signalled the arrival of the police. Two officers stood on the doorstep – one was a broad man with tired creases across his face, as if he had been doing this a very long time; the other was brighter, younger, with eager eyes that made him look like a stoat.

The older man took his helmet off, revealing a balding head. 'Good afternoon, young man. I'm Sergeant Brady, and this is Officer Burton. Our sympathies to you and your family.'

'Thank you, officer. He's upstairs,' I said. I gestured for them to come inside. The younger one gazed around the hallway with an awestruck expression.

'Would you be able to tell us what happened?' Brady asked.

'There's a decorative shotgun in his study,' I said. 'It came loose from the wall and discharged . . . through his head.' I touched my own head at the back. The officers grimaced simultaneously.

'Can you take us to the body?'

I walked them up to the study. 'He was in the war,' I said before opening the door. 'His face was injured. That's why he has the scarf.'

'You don't need to come in again.'

I wondered if Sergeant Brady had a son of his own. I closed the door behind them and listened with my ear pressed up to the wood.

'What a mess,' Burton was whining. I should have warned them I'd vomited. 'How does an accident like this even happen?'

My heart began to thud. Of course they were bound to be suspicious. It seemed so improbable.

'I think we're looking at a suicide,' Brady replied. 'Terribly sad. A lot of these soldiers can't cope with life any more when they come home. Makes the difference between their life now and their life then all the more stark, you know?'

Suicide. Perhaps it was for the best if they drew a conclusion that meant it would all be resolved swiftly, without further questions.

I shuffled back from the door and waited for the officers to reappear. As the younger one went to collect a body bag from their vehicle, Brady cleared his throat. 'I need you to tell me the truth. Did you mount the gun back on the wall, so it would look like an accident?'

Panic flooded through me. He was asking me to confirm that my father killed himself, and that I had tampered with the scene to make it look like an accident. My mouth gaped and closed as I reached for a response that wouldn't form.

Ultimately, if Father's body ended up in front of a coroner, there would be questions asked – the angle of the entry wound was strange, and the story that a decorative gun broke away from its frame and discharged itself even stranger. Yet another bizarre accident at Pitch House. How could a supernatural death possibly be understood by the law? I needed to make sure that it didn't turn into a murder investigation, so I had no choice.

'Yes. He did it himself,' I said.

'I know.' Brady's mouth twisted. 'You meant well, and it's a real tragedy. I can't lie in my official report, but I can promise that I'll be discreet. We can arrange a swift cremation.'

Cremation. The modern way. More efficient in terms of turnaround. I nodded. This was for the best.

Burton returned with a thick black bag. My stomach heaved at the idea that Father's body would leave our home inside it.

I turned away, wishing I could block my ears against the sound of their clumsy movements and grunts as they hefted his body out of the study and down the stairs. I felt as though I'd been hollowed out.

Once they had gone, Mother made a telephone call. 'He's dead, Geoffrey,' she managed to choke out. 'You must come at once.'

We waited for him in the drawing room. The delicately striped curtains were drawn tight, and the fire in the grate was alive, but only just, and the combination of the two made the room seem almost cosy. Setting down the herbal tea that Lydia had thoughtfully brought her, Mother opened up the disguised liquor cabinet that appeared to be a globe at first glance. She poured a glass of brandy from her secret stash. She'd found a way of keeping her stocks replenished despite Prohibition, and I was certain that Simpkins, the groundskeeper, had something to do with it.

Mother's eyes were swollen and her lipstick was haphazard and bleeding. I sat waiting with her, the pair of us silent.

When Geoffrey arrived, he offered her comfort instantly.

'You can't blame yourself,' he said. 'It was a terrible accident. The timing is just awful – home for fewer than twenty-four hours . . .'

I left her sobbing in his arms and went to find Nick. Once again, my attempts at creating a delicate peace for my little brother had been blown apart.

'Father's gone again, hasn't he?' Nick asked, slipping his hand into mine.

'Yes,' I said. 'He's gone.'

'I saw the black bag.'

'You did, huh?'

'I shouldn't have been looking, but I was.'

'I'm sorry I yelled at you,' I said, looking at my feet. 'You know I wouldn't normally.'

'He's dead.' Nick's voice was stark, cold.

I didn't know what to say to that, besides making a noise that confirmed it. I had nothing left to give him of myself. I was utterly drained.

In my pocket, crumpled, was the slip of paper prised from Father's death grip. In the horror of the aftermath I hadn't come to terms with what it seemed to mean. It was decorated with the insignia of Imperium Mortis, and it accurately recorded the exact moment of Father's death – which meant that somehow they had known that this was going to happen.

The dark magic that haunted our family wasn't finished with us yet.

And, unless I could uncover a way to defeat it, it was going to claim me, and Nick, too, as time inevitably passed.

I determined then and there, with Nick's little hand in my own, that I was going to find out more. I would get to the bottom of the darkness and find a way to free our futures from its clutching grasp.

11

That evening, I sat with Leery's journal on my knee, flicking through it, looking for recurring letters.

'A good place to start with ciphers is substitutions,' I recalled Father teaching me. *'The most simplistic being the monoalphabetic.'*

Monoalphabetic substitution was where each letter of the alphabet had been replaced with another, but still in order, so you could write side by side; for example, A is B, B is C, C is D would be the first option out of twenty-six. The key was finding out which option was being used.

As most people probably realize, the most common letter in the English language is E. If Dr Leery had used a monoalphabetic substitution, then the letter that appeared most frequently throughout the notebook was most likely standing in for the letter E, and from there it would be a simple process to decipher the code used and then begin the long process of transcribing, which could take hours and hours.

But I found no single dominant letter. Dr Leery must have used something more complex. He'd created a deeper layer than the purest cipher of replacing one letter with another. Too easily solved.

'The next thing to try is a polyalphabetic cipher.'

Father's voice was so present, it was as though he were sitting next to me, coaching me through the process. I could almost smell his wood-sage cologne.

'People use a keyword, several letters long, and that acts as the key to which set of substitutions to use for each letter. So, if I were to use your name, Felix, then I'd begin with my first letter using an A/F substitution, my second an A/E, my third an A/L, my fourth an A/I and my fifth an A/X. Then I'd start again from the beginning. Do you follow me?'

I remembered him writing out six versions of the alphabet, one ordinary alphabet, and one based on each of the letters in my name, side by side. He showed me how to encrypt and decrypt a simple message. 'Most people use something they love, or the names and places important to them, as a keyword for their own ciphers,' Father had said.

But I didn't know anything about Leery. I certainly couldn't anticipate what sort of word he might have used. I scribbled out the alphabets I would need to use if the keyword were LEERY, just as an experiment, but all that gave me when I used it to decrypt the first line of the journal was a string of gobbledegook.

I closed the journal again. It would take a long time to work out what it said. Time I didn't have.

Running my hands over the leather cover, I noticed it was a slip concealing an ordinary notebook. I peeled the slip away, releasing the journal from its skin, and out fell several sheets of patients' notes. I felt a thrum of excitement. This appeared to be progress.

The notes were not in code; they looked like they had been torn from an inpatient record – name, date of birth, last-known address, next of kin, rank or role in the war. There were four such pages in total, with one belonging to Father.

And, finally, the last sheet behind the patient records was a list of names and dates and times.

- Alfred Ashe – 15 November 1920, 12 p.m.
- Bradley Cooke – 16 November 1920, 12 p.m.
- Chuck Hardaway – 17 November 1920, 12 p.m.
- Vaughan Jenkins – 18 November 1920, 12 p.m.

Apart from Father's, I didn't know any of the names. The image of the other veterans stumbling off the boat with Father, all in differing but severe states of injury, came flooding back. Could they be the other men on this list?

I was collecting pieces of evidence bit by bit, and I laid out what I had found: the slip of paper that Father had died clutching, with the exact moment of his death inscribed upon it; the list that followed the same pattern – four men, four dates and the same time; a small sheaf of papers with what were probably confidential patient records for each of the men; and the journal, its secrets locked behind what I assumed was a polyalphabetic cipher, with a keyword I would have to discover if I wanted to know what it said.

Father had wanted me to see these notes, had brought them across the ocean for me so I could find out the truth. He'd only followed Leery into the war in the first place because he trusted that he was going to find a way for Nick and me to survive the grip of the magic.

It looked as though Dr Leery had been able to accurately predict the moment that each of his patients was going to die. If I was right, then the list with the names on was a guide to who would die next. They were all lined up like dominoes, each of them waiting their turn to fall. It all seemed so calculated, as if designed to send a message. People don't just die in a row like that, in a predetermined fashion. It was *more* plausible to believe there was some invisible magic hand playing the game. I snorted. My understanding of the word *plausible* had been stretched so far that it seemed an odd bar to hold things up against.

But I had a feeling.

Dr Leery had not just predicted when these soldiers would die, he had *dictated* it. I was sure of it. They were like mechanical toys sent out into the world, waiting for their clockwork to wind down and stop. And somehow it was all connected to Imperium Mortis, that secret society of dark magic.

I looked at the next name on the list. Bradley Cooke. I shuffled through to find his patient notes – a quick check told me his last-known address had been an apartment in a Brooklyn tenement.

I would go and find Bradley Cooke. I would ask him my questions.

If Dr Leery had the power to manipulate death itself, then I needed to know, and I needed to find him, because that skill was perhaps the only thing that could save me from the curse. If Leery was able to control death – well then, why shouldn't he be able to control mine? Why shouldn't he be able to release me from the curse counting down to my birthday?

I would not wait one second longer for life and death to just happen to me. I was going to take matters into my own hands.

Even though it was getting late, there was one person I longed to speak to, and if I was going to tell her everything, then I had to act immediately, before I began to second-guess myself. I needed to share all this with Lois. I needed to know if she would draw the same conclusions I had drawn from the evidence. Whatever she made of it, I was certain her perspective would help me understand what I was in the middle of. More than that, though, it would be good not to feel so alone.

I went downstairs to the telephone, remembering the late-night phone calls that Lois and I had shared during the summer when we were at our closest. Her father was nearly always away on business trips, meeting with his clients or doing research, so we were never interrupted or prevented from talking for as long as we wanted.

The operator connected me, and it was Lois's brother, Conrad, who answered.

'I thought you and Lois broke up,' he said when he realized it was me.

'No . . . I . . .' I stammered, lost for words. I wanted to explain that you couldn't break something that hadn't been put together in the first place.

'Well, that's good news,' he said. 'I always thought you were right for each other.'

The chord that comment struck within me was significant, but all I could do was bluster. Conrad handed over the receiver.

'Felix,' Lois said. 'Have you changed your mind about the tutoring?'

'Father's dead,' I blurted.

'What?' There was genuine horror in her voice.

'It's true. And what I'm going to say next will sound very strange, but you just have to listen until I've explained it all.'

'Haven't I always listened to you?' she murmured. I thought of the hours we'd talked. She'd never been judgemental before. 'Go on,' she said.

I didn't know where to start. I cleared my throat and told her about the encoded journal that Father had given to me. I told her about Imperium Mortis, and magic made from death, and how everything fit together, tracing back before I was born to that fatal moment in the factory and the wallet.

'If I don't get to the bottom of this, then I'm going to die too.' I was desperate.

But Lois sounded doubtful. More than doubtful. 'You're scaring me, Felix. Death and magic and secret societies . . . ?'

'It's all true. Don't you see? What happened to my brothers . . .'

'What happened to your brothers was horrific, but it was just an awful series of accidents. You can't really believe that you're going to die on your birthday,' she said. 'It's just your mind playing tricks on you.'

'This is what I was frightened of,' I said. 'You think I'm insane.'

'No, I don't,' she insisted. 'I just think this is your brain's way of trying to cope with the bad things that have happened. And they are terrible, awfully sad things, Felix. I'm not trying to diminish that.'

'You don't understand,' I said. 'I found Father's body. He died in an accident that shouldn't have been possible, and he had this slip of paper in his hand that had the exact moment he died written on it, like a prediction.'

'I see,' Lois said. 'But couldn't he have created that himself if he was going to take his own life? Are you sure that isn't what happened?' She spoke as if I were some kind of animal she might spook.

'I'm sure,' I said. 'Let me show you – you just need to look through these documents and you'll see. Come tomorrow afternoon, and you can draw your own conclusions.'

I knew, though, that by the time Lois came the following day the next soldier would already be dead. I had to track him down first, gather more evidence. I had to find proof that this dark magic was real, and from there perhaps it would be possible to release Nick and me from its twisting, grasping tendrils.

16 NOVEMBER 1920

TWENTY-SIX DAYS LEFT

12

I reread Bradley Cooke's patient notes early in the morning while crunching through a delicate French pastry. He had just turned thirty. A wife was listed as his next of kin. I weighed up my options, hoping to ascertain whether my late-night logic still carried the same significance when I appraised it in the clear light of day.

Dr Hugo Leery and, by extension, Imperium Mortis were the only people who could tell me what had happened to Father. They were also surely the only people who could tell me how to relieve the burden of the curse, if it were even possible. It was clear to me that they had ways of manipulating death itself – and that was something I desperately needed, as my eighteenth birthday drew closer by the day.

When the thoughts started up their chorus – *it's too dangerous, you don't know what you're getting yourself into, this road leads to ruin* – I tried to remember what Dr Albass had told me. As I breathed deeply, the effects of the fear started to wear off before it had a chance to reach the sort of peak that sent me completely to the point of no return.

I couldn't unknow what I knew, and the combination of curiosity and hope was a heady one. Imperium Mortis had the answers, and my life depended on them. Finding the other soldiers was the first step. I needed them to tell me exactly what they knew about Dr Leery and how I could find him.

I planned to set off in the car straight after breakfast and head directly to the address in Bradley's patient notes. I was painfully aware of my time being limited, and that every second was counting down to the moment when Bradley was scheduled to die. Earlier that morning, when I had dressed, I had strapped on a gold-faced wristwatch. I'd need to make sure my timings were accurate.

My plans were disrupted by the sound of a cold, businesslike voice bleeding through the door to the dining room. I heard the words 'police department', and my nerves were set on edge. They weren't supposed to be asking questions. Brady had promised to be discreet.

Brushing the crumbs from my lips, I gathered up the patient notes and tucked them away inside my blazer. I headed out into the hallway, where it was clear that Mother had been summoned from her bedroom before she'd had the chance to properly prepare for the day. She was wrapped up in a silken robe, and her face was bare of make-up for a change. I didn't often see her like that, and it made her look younger and fresher, although her eyes were still swollen from crying the night before.

Mother was speaking to a striking older woman, with hair the colour of white-hot cinders. 'This is Detective

Jones,' she said, gesturing as if she were introducing us at a party.

Jones wore a black shirt with a white collar, and her NYPD badge glittered where it was pinned to her chest. I'd heard that female detectives had been recruited to the force, but I'd never seen one before. She looked as if she were made for the role – her stance was assured, her expression inscrutable, and she seemed utterly at ease with the firearm at her waist.

'You must be Felix,' she said, appraising me with her cool gaze. 'I have some questions to ask you.'

I swallowed, my mind racing.

The police are suspicious about what happened, and there's no way you can tell the truth because then you'd have to start talking about magic, and you'll be branded completely insane . . . But there is no way to explain! There's no way out of this that doesn't end with you being arrested and investigated for murder. This is the way the curse gets you, in the electric chair for your father's murder.

'What do you want to know?'

I tried to keep my voice even and steady, even though beneath the surface I was panicking. I snuck a look at my watch, feeling the pressure of time. Not only did I need to clear our family of suspicion, I also had to reach Bradley Cooke before it was too late.

'I want to hear your account of what happened here yesterday.'

'Of course,' I said, but my thoughts were tangling, struggling, fighting – Brady's official report would say

97

suicide, and so I had to recount a version of events that remained consistent with that.

Mother's gaze flitted around the hallway. She was thinking of the staff, of whether anyone might be listening. 'Why don't you both take a seat in the dining room? I'll have some coffee brought to you.'

Jones took a seat at the table. Stray pastry flakes were strewn in front of her, escaped from my breakfast. I sat down opposite, my chair creaking as I lowered myself into it. Jones watched me, her eyes narrowing slightly. I felt as if she were trying to see inside me, right to the bone and sinew and blood. She produced a small notebook and a pen from her breast pocket. She seemed incredibly comfortable in silence.

Mr Reed arrived with a small trolley, a scalding coffee pot rattling on top of it. He rolled it alongside the table, gave me a reassuring hint of a smile, and then swiftly made his exit.

'None for me,' Jones said.

I poured one for myself, hands shaking.

'Tell me, in your own words, what happened here yesterday.' There was no offer of sympathy, no gentle easing in.

'We heard a gun discharge in Father's study. I went by myself so that Mother and my little brother Nick wouldn't have to see. Father had shot himself using the shotgun that's usually mounted on the wall. I vomited. I called the local police, and they came and took his body.'

I surprised myself with the fluidity of the lie, the way it interwove with the truth.

'Had he given any indication that this was what he intended to do?'

'No,' I said. 'It was a horrible shock. Although, when you consider what he went through, maybe we should have seen it coming.'

'Elaborate.' Jones's eyes glinted.

'He was a soldier during the war. He was injured and was kept at a specialist sanatorium in England for two years. He couldn't speak because of his injuries, and he couldn't write because his hands shook so badly.' I was surprised by the prick of tears at the memory of buttoning my father's shirt.

'How awful. I'm so sorry. What do you know about the sanatorium where he was based?'

I shrugged, a performance of nonchalance. 'Very little. We received a telegram informing us that he'd be staying there, and then a telegram more recently from his doctor, saying that he was being sent home, but that's all.'

'Who was his doctor?'

'The name given was Leery.'

She wrote that down. 'What do you know about this doctor?'

'Nothing,' I said.

I wondered if she sensed that there was something unusual about Leery, about the sanatorium. If so, she didn't give anything away.

'And your father – did he leave anything behind? A note?'

'No,' I said, thinking of the slip of paper that dictated

the exact moment of his death, of the encoded journal and the patient notes. These were clues that Father had left for me and nobody else, and I was determined not to reveal any of this to Detective Jones. I wouldn't let Father down. I would follow the trail he had left me.

Perhaps my discomfort at lying was beginning to show on my face because Detective Jones's expression became even more severe. 'You're certain of that?'

'He left nothing,' I said, hoping I sounded convincing.

'I think that's all I need to ask for now,' she said, slotting her notebook and pen away and standing abruptly.

After she left, Mother was panicky. 'There's something going on, isn't there? What did that detective want with you?'

My eye caught the grandfather clock, its pendulum swinging back and forth and reminding me that I had a limited window in which to find Bradley Cooke. I was experiencing a new sensitivity to time. Every second had acquired a gravity that it didn't have before.

'I need to go.' I cut her off and slammed the door behind me as I stepped out into the freezing cold. A layer of frost twinkled like a constellation of stars captured and anchored in the ground, and, when I breathed out, a hot plume formed in the air.

The wooden doors of the garage were fastened with a hefty padlock. I slid the key inside, and the lock opened with a thick, satisfying clunk. The cars were lined up as if they were sleeping in their stalls, just waiting for me.

I picked out the Abbott-Detroit roadster. Shiny. A deep ocean blue. That one had always been my favourite. It had *character*. Luke had taught me to drive in it. The polished leather seat squeaked beneath me as I got comfortable and forced myself to try and shake off any images of death or destruction that might await me on the roads. I eased out of the garage and along the drive. As I pulled up to the gates, the groundskeeper, Simpkins, opened them wide for me to pass through.

I was beginning to accelerate when a black stain on the grass caught my eye, and I slammed on the brakes. Fear prickled at me as I took in the image that had been painted in a tar-like substance at the foot of the pitch pine nearest to the gates.

A pair of wings. An uneven lump with two stalks poking out from the top – a crude rendering of a heart.

The symbol of Imperium Mortis.

Had they been here and marked our home? What was the meaning of it?

I rolled down the car window and yelled back at Simpkins. He came running over.

'Where did this come from?' I demanded, pointing at the paint. My voice was high and shrill.

Simpkins looked at the grim symbol, astonished. 'I . . . I don't know. I never saw it before, Mister Felix.'

He was frightened, an emotion I'd never seen cross his gruff features before, although I couldn't assess whether he was afraid of my anger at his failure to protect our grounds from defacement, or the implications of the stealth the perpetrator must have had in order to get past his eagle eyes.

'Get rid of it.'

Before he had a chance to reply, I rolled the window back up and began to drive, aware of the nagging sensation that Bradley Cooke's time was running out.

13

As I drove towards Brooklyn, my hands gripped the wheel so tight that my knuckles went white. A hard knot sat in my gut, and the city didn't appear to care. It just ate up the cars flowing into it, swallowed them whole like a child gulping down candy.

And then the images began to press into my mind.

... Something is about to fly into the windshield, and I'm flailing in response and twist the vehicle right into the path of another automobile ...

My heart rate rose. I pushed the picture away. But my brain produced another, like a terrible magician with a never-ending trail of scarves.

... The gas pedal gets jammed, ramming my car into the back of the one in front, the steering column spearing me ...

... Or a crazed driver comes down the wrong side of the road, and my only option is to swerve out of his way ... and skid on ice, flipping over the car, so that I'm crushed inside it ...

It was the same writhing terror that had taken to hounding me in the middle of the night, making me fling my body from one side of the bed to the other, as if I might be able to shake it loose. From somewhere deep in the recesses of my brain came the voice of my old school principal the day I had that 'funny turn'. *Snap out of it.* As if it were a choice.

In twenty-six days' time, I was going to be killed by a twist of fate – and my brain seemed to have snagged on the imagining of every possible way it could happen. As if the imagining itself could ward off the event.

The journey shouldn't have taken me long, but I got caught in the worst of the morning rush. Those who weren't driving were darting along the sidewalk towards their workplace prisons ready for the daily grind.

I was brought to a complete standstill at one point, which gave me time to take in the sight of a towering structure in the midst of its growing pains. It must have been sixty floors at least, the tiny figures of men moving on rust-coloured girders at the very top. I was still gawping at their fearlessness when a sharp honk roused me, and I saw that the cars in front had long since pulled away.

I had to hope that Bradley and his wife were still living in the same tenement building they'd resided in before the war, and that he was at home. The row houses were a depressing sight, the once-white paint turned grey from the layer of damp mould that had grown and spread. The windows glared down from up high, as far as I could see down the block, and maybe a quarter of them were boarded up or cracked.

This was the neighbourhood where Father grew up. I could see why he had been so desperate to rise above his station, to chase down a new life. The desire in him had been so strong, and it had originated in a sad tenement just like the ones I was driving past. He had toiled away in a factory like the one that was casting a shadow of smoke over the rooftops, and then he'd laboured on the railways, saving every penny until he had the chance to invest ... It didn't surprise me that he'd given in to the strongest of dark temptations, that when given a taste of another life it was magic indeed that had promised Father a way out forever, a life of luxury for his descendants, so that they might inherit a fortune and would never know what it was to live in poverty the way he had.

I got out of the car, feeling uncomfortably conspicuous. The roadster was completely incongruous with the scene of poverty around me. I locked it and headed up towards the tenement building where I hoped Bradley Cooke still lived with his wife. It had a squashed appearance like every other house on the street. They were like plants, crowded together in one pot, cramped and straining for the sun.

There was a tiny square of garden at the front of number 37. It was overgrown with weeds, and the gate was hanging off its hinges. Even the steps leading up to the door had given up doing their job, crumbling at the sides. The only glimmer of hopefulness was a box of evergreen herbs – thyme, rosemary, bay – that had been set out on the window ledge of the first-floor apartment. Their fragrance seemed to promise better times ahead, their green leaves standing strong against the harsh wind. The sight of them encouraged me.

By the door, there was a little metal frame with sections for each of the apartments inside and the family name of the current residents. In this three-storey tenement, there were six households that shared the front door. Cooke was there, I spotted with relief. Apartment A on the first floor.

I knocked on the door. When there was no response, I knocked again, a little louder, and that was when the curtains behind the herb box twitched. I saw a pair of dark brown eyes set in a pretty face peering to see who was there. I offered my most encouraging smile, and the curtains flicked closed again.

I waited, hopeful that she would come meet me.

The main door opened slowly. 'Hello?' asked the woman. She had hair coiled elegantly on top of her head and wore a concerned expression.

'I'm looking for Bradley Cooke,' I said.

'He's not home,' she said, shaking her head. 'What do you need him for?'

She sounded suspicious of me, and I felt desperate to alleviate her concern. If she was, as I suspected, Bradley's wife, then she had no doubt experienced enough turmoil since his return to set her on edge. I wondered if she'd had the same letter as us, out of the blue. If she'd suspected he would never be coming home to her, begun to build a life without him, only for it to be turned on its head? I wonder if he'd confessed to her that he was going to die.

'I just wanted to talk to him,' I said. 'My father was at the same sanatorium in England after the war, and he just came back. I think they would have been on the same ship.'

She was nodding a little now, but she still seemed wary.

'I'm Felix,' I said, holding out my hand. 'Felix Ashe.'

'Charity,' she replied and shook my hand. Her fourth finger was looped with a thin gold band.

'I wanted to ask Bradley about the sanatorium. My father . . . he couldn't speak.' I stumbled over the past tense. It seemed wrong to consign him to history. 'He passed away yesterday.'

Charity seemed to swell with empathy. 'Oh, I'm so sorry.' She shook her head and pressed her fingertips to her lips.

'I just wanted to know a bit more about where he'd been for the last two years.'

She nodded, and understanding was written across her face. 'We lost so much time with them. I've asked Bradley, but he won't talk about it. He says that he just wants to forget. I've been thinking that they had a very terrible time of it over there, and they've all made a pact not to let us know how awful it was.'

There was nothing in the way she spoke that suggested she had any notion of a secret society or dark magic.

'We're the lucky ones,' she said, a firmness creeping into her voice. 'We got to see them again. I'm so sorry you didn't get to keep your father for longer.'

'Was Bradley very badly injured?' I asked.

'His legs,' she said. 'He walks with crutches now.'

Without meaning to, she'd confirmed my suspicions that the soldiers weren't confined at the sanatorium because Dr Leery was a specialist in facial injuries, as we'd been told.

It had always been about the magic – about using it with these soldiers, for some reason.

'Will Bradley be home soon?' I asked, glancing at my wristwatch. If it could have yelled at me that I was running out of time, I'm sure it would have.

She shrugged. 'I'm on the evening shift at the factory and Bradley told me he wouldn't be back before I had to go.'

I figured he knew he was going to die. He didn't want her to see and he didn't want her to find him, so he was staying out of her way. I wondered if he were clutching a piece of paper that had his date and time branded on to it, like Father had been.

'Where is it that he might be now?' I asked, aware of the urgency that had crept into my tone.

Charity's eyes went wide, and she took a step back from me, into the safety of the entrance hall. She put her hand on the edge of the door, a defensive move.

'I'm sorry,' I said quickly. 'I'm just a little on edge at the moment, what with my father and all. My mother, she's just so desperate for answers, you see.'

Charity seemed to debate whether to tell me or not. I'd certainly spooked her. But maybe I'd convinced her too.

'Prospect Park,' she said eventually.

We weren't far from Prospect Park at all; it would be easier to walk there than to get back into the roadster, but the park itself was enormous. How on earth was I supposed to find Bradley with less than an hour to go? I was certain I'd be able to recognize him by his crutches, but over five hundred acres was an impossible amount of land to cover.

'You might find him at the Boathouse . . . or the Peristyle,' Charity added as though she could read my mind. 'He likes the buildings in the park far more than any of the nature,' she said with fondness. She twirled the wedding band on her finger and seemed lost in a memory.

I wanted to warn Charity. Whenever she had said his name, it was as though it tasted like honey. Later that day she was going to go work a gruelling evening shift in that factory that belched fumes all over the row houses, and she was going to come back a widow.

'Thank you for your help,' I said instead.

'No problem,' she said.

As I was heading back down the pathway towards the broken gate, Charity called after me. 'If you find him, be gentle with your questions, okay?'

'I promise,' I said, and I drew a little cross over my heart. As soon as she was back inside the house, I broke into a run.

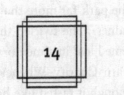

14

The lake in Prospect Park had a thick layer of ice on the surface, appearing like a beautiful illusion. Camperdown elms stretched their spidery fingers out in desperation as though they would love to get hold of me and suffocate me in their arms, needy and intense.

The wide pavilioned Boathouse rose out of the ground, palatial, its white terracotta catching the daylight. The smooth soles of my brogues skidded on a patch of black ice and I almost lost my balance, flinging my arms into the air in a wild motion in an attempt to steady myself. I struggled to squash my embarrassment at nearly kissing the ground and looked around, to see a courting couple trying to stifle a snigger at my expense as they looped around the lake, arms linked, heads bowed together. That could have been Lois and me in another life, I thought, but my motives for circling the lake today were much darker.

A man was going to die.

Until that moment, I hadn't really considered what it meant if I found Bradley. I was going to *see* a man die.

I jogged up the stairs at the front of the Boathouse. Bradley Cooke was nowhere to be seen. I clasped the rail and leaned over to squint out across the lake, using the balustrade as a vantage point. The Peristyle was opposite the lake at the southern edge, maybe a mile away – a fifteen-minute walk?

Bradley Cooke had twenty minutes to live. It had to be worth a try.

I took a deep breath and committed to running again. That was easier said than done in my pleated pants and lace-up patent brogues, but if I walked I might as well have admitted defeat. The icy air stabbed on its way down into my lungs and puffed out in smoky curls that wouldn't have been out of place in a speakeasy. I was already starting to get uncomfortable stretching sensations in the back of my legs, and I'd barely gone a quarter of a mile.

You're not going to make it. You're going to see a man die, taking with him all the information that you need.

Keeping my eyes fixed on the Peristyle, I focused on my breathing to push away the thought.

In.

Out.

In.

Out.

With each breath, my legs pumped and the distance between me and the Peristyle shrank. The nearer I got, the more it began to take shape – the columns and the triangular roof looked transported from Ancient Greece. While the Boathouse seemed to capture light, the Peristyle was more foreboding, the edge of the roof lined with a jagged row of icicles, looking for all the world like dangerous teeth.

I spotted someone sitting on the stone steps of the Peristyle, using a brush on the end of a long stick to deface them. As I came even closer, I noticed a pair of crutches lying next to him on the ground. The way that his clothes seemed to hang off his frame, as though they belonged to a larger person, reminded me of Father and the way the war had shrunk him.

I plunged all my efforts into reaching the figure, and, as I ran the last few yards, I debated with myself – if I only had the chance to ask him one question, what would it be? What was the most pressing thing I could glean from him?

'Bradley?'

His head jolted up in recognition of his name and, although he looked younger than my father, his face less lined, I noticed that his eyes were just as haunted. What a sight I must have been – my unnatural gait, and trussed up in clothes better suited to a dinner party than a sprint across a park. He reached for his crutches and shoved them under his arms, using them to lift himself back up to standing.

I came to a halt, breathless and lost for words. The image he had painted on the steps was striking and horribly familiar. It was the same symbol that had been left outside my own house, the insignia of Imperium Mortis.

'Do I know you?' he asked. His voice was rich, and his eyes had the same sad quality that I had seen in Father's.

'My father, Alfred – he was at the sanatorium with you. He died, yesterday. Please – I have to ask you some questions. What can you tell me about Imperium Mortis?'

I settled on that question because it was short, it was to the point, and yet it encompassed what I needed Bradley to know – that I was already a believer. He didn't have to convince me about magic and secret societies. In the wait for his reply, I could hear a *tick tick tick*ing that chilled me. Just like with Father.

Bradley wedged his crutch beneath his arm to free it up so he could reach into his pocket and pull out a slip of paper. 'If you know that name, then you already know too much,' he said. 'And you would do best to put that knowledge in a small box at the back of your mind and forget about it.'

Behind us, there was a cracking sound followed by a great shattering. I turned to see the remains of those vicious-looking icicles resting like a discarded sword lost in battle on the base of the Peristyle. Its tip had smashed away and fragmented into hundreds of skittering crystals. It was simultaneously beautiful and slightly horrifying, as what was left of the icicle was still at least ten inches long and as thick as a candlestick. Put simply, the frozen dagger would have been lethal if somebody had been standing underneath it.

The moment I thought the word *lethal*, I wondered if Bradley's mind was making the same connection as mine, if he'd thought about the way the tip of a falling icicle could puncture the soft spot at the back of your neck. A terrible accident . . . or a twist of dark magic.

I resisted the urge to look at my watch, but I couldn't help but feel that the icicle was a warning from the darkness – it was here, and it wanted Bradley.

Bradley had a strange look on his face, a sort of knowing grimace. I wondered if he could feel the darkness like I could, its presence hovering over us like a thunderous cloud, pregnant with rain and threatening to burst.

'What are you painting that for?' I asked, pointing at the symbol on the ground. It was still tacky and shiny.

'We're exposing –' he started to say, but a sinister cracking sound began above our heads as another icicle began to release its grasp on the edge of the Peristyle.

I backed away, down the step, and, as I went, I instinctively took Bradley by the arm to pull him out of harm's way. I didn't see the black ice on the ground.

'Watch out!' a voice called. A young woman, with a brisk British accent, was rushing over to us, pointing at the falling icicle. But it was too late.

Bradley's shoe slid out from underneath him, like a dancer doing the Charleston. His face was all surprise, and his mouth went slack. Then he was down, like a felled tree.

The noise his head made when it hit the step was an almighty dull *thwack* that echoed around the Peristyle. I stared into his eyes, and they looked so strange as the life left them. It was as if the pupil of his eye began to bleed, expanding across the entirety of the brown of his iris and then into the whites of his eyes. It seeped and spread like a plague until his eyes were like bottomless holes.

Blood pooled behind his head, sticky and glistening and so, so red.

Even though I didn't want to see the proof, I couldn't help myself . . . I felt an awful detachment as I looked at my watch. It was midday. Exactly twenty-four hours after the death of my father in a terrible accident, here was another soldier meeting an awful end. It was exactly what had been predicted on the slip of paper inside Dr Leery's notebook. I had no doubt that this was the work of the magic – the magic that had now claimed Bradley.

I knew he was already dead, and there was nothing that could be done for him. But I screamed for help and tried to rouse him nonetheless, even though I knew it was hopeless, because it was overwhelming, because one moment he had been speaking to me, and the next moment his blood was pooling on the ground. My own life had never felt so fragile. I felt as if I were just clinging on by a thread or by chance.

'He's dead,' said the girl. 'We can't save him.'

I looked at her properly for the first time. She was slight and couldn't have been more than eighteen, with pointed features that could take your eye out – sharp cheekbones, an even sharper chin. Her sleek black hair, gathered by a tie at the top of her head, was a long dark waterfall. It swished like the tail of a horse when she moved her head, which she did a lot when she spoke.

I gulped. 'I don't know what to do,' I said. 'We need to help him.'

'I told you – it's too late for that. Listen to me: the questions you're asking are dangerous. You need to ask them more discreetly – not loud enough to be overheard by strangers in a park. I can explain, but we need to go, and we need to go now.' She pointed over my shoulder then, and I turned and saw two figures, dressed in pristine black suits, who were making their way over to us in haste. They both wore their hair slicked back from their faces and had darkened glasses so that you couldn't see their eyes. They could be anybody and nobody, and if I'd been asked to identify them after the event, I wouldn't have been able to.

The girl tugged at my sleeve, but I felt rooted to the spot. 'There's nothing more we can do for him,' she said, firmly now.

I allowed her to pull me away from the scene and on to the path, where we were quickly swallowed up in the crowd. I peered back in the direction of Bradley's body and saw the two figures were going through the pockets of his jacket with swift, sharp motions.

They were not behaving the way you would expect people to in an emergency. They lacked both the care and earnest dedication of medics, and the thoughtful consideration of the scene required by the police. Neither of them had even tried to feel or listen for a heartbeat, or ask me what had happened to Bradley ... No, I had the odd sensation that these were not public servants performing their civic duty, but individuals who had an altogether different agenda, swooping in on the scene.

It was uncanny too, the manner in which the pair of them assessed the death and were able to have no emotional response at all. Icy fear speared my guts, and my body had begun to shake with the shock of it all, the movements uncontrollable. I tried to remember to breathe.

'We need to be quick. Follow me!'

Before I had any chance to respond, the girl had turned on her heel and taken nimble strides away from me. She glanced back once and jerked her head in the direction she was walking.

I needed to move. I took some big, deep breaths, feeling their flow loosen the grip of the fishhook deep in my belly, easing it out, until I was no longer pinned. I began to walk, as if in a daze, feeling as though I'd slipped into some sort of dream.

I began to follow the girl with the long dark hair. As I emerged on to the pathway by the road, a police car pulled up. I glanced over at it. Out leaped Detective Jones. If she saw me here, at the scene of the death of another soldier, it wouldn't take her long to discover the connection between Bradley and my father. A new fear raised its head – if she connected those dots, could my presence here be incriminating?

I ducked my head down and sped up to catch the girl. I think I knew even then that I'd already immersed myself in the waters of this dark world, so that even if I tried to clamber out now I'd be sopping wet . . . So there was nothing left to do but embrace it, swim with the current and hope not to drown.

15

I followed the girl, watching her hair swing from side to side with every step she took. She moved effortlessly through the bustle of the Brooklyn streets, and I was struck by the impression that you would only notice her if she wanted to be noticed. She seemed capable of performing a disappearing act, slipping between shadows.

What was I getting myself into? It felt like I was playing a version of chess where the pieces moved in ways I'd never seen before. Who were the men that had descended on Bradley's dead body with such speed and efficiency, like vultures? Who was this girl, and how did she fit into the picture?

She finally came to a halt outside a little cafe with doors painted a cheerful yellow flung open to welcome customers. The bottle-green canopy over the entrance declared it to be *Jenny's*, and the girl paused for a second, appraising it, before heading on in. It was the sort of nondescript cafe that could have been on any corner on any block in the city – and I was certain that was exactly why the girl had picked it.

Inside, the smell of hot fat seared my nostrils. The flat-top grill behind the counter was sizzling under the watchful eye of a formidable woman with black flyaway hair barely contained by the net she wore over it. A badge proclaimed her the eponymous Jenny, and she had a satisfied grin as she determined the bacon and eggs cooked to perfection and ready to be delivered to the four hungry young men in hard hats, clothes sweaty and dusty, no doubt on a lunch break from a construction site, who lined the counter on swivel stools.

The girl took a seat in the corner at a table with a cheerful floral cloth. The wooden bench squeaked as I sat down opposite her. Her intensely green eyes were fierce and intelligent, and her smile was disarming in the way it played at the corners of her mouth. I couldn't tell what she was thinking.

'You saw the icicle. You tried to warn him,' I said. 'To save him.'

'For all the good it did.'

'I don't think you could have prevented it.'

'No, I don't think so either,' she said. 'I'm Violet. I think we have some things to discuss.'

'I'm –' I started, but she interrupted me before I even had a chance to get my name out.

'– Felix Ashe, I know,' she said.

She pulled off the crossbody satchel she was wearing and rummaged inside, bringing out a copy of *Disclosed*. She skimmed through it until she landed on the article she was searching for, and I immediately recognized the figures in the inky rendering – it was a photograph of Mother and me, looking out towards the liner that had brought Father home.

'Give that to me,' I said, snatching it out of her hands.

TWO YEARS TOO LATE! yelled the headline. *Soldiers return from British sanatorium, including the husband of retired tennis ace Gracie Ashe, pictured here with her son Felix.*

I skimmed through the rest of the article. A second picture showed the soldiers huddled together in their various states of injury as they shuffled down the gangway. The writer of the piece had strayed from the remit of celebrity gossip to explore the sad parallels between our wealth and the destitution that faced many war veterans on their return. No doubt he thought himself a journalist on some sort of mission. I tried to bring the pushy young man's face to mind again, but all I could remember was that thick Boston accent and the way he tried to get a quote out of Mother.

The writer, Flatt, had named each of the soldiers, and even interviewed one of them – Vaughan Jenkins, now homeless, destitute. I shivered as I recognized Vaughan's name from the list I had. He was going to die in two days' time.

The writer had also learned the name of the sanatorium and the doctor that had treated them. St Anthony's. Dr Leery. No more information than that had been forthcoming, he lamented, hinting that something sinister had happened at St Anthony's that they weren't allowed to discuss. He expressed concern at the length of time the soldiers were kept in England, implying that it was against their will, that they'd been incarcerated there. Interesting. I would never have thought a gossip rag could house legitimate journalism, let alone snippets that could aid my understanding of what had happened to my father.

'So you know about Doctor Leery and the sanatorium.' I closed the magazine and pushed it back across the table to Violet. A question was brimming on her lips.

'What happened to your father when he came home?' she asked, her eyes narrowing. It was a simple question, and yet it was intensely loaded. I felt as though I were under a spotlight, being interrogated.

'He passed away,' I said, picking each word carefully. 'It was an accident.'

Violet raised an eyebrow.

'An accident,' she repeated, and her nose wrinkled where it met the severe slant of her brows. 'An accident, just like our friend Bradley?'

It was a test. She wanted me to be the one to break the illusion of normality. She wanted me to admit that when we used the word 'accident', we both really knew that there was a dark magic responsible. We were having two conversations. One was simple, brief and surface-level, filled with caution. The other, rippling beneath the surface, was full of questions that hadn't come up for air.

Yet.

I caved first.

'He was holding this when he died.'

I reached into my pocket, feeling for the slip of paper my father had died clutching. My hand was shaking as I held it out to show Violet the date and the Imperium Mortis symbol.

'It predicted the exact moment that he was going to die. My father also left me a list of the other soldiers that Doctor Leery was treating, and when death is going to get them too, one after the other. They're all so close together. Why would they all be in a row like that?'

Would she draw the same conclusions as me, that Leery was machinating it all, manipulating the deaths?

'Perhaps to send someone a message?' I got the sense that Violet knew exactly who would be on the receiving end of such a message.

'You think he's behind it all?'

'Not just him. Imperium Mortis,' she said, running her finger over the insignia.

'What do you know about them?' I asked. The question broke free, gasped for breath. 'And what did they do to my father?'

She hesitated. 'Are you sure that you want to know this?'

'I already know enough that I'll never be the same again,' I said.

A strange sadness crossed over her features. I felt as though she understood, somehow, and I couldn't wait to know more about her.

'The society began in the fifteenth century, with a group of students in York in England. They were a small, very intimate sect, and the story goes that they became fascinated by the precise moment of a person's death. They thought that it had power attributed to it, especially in certain circumstances where the death was accompanied by intense emotional stress. They had a conviction that this power could be harnessed, creating a kind of magic. Death Magic.'

Everything inside me tensed up. *Death Magic*. It was the same phrase Mother had used.

We were interrupted by the appearance of long, gangly limbs and a cowed expression. One look behind the counter showed that Jenny was keeping half an eye on this particular waiter. 'What can I get for you?' he asked.

'I'll have a strawberry malt,' Violet said without missing a beat. She was no longer my sombre guide to the world of fifteenth-century students dabbling in the darkest of arts; she was acting the part of a girl on a date, coy and flirtatious. She grinned at me.

'Just a black coffee,' I said. I couldn't shake the image of Bradley's eyes, the spreading darkness, and the blood pooling on the stone step of the Peristyle.

The waiter sloped off to fill our orders, and I willed Violet to continue, clinging on to every word.

'Of course, there's only one way to truly experiment with death,' she continued, and then she paused. She was talking about murder, I realized with a shiver. 'Even at a time when life was cheap, eventually the students were discovered. Half of them were arrested and publicly executed for their crimes, and the others fled and went underground with their research. They've operated under the banner Imperium Mortis ever since, thriving on working in secret, protected by wealthy benefactors, passing down their discoveries through the generations.'

'But why?' I asked. 'Why would anyone be interested in messing with this kind of dangerous, supernatural world?'

Violet laughed. 'Why do you think? Power. In this case, the ability to wield actual magic – magic that can manipulate people, among other things. In their history, they must have killed thousands, attempting to get this magic to work. And only once in a generation did someone manage to create something powerful. It seems that most of their endeavours fail, that most of their victims die in vain, but then sometimes – just sometimes – the most skilled practitioners of Death Magic have the ability to capture the energy inside an object. It seems to be related to the height of the emotion involved.'

I felt as though I had fallen off a wall and winded myself. There was a heady relief in the realization that I wasn't insane, that somebody else could validate the things I had discovered – or at least believed in them too. It felt like a homecoming. It felt like being understood.

'I think I know something about that. The magic in the objects, I mean. And I know the magic gives the user power, but they have to pay for it,' I added.

Violet nodded. 'It seems that's always the case. Death Magic creates powerful objects that can do incredible things. But for every positive action there's a negative reaction.'

'It balances the scales,' I said, my understanding growing so quickly it felt as though my head were cracking open.

Just then, the waiter reappeared with our drinks. He placed a cup of deep black coffee as thick as motor oil and just as pungent before me. The heat of it radiated through the cheap ceramic. In front of Violet, he placed a pastel pink milky drink topped with a perfect whip of cream.

Violet picked up a spoon and shaved off the top of her cream, devouring it as though she were on the clock. Who was this strange, hungry British girl with all this knowledge of dark magic, and how had she ended up in New York? She had shared with me the origins of Imperium Mortis, but I was no closer to finding out what exactly Father had been involved in, how Dr Leery had been able to predict – or decide? – the moment he was going to die. And that was what I needed to know. It was the only hope I had of finding a way to extend my life beyond my birthday – and therefore, I hoped, breaking the curse, taking back control of my life, and freeing myself from the grip of the darkness . . .

'You obviously know about my family,' I said, gesturing at the copy of *Disclosed*. 'So I'm sure you know the kind of life we lead . . . our wealth, our privilege.'

Violet gave a small, almost ravenous, nod.

I looked her dead in the eye. 'Well, it seems my father's fortune came from Death Magic.'

Violet's eyes shone with an odd excitement.

'What was the negative reaction?' she asked, a little breathless.

'No line of inheritance. My three older brothers all died on their eighteenth birthday.' My voice cracked. Would it ever not hurt to talk about them?

'Aha! It always works like that!' I was perturbed by how excited she sounded, gesticulating with her hands. 'The magic seems to have this heavy dose of irony. As if . . . as if someone is playing a very clever game, but wants to prove that you can never win against them. So it gives your father an inheritance, but it robs him of anyone to . . .'

She trailed off as she realized the implication. Father's fortune was a gift from Death Magic, and I would pay for it. It was like something from a fairy tale, the type told to frighten children, with grim punishments for moral transgressions.

'I turn eighteen next month,' I said. 'I thought that if Doctor Leery was able to manipulate death like that, then . . .'

'Then there might be a way for you to escape it claiming you.' Violet sighed and took a big sip of her sickly-coloured confection.

It was like saying I believed in wishes on a birthday cake. I needed a way to cheat Death Magic, beat it at its own game, and I had hoped that the trail of soldiers would lead to Dr Leery and the answer. Admitting that was embarrassing.

'Do you think that might be possible?' I sounded pitiful.

'Well, one thing's for sure: I want you to be under no illusion that Hugo Leery is going to save you.' Violet tossed her hair over her shoulder. 'He was born into Imperium Mortis. Hugo and his twin sister, Ada, are extremely naturally talented at using Death Magic – I mean, as in they have an extraordinary capacity for success in creating objects, like nobody has been able to do before. As I said, it's not as though every time somebody is killed by Imperium Mortis Death Magic happens. Before Hugo and Ada, they saw success maybe once in a generation. The Leery twins are ... something else. And Ada is the newest director of Imperium Mortis.'

It was dizzying, so much new information all at once. All the answers I'd been certain would reassure me made me feel as though I were standing on a window ledge thirty floors high, teetering in the wind. I noticed, though, that Violet spoke about Hugo and Ada as if she were deeply acquainted with them. Maybe even admired them.

'You sound like you know them,' I said.

'I did once,' she said coolly. 'And I'm telling you that Ada and Hugo Leery are not going to be interested in saving your life. If they've created an object that can predict the moment of death, or even cheat it ... they're not going to hand it over to you. You'll have to take it.'

16

We had been talking for hours, and the sun was beginning to leech away from the sky, the darkness of November stealing precious daylight hours. I needed to leave. I had not forgotten that I'd invited Lois over to the house, knew she might even be there already, waiting for me. Lois was coming to look at the evidence for Death Magic being involved in my father's death; Violet had needed no such convincing. And yet there was something I had left unsaid. I had the encoded casebook that had once belonged to Leery, and it was an important piece of the puzzle, but I felt that Violet was keeping things from me, and it wouldn't be wise to reveal everything in my hand. I left a bill on the table to cover our orders and tip the browbeaten waiter.

I still had so many questions. But I felt certain this would not be the last time I saw Violet.

'Who do we need to find next?' Violet asked when we were out on the street.

'Chuck Hardaway.' I'd memorized the names, their order.

'I found out a bit about him using the limited information in that article. He's working at The Pet Store.'

'A pet store called "The Pet Store"?' I raised an eyebrow.

'It's a speakeasy,' she said, confirming what I feared.

The store itself would just be a front for an illegal bar selling alcohol, no doubt with some connection to more sinister criminal activities.

'It's owned by the Spencer family.'

She said their name like I should know who they were. As it happened, I knew nothing of the Spencer family, but I had heard of families who ran this sort of racket, and I did know they tended to dislike people snooping around in their business.

'He's supposed to be working there tomorrow,' Violet said. 'If you want to go together?' She sounded hopeful. I supposed there was safety in numbers.

'Why are you tracking the soldiers?' I asked.

'The same reason you are: I want to find Imperium Mortis – and whatever the hell it is they're using to kill the soldiers like this.'

'But why? How do I know you're any better than them?'

'I don't want to *use* it,' she said with a sneer. 'I want to take it from them. The things they've done . . . People like that should never be allowed that kind of power. I'm here because I'd heard rumours that Hugo was conscripted like everyone else during the war, but, being the kind of man he is, he'd used it to his advantage and created some sort of new and horrifying object while he was working in a field hospital in France. Plenty of pain and suffering and emotional stress there, I guess. And meanwhile Ada travelled over here to start a US faction of Imperium Mortis . . . It's too much. I want them stopped. And somebody's got to try.' She kicked her shoe against the sidewalk.

Once again, I had the feeling that her involvement in all this was more personal than she was letting on. She might be on a noble quest, but Imperium Mortis had done something to her, or somebody she loved. I was sure of it.

Violet suddenly shivered in the cold and wrapped her arms around herself. I realized she didn't have a coat, just the thick woollen dress she was wearing and a sturdy pair of winter boots that looked like they'd been long battered.

'Do you need a ride someplace?'

'My place is in Queens,' she said with a shrug of nonchalance, though I could tell she was more than a little keen.

'I can drive through that way,' I said, and a little smile ran across her mouth, but didn't reach her eyes. 'Do you live with family?' I asked.

'Don't have any. I'm staying in a women's boarding house. Look, if you're going to keep asking personal questions, then I'm taking the train,' she said. 'I don't want to talk about it.'

'Okay, okay,' I said, letting it drop.

We walked in silence to the roadster. Violet's eyebrows nearly disappeared into her hairline when she saw it.

'*This* is your ride?' she asked, eyes widening.

Once, I might have felt proud of the car. Now I knew its true cost.

'Get in,' I said, unsettled by this new sensation of shame.

Violet directed me to a smoggy and industrialized area of Queens dominated by an ash dump created by the factories, a vast and sprawling mountain of dust and decay by the Flushing River. The boarding house looked like little more than a shack cowering in the shadow of the giant ash heap. It was next door to a long-deserted store whose glass front had been smashed and the insides looted, leaving it looking like roadkill pecked by buzzards.

'Well, now you know where to find me,' Violet said. She sighed a deep sigh that seemed to be dredged from the bottom of her boots, and then added, 'I'm not very good at opening up, but this means a lot to me, and I'm grateful for your help.'

As if she couldn't bear to hear my response, she clambered out of the car before I had the chance to say anything.

I waited to make sure she got inside the pathetic, splintering door of the boarding house before starting the engine again. She didn't look back.

17

Lois was already at Pitch House by the time I returned. Her golden hair was a little longer than it had been the last time I'd seen her, but her dress was familiar, adorned with a striking floral pattern that I recognized from the time we had gone to see a show together on Broadway. Had she worn it deliberately? It was hard enough to look at her without imagining the way her head had rested on my shoulder in the darkness of the theatre. Not for the first time, I felt the pang of regret that I had never been bold enough to ask her if we could go steady, or if she would mind if I kissed her.

'It's good to see you,' I said, and noticed her cheeks turn pink.

'I wish it were under happier circumstances,' she said, placing a gentle hand on my arm. 'I'm so sorry, Felix. There should be a limit to the amount of tragedy one family has to endure.'

'This curse seems to have no limit,' I said solemnly. 'But I'm beginning to think it might have an antidote. Come with me.'

Lois didn't try to hide her scepticism, but she followed me to the library, where I gathered up all the evidence I had and laid it out across the table.

'It's like watching my father in court,' she said with a wry smile.

'Ha ha. Just hear me out,' I said.

So I went through it all, piece by piece, starting with the slip that I had found in my father's hand. Then I showed her the patient notes, the encoded casebook, and the list of names and dates.

'I tracked down Bradley Cooke today, using the patient notes,' I said. 'He died at the exact moment it said he would, just like my father did, in another terrible accident. But I wasn't the only person who had been following him. There was a girl, Violet, about our age . . . and some men. They looked . . . strange. Sinister.'

Lois's eyes narrowed. 'Do you think it's a good idea to keep probing?' she asked. 'They sound dangerous, Felix. Why don't you just leave it alone? Your father's dead – even if they were involved somehow with what happened to him, what good can come from risking getting on the wrong side of these people?'

'I can't stop now,' I said. 'It's less than a month until my birthday. Look what happened to my brothers, Lois. The same will happen to me.'

She paused. 'You really believe that you're going to die?'

'I do. And I need you to believe me too.'

She looked at me closely. 'I do believe that you believe it. But there must be a more rational explanation. You're talking about magic!'

I shook my head. 'With everything that's happened to my family, it's easier to accept the idea of magic than to think that it's all just been coincidence. That's so ... meaningless.'

'Isn't that why people believe in anything?' Lois asked, earnest and measured.

'If you can't believe in the supernatural element of this, surely you can at least see that these were my father's last gifts to me, and there's something he wants me to know? To learn?'

'Absolutely,' Lois said. She clapped her hands together. 'So, where do we begin?'

'We could try some ciphers?' I asked, keen to focus our attention.

'What did you have in mind?'

That felt like progress. Perhaps she was still dubious that the cause of all this was dark magic, but at the very least she saw that there was something worth investigating.

I now knew a little more about Leery than I had before, so I also had a shred more of an indication as to what keyword he might use. DEATH was unsuccessful. We tried HUGO and LEERY and finally we tried ADA. How much closer or more important could you get than a twin?

But the exercise was futile. Each of the attempts created a string of nonsense. We could try for years and make no progress, but at least Lois's company made it bearable.

'Tomorrow I'm going to find the next soldier,' I said as we finally admitted defeat and began to pack up. 'He's due to die at the stroke of noon, just like the others. Maybe he can tell us something useful before then.'

How quickly I'd given up on the idea of helping these people.

'I'm coming with you,' Lois said, and she pursed her lips. I had never seen her look more determined – and that was saying something. 'You *can't* go alone,' she added, by way of explanation. 'It's too dangerous.'

'I won't be alone,' I said. 'I'm going with Violet. And precisely *because* it's going to be dangerous, I'd really rather you didn't come.'

'Uh-huh. And what do you really know about this girl exactly?' Lois asked, her back straightening like a rod, and pulling her legs out from underneath her.

'I know that she's going to be able to help,' I said. 'She knows a lot more about Imperium Mortis than I do.'

'Still . . .' Lois said. She cleared her throat and looked up at me. I could have sworn a blush had crept into her cheeks again. Her chin lifted slightly, and – for a second – I thought that the most natural thing in the world would be to dip my head down and kiss her . . .

But I didn't.

My feelings for her swirled chaotically inside me – as did the unbidden image of Bradley Cooke falling.

'Are you sure?' I said. 'The soldier is going to die. Possibly right in front of us. Are you certain you want to see that?'

'That would be horrible,' Lois admitted. 'But I want to get to the bottom of this with you.'

In spite of the spark of hope her words sent through me, a note of dread plucked at me too. What would happen to me if I didn't manage to unravel the curse before the Death Magic took hold? My own eyes taken over by the darkness, the pupils spreading . . . The very idea started a quiver in the corner of my eye and made my jaw clench and my nerves begin to jangle. It had already taken my brothers. I wondered if their eyes had gone dark too. And my father . . . His eyes were closed, but, if I could have looked at them, would I have seen that horrifying emptiness?

I didn't say any of this to Lois. I just squeezed her hand tightly.

*

The light was still on in Nick's bedroom after I'd said goodbye to Lois and headed up to bed. I gently opened the door, and saw that he was sleeping, all curled up on top of his quilt, his hand clutched around a book. He stirred slightly as I lifted the book out of his hand and placed it on his nightstand, where a row of glasses had been arranged by level of water. He seemed so peaceful that I was loath to place him under the quilt in case I roused him, so instead I fetched a blanket from my room and tucked it around him so he wouldn't get cold. I turned off the light, but hovered in his doorway for a moment longer, listening to the sound of his breathing, soft and with just a slight catch at the start of every inhalation.

The snuffling noises of his sleep warmed my heart, and I couldn't help but feel the same fierce protectiveness that had overcome me when Mother invited me into her room to see the sweet, milky-smelling bundle, and first placed him in my arms. I learned fast how to support his neck in the crook of my arm, how he preferred to be held upright against my chest, how I could soothe him by rocking and humming . . .

I needed to keep him safe from the darkness of Death Magic. I would not let it steal him away from the world. I would do whatever it took to find a way to break the curse, to save his life and mine, and secure us time to decide what to make of our lives.

And I swore then that Nick would never learn that I had needed to do it at all.

17 NOVEMBER 1920

TWENTY-FIVE DAYS LEFT

18

The following morning, Mother's face lightened a little when I told her I was going to spend the day with Lois. I spared her the worry of the truth of our destination, crafting an easy-to-remember but difficult-to-verify alibi in the form of a shopping excursion.

'We'll be gone all day,' I said, deceptively cheerful.

I took the black Ford model T, so there would be enough space for three of us, regrettably leaving the gorgeous navy roadster, and drove across to Lois's mansion – a bright and light structure, with white columns and so many windows framed by pristine balconies. She was ready and waiting for me by the gates.

'Tell me more about Violet,' Lois asked when she got into the car. 'I really don't know what to expect.'

'She's like you in a lot of ways,' I said, after thinking about it for a moment. 'Fierce, intelligent, determined. But she's harsher. You can tell she's been hurt. She's not an easy person to talk to, and she's not particularly friendly or warm.'

'Do you think she'll mind that I'm coming?' Lois sounded a little nervous for the first time.

'It doesn't matter if she minds,' I said, though I felt a little apprehensive about that myself. Violet did not strike me as the kind of person who would take surprises well.

As we passed the ash dump, Lois gawped at the mountainous heap. Grey fragments circled in the air like butterflies, dancing with the wind. Tiny specks and larger clumps alike were scooped up on the gusts that provided an accompaniment with their song of fervent whistles and howls. Everyone we passed appeared to be on their way to long, laborious days, kitted out in heavy work boots, aged shirts with stained pits and trousers that had been patched a time too many. They all seemed so weary, so stiff, moving in the direction of the factories as if they ached.

I parked up a little further down the street. 'You wait here,' I told Lois. 'I want to give her a bit of warning that you're coming with us.'

She nodded and plucked at the end of one of her gloves, nipping the fabric at the tips of her fingers.

In the clear morning light, the boarding house looked an even sorrier sight than it had in yesterday's late-afternoon gloom. The paint on the door was peeling off like dead skin, revealing the rotten wood below. Ash and dust danced in the air as I waited for a response to my knock.

The door swung open, and Violet's eyes were as vivid as I remembered them from the day before – they reminded me of the way an opal could catch the light and flicker with fire. She was wearing a peachy-pink dress with long sleeves and a skirt that fell in pleats around her calves, and she had traded the exhausted winter boots for a pair of flat black pumps. Her hair was fastened in a chignon and accented with a little bow in the same colour as her dress. It was a striking change in her appearance – she was elegant and yet understated.

'Let's go,' she said, brisk and to the point.

'Wait – I have something to tell you,' I said. 'My friend Lois is coming with us.'

'What?' Violet hissed, stopping dead.

'I would have told you before we came, but I didn't have a way to call.'

'I see.' Her tone was icy cold. 'So, who is she?'

'She's an old friend. She'll be incredibly useful – she's very smart,' I said, certain that was the way to get Violet on board, convince her that Lois was indispensable to the success of the things she hoped to achieve.

'And how long have you been in love with her?'

'Quit it,' I warned, feeling a flush of embarrassment.

Violet rolled her eyes. 'Well, you've done a very stupid thing involving her in this. The best thing you could have done for her safety would have been to ensure she never heard the words "Imperium Mortis", but it's too late now.' Violet sighed and began to march in the direction of the car. 'Let's hope she's as useful as you say she's going to be.'

When we got back to the car, Lois had moved to the back seat, making way for Violet to sit up front. There was a heavy atmosphere in the car, like the moment before a storm breaks.

'I'm Lois Bouwmeester,' said Lois, leaning forward. She sounded a little tentative.

Violet ignored all pleasantries and shot a cold look at Lois over her shoulder. When she spoke, her voice was harsh, dismissive. 'Have you ever seen someone die before?'

Lois startled at the abruptness of the question and the hostility of its delivery. But if the question was meant to unsettle her, it failed.

'Yes,' she replied. 'I was at my mother's side when she took her last breath. If you're trying to prepare me for today being unpleasant, you needn't concern yourself.'

Violet snorted. 'If you think that's comparable to what we might see today, then you really are in the wrong car.'

I couldn't help but agree, images of my father and Bradley flicking through my mind.

Lois's eyes turned steely. 'Are you in the habit of underestimating people?' She was more than capable of holding her own, so I kept quiet. 'Because that can be dangerous.'

'And you know a lot about danger, do you?' said Violet, sneering. 'I'm sure we can rely on you in any emergency that might unfold.'

Lois gave a small breath of laughter in the face of Violet's onslaught. 'Well, you can count on me to do my best.'

' "Your best" ,' Violet repeated, loading the phrase with sarcasm. 'Well then. Lucky us. Felix, The Pet Store is on the Lower East Side.'

I took that as my cue to drive. We were up against the clock – again. Time had gained such an intense quality. It was a striking contrast to the slow pace of my life before, when my lessons with Geoffrey seemed to drag, or I could while away a whole afternoon immersed in a detective novel, finishing one just to pick up the next immediately.

As we travelled, Violet told us that the Spencer brothers had the police chief in their pocket, and all manner of dealings went on in their club. Since reading the article about Leery and the soldiers in *Disclosed*, Violet had been trying to gather as much information on all of them as she could – Chuck Hardaway had been the easiest to learn about besides my father, but he had been tricky to pin down and speak to. He'd been indispensable to the Spencer brothers before the war, and now he was back. If he wasn't in the club, he was out on an errand for them. It turned out he was the perfect messenger.

'I heard that he thinks he's bulletproof,' she said. 'He's completely unafraid of death.'

'Because he knows when he is going to die,' I murmured in realization.

Was that the way it worked? Were the soldiers protected from death until the exact moment Hugo Leery had dictated they would die?

I wasn't familiar with the Lower East Side. Violet had a better idea of where we needed to go, and she directed me past the blocks of tenement buildings, until she instructed me to park up in a little shopping district. As we wandered down the street, we headed past a bakery whose windows were full of tightly knotted pastries. The buttery smell that wafted out from the doorway made my stomach grumble – I'd been in such a rush that I hadn't eaten breakfast.

'There it is,' she said, nodding at a store whose windowed front held a great iron bird cage filled with yellow canaries. THE PET STORE, the sign proclaimed.

'We're going round the back. Just follow me. I've seen what they do.'

Violet led the way down a little side alley, and, when we reached the back of the store, she rapped on the door in a precise fashion. A code, I realized. Sure enough, a slot at eye level opened, and a pair of tired eyes appeared. They looked like they hadn't slept in a week.

'We're here to see Chuck,' Violet said.

'That's a fancy accent,' the voice said. 'You've travelled a long way. Does the boss know you?'

'Warren?' Violet replied without hesitating. 'He said he was expecting a new delivery of goldfish on Thursday.'

It sounded like nonsense, but I got the sense this was one of the coded entries I'd heard about, designed to keep the speakeasy under wraps. If you said the right thing at the door, you were allowed in.

'All right, all right,' the voice said, satisfied. 'But I've not seen Chuck today. If you want to wait, I'm sure he'll be along sometime. We've got a table. You'll have to order.'

'Of course,' Violet said. 'It's not like Chuck's ever on time anyway.'

The lies just slipped off her tongue like honey from a spoon. She should have been an actress.

'Sure thing.'

The slot slid shut again with a clunk, and the door opened properly. The eyes were set in the face of a man in a suit with a thick neck and broad shoulders. I spotted the gun in his waistband, and my nerves started to jangle. The guy shut the door behind us, and my eyes strained to adjust to the dimmer light inside.

'You won't have heard what Chuck did last night,' he said, chuckling as he crouched down and began to lift a segment of the carpet, revealing a trapdoor.

'No?' Violet said, turning the word into a question.

'He went up on top of the building here. We're talking on the roof. And, get this – he jumped, literally *jumped* from this roof, over the gap, on to the roof of the store on the other side of the alley. I mean, that's a sheer drop three storeys high. If he'd failed, he would have just been dead. Splat.'

'That's a feat indeed,' Lois murmured.

'How do you know Chuck?' asked the doorman, a slight suspicion creeping into his tone.

'He's an old friend from before the war,' Lois replied without missing a beat. I caught Violet smiling approvingly.

'Well, you might find him somewhat changed.'

He lifted the trapdoor. The underside was heavily padded with some sort of insulation material. Strains of jazz music that had been muffled by the soundproofing rose up to greet us.

'Good luck.'

Violet lowered herself to the floor first, down on her hands and knees. She shuffled to the edge of the drop and got purchase on the ladder, before starting to climb down. She winked at me as she went. Lois followed, a glint in her eye, which might have been nerves or excitement. And then it was my turn.

I dropped one foot over the edge until it landed on the top rung, then the other. I made my way down the ladder, into the darkness, guided by the sound of saxophones that vibrated through the rungs and into my body.

I squinted to see as I oriented myself on the ground. The stage captured my gaze, a spotlight drawing a halo around a singer in a dark green evening dress. When she sang, her voice was a rich rumble, and she swayed her hips from side to side. The musicians behind her seemed rapturous, holding their instruments like lovers.

Round tables and chairs were angled to face the stage, creating something between a theatre audience and a dinner party. The place was lit by candles and the tiny red embers of cigarettes. The air was full of their smoke, which caused me to splutter and screw up my face at the stale taste. Each table was occupied by women in short dresses, with pearls and bobbed hair, and men with white bow ties and oiled hair raising their voices above the music.

There was an empty table at the side of the room, tucked into a little nook. Violet pounced on it and the three of us sat, squashed together, elbows brushing. At the next table a group of gentlemen were playing a game, and their cards jostled for space with appetizers – plates of little pancakes and crisp bacon. Even though it was still before noon, everyone had a drink in their hand. The atmosphere was intoxicating, and everybody seemed soaked through with a warm thrill from their drinks.

When a waiter came to take our order, I asked for a platter of the pancakes that had caught my eye, and he swiftly returned with the golden treats, hot and steaming, and three complimentary shot glasses with a viscous green liquid inside.

Lois pushed hers aside, but Violet smirked and threw one down her neck with a gulp. The differences between them were becoming more striking. In fact, Violet was like no other girl I'd ever met, and I found myself wondering again – who was she really? What sort of life did she come from, and how had she become embroiled in the world of Death Magic?

'How did you find out about Imperium Mortis in the first place?' I asked. 'How do you know so much about them?'

Violet scrunched her nose up. 'I knew this was coming.' She screwed her eyes shut and took a couple of deep breaths. 'Don't judge me too harshly.'

'I won't,' I said, although I wasn't sure that was a promise I could keep.

'It's a long story. I don't really know where to begin.'

She glanced around the room, looking truly nervous for the first time. The card players at the table next to us were only an arm's reach away.

'Maybe this isn't the place,' Lois said, and I realized my misstep.

This was clearly not the sort of thing Violet wanted to delve into in public, let alone in a place where she had to raise her voice to be heard. 'Why don't you tell us where you grew up instead?'

Violet smiled gratefully. 'It's a little market town in the north of England.' She paused. 'I will tell you the other thing. Just not here.'

'It was stupid of him to ask now.' Lois looked at me, pursing her lips.

I bit the inside of my cheek. 'Sorry.'

'No, it's only fair,' Violet said. 'You've told me everything.'

Not everything, I thought, thinking of the casebook. She still wasn't going to tell me everything yet, so I wasn't going to either.

There was a whoop from the direction of the entrance. A young man dressed in a pinstripe suit jumped from halfway down the ladder and, when he landed, pulled out a lighter, dancing with the flame above his head. He had thick blond hair in a dramatic swoop across his forehead, skin so pale that he seemed like a ghost, and an eyepatch over his left eye.

I knew, without needing to be told, that this was Chuck Hardaway.

19

There was a frantic wildness about Chuck Hardaway. One moment he was drawing a pretty blonde in for a kiss, full on the mouth, and the next he was standing on her table, calling for a glass of something syrupy and brown, which he drank in one gulp.

Violet immediately dropped off her chair and negotiated the crowd to approach him. The more time I spent with her, the more I noticed her total lack of fear. I wanted to be like her. It was so tiring being afraid all the time. She dipped and swerved through the crowd with ease, Lois and I trailing in her wake. Chuck had dropped down off the table and was holding court, telling the story of his leap from the roof the night before. He talked with his hands a lot and appeared to have no difficulty projecting over the music. The girls seemed enraptured by his storytelling, and the blonde he'd kissed kept touching his arm affectionately.

'Chuck Hardaway?' Violet asked as she marched up to him.

He stopped mid-sentence, and there was indignation in his face, as though he couldn't believe somebody would have the nerve to interrupt him. When he spotted Violet, he softened just a little.

'The man himself,' he said with a wide smile, running his hands down the sides of his body. 'And who might be asking?'

'I need to talk to you about Leery,' she said.

Lois and I exchanged a nervous glance – Violet was so bold, much bolder than we would have been. I hoped it would pay off.

Chuck's expressive face went very still. His eye narrowed, and he flicked his cigarette lighter, the flame leaping out, eager and ready to do his bidding. He licked his lips before speaking.

'I don't want to talk about him,' he said.

He turned his back on Violet, as if she were nothing more than an annoying bug he could flick off his skin.

'Chuck,' I said, and he turned, even more visibly annoyed. 'I think you knew my father, Alfred Ashe. He came back from the sanatorium and died a couple days ago. I want to know what happened to him over there.'

'I said I don't want to talk about Leery,' he said, his jaw tensing with irritation.

I was beginning to feel desperate. On the one hand, I didn't want to rob Chuck of his final moments, which he clearly wanted to spend in hedonistic delight, but on the other we were running out of time before the things that he knew died with him. I couldn't bear another failed attempt at understanding what had happened in the sanatorium, and how it could be the answer I was looking for.

I had tried appealing to Chuck's sympathetic nature, but it seemed he didn't have much of one.

Then it dawned on me – what sort of person, who knew they were going to die, would spend their final moments working for somebody else? Doing dangerous but well-paid work? A person who was trying to provide for somebody they were going to leave behind.

I reached for my wallet. That was something I knew how to do, and it had provided me with the answer to my troubles so many times in the past.

'I'm sure the people closest to you might benefit from you loosening your tongue,' I said, allowing the bills to flash.

A moment of indecision shot across Chuck's face. He looked from the wallet to the elegantly manicured hand of the blonde resting on his bicep and then to a clock behind the bar. Then his eyes settled on the wallet again.

'All right, all right,' he said. 'Up there.'

He gestured back to the ladder. Making excuses to his friends and planting a kiss on the neck of his girl, he made promises to return before leading the way back to the ladder. We climbed up behind him, the sounds of the speakeasy fading away when he shut the trap door, and laid down the insulation and the carpet. It was in this quiet space, this dark in-between room, that I heard the ticking sound emanating from Chuck – just like from Father and Bradley, and no less horrifying.

Out of the speakeasy, Chuck walked us right down to the end of the alleyway, and, as we emerged, the adjustment to daylight was so bright that my eyes ached with it.

'We haven't got a lot of time so let's get straight to it,' I pressed. 'What sort of Death Magic was Leery using on you all? What kind of object?' I added, cutting straight to the chase.

Chuck shook his head. He opened his palm and gestured for the money. 'I've got a sister. She's got three kids. I've been working for the Spencer brothers to make sure they're well taken care of. They even gave me this car,' he said, patting a beat-up orange buggy affectionately. 'It's not honest work, but I don't see how dispatching members of the Toombs Gang is any different than what they asked us to do in the war. At least I know the people Toombs employs are criminals.'

My skin crawled as I handed him a few folded bills. He'd spent his last hours making money as a hitman. Even if he had his reasons, Chuck Hardaway was a dangerous, damaged individual to have considered such a scheme. He tucked the notes in his pocket.

'So you know about the magic, huh?' Chuck placed a cigarette between his teeth and lit it, filling the air around us with a toxic plume. I managed to hold in my splutter. 'Well then, I guess I can tell you the whole thing without you thinking I've gone mad.'

'Tell us as much as you can,' Lois said without a waver in her voice. Was she becoming more convinced now?

'Your father was a good man,' Chuck said, gesturing at me. 'He'd work tirelessly for hours, stretchering injured men from the trenches to the dressing station, or driving a horse and cart loaded with casualties on to the field hospital further behind the front line.'

154

Although I'd hoped he would, it was a shock hearing him speak about Father. It was like getting a tiny glimpse into his life in the war. I wanted to know more, felt a tugging inside to ask questions related only to my father, but we had more pressing matters.

'Your father and I had got to talking a few times. I helped him carry the wounded from the front sometimes. He was the one who told me about Leery, said there was this doctor in the field hospital who could do things you never dreamed of. And I remember his voice was shaking when he told me that Leery had told him he thought he could bring the dead back to life.'

My breath caught in my throat.

'It's unbelievable, right?' he continued, staring past us out towards the busy street.

It was as though he were seeing a different time, a different place, in his mind's eye, not the day-to-day activities of the Lower East Side. He was in France, in the trenches. The look on his face was terrible. Haunted.

'I told him he'd finally lost his marbles if he believed all that. I said this doctor ought to be struck off if he was going around saying that sort of thing. But your father said he'd seen Leery do things that shouldn't be possible.'

'So what happened?' Violet asked. She seemed mesmerized.

'I died,' he said simply. 'I was in the dugout when it exploded, and a piece of corrugated iron from the roof sliced across my face. Right into my damned eye.' He gestured at the eyepatch. 'I was dead. Until I wasn't. There was Doctor Leery, peering in my face, telling me that he'd given me a few more years to live.'

'How did he bring you back?' I asked, my voice shaking. I was desperate to know.

Chuck shrugged. 'I don't know. And I don't want to either. We should have died, and we should have stayed dead. That was my moment, my fate. Afterwards, he looked after us well – I'd never say he didn't. But this isn't . . . this isn't life, the way we are.'

'What do you mean?' I asked, at the same moment as Violet whispered, 'The reaction.'

Chuck leaned up against his vehicle, and out of the corner of my eye I spotted the Imperium Mortis symbol painted by the edge of the wheel hub.

I was filled with an immediate sense of dread – was it a warning from Imperium Mortis? Were they here, lurking around a corner? Then I remembered that Bradley had been painting the symbol too, right before he died.

'Did you do that?' I asked Chuck.

He nodded. 'The last thing Imperium Mortis want is attention. It's sending them a warning. We're dying, and we want the police to notice, start asking questions. It's not as if we can walk up to them and talk about magic.'

If all the soldiers were painting symbols in the hopes of exposing Imperium Mortis, then perhaps it was Father who painted the one by our gate, the one I'd asked Simpkins to destroy all evidence of. What I didn't understand – *yet* – was why Leery would let them go without being certain of their silence. Surely he wanted to protect Imperium Mortis and ensure their work remained under wraps, so why didn't he keep the soldiers locked in the sanatorium until their dying day? Why would he risk them exposing the secret society he was part of and the terrible things they'd done?

Before I had the chance to ask Chuck about this, something caught his eye, and his face fell. I spun on my heel to see what he was looking at and saw a jewel-green vehicle turning down the alley, a man leaning out the window.

'Toombs,' Chuck spat. 'Sorry, kids, time's up. You'd better get out of here.'

He muttered a curse under his breath and started rummaging in his pockets for the keys to his car, but fumbled and dropped them as a loud rat-a-tat sound startled him. Chuck's face was a mask of terror, Lois screamed, and Violet ducked for cover behind the buggy, and it was only then I realized that the noise came from guns, from bullets heading in our direction. I didn't know what to do – the panic that flooded me had a tangible cause for a change. Fear speared my limbs, pinning me in place like a decorative butterfly. Chuck scrabbled around on the ground, blindly picking up his keys and leaping into the front seat.

I yelped as a bullet cracked past my ear.

This is real. I might actually die. It just takes one of those bullets to ricochet, one bad aim and we're done for.

The thoughts were galvanizing. A powerful exhilaration loosened my body, and I was able to use the rush to do what I needed to do – I grabbed Lois and pushed us both up against the wall, and the green car sped past us, the man with the gun screaming something that I couldn't hear before he was gone, in hot pursuit of Chuck's vehicle. Chuck must have stomped on the gas. He was fast, but the other car was faster. He swerved right, skidding round the corner, invoking the wrath of another driver who smashed down on their horn. The noise blurred with the squeal of tyres.

Lois was breathing heavily, her chest pressed up against mine, her eyes wide. Over her shoulder, I met Violet's gaze. Her jaw was tense. In the moment of danger, I hadn't given her a second thought, and she knew it.

'Follow them,' Violet said with grim resolve.

20

We breathlessly ran in the direction the cars had gone, expecting to see Chuck's orange buggy and Toombs' green roadster speeding away. But there was just utter chaos. As if from nowhere, a street lamp came crashing down. It slammed in front of Chuck's car, and he veered off the road. He was spinning and wheeling, round and round, until the front end of his car rammed straight into the front of a little grocery store. The window smashed, and Chuck's car concertinaed up on impact. Meanwhile, Toombs' car screeched, tilted and skidded sideways.

Lois turned to look at me, and all the colour drained out of her shocked face. Violet drifted towards the carnage, as though she were hypnotized and unable to keep away. My body started to shake again, just like it had done after Bradley died. Even my toes were quivering in my shoes as we joined the small crowd that had started to gather around the scene. Somebody was pulling a silent, still Toombs from his car, and, as we drew nearer, I saw a glint of something pearly that must have been bone.

There was shattered glass everywhere. The front of Chuck's car was crumpled like tissue paper. I stepped towards him, knowing what I was going to see, but my breath still pulled in tight and involuntarily. I gasped, mouth agape, because there was no other response to have.

Chuck was half in, half out of the windshield of his car. His torso was spread across the hood, face down, his arms spreadeagled and surrounded by shards of glass that glittered like diamonds. Where his waist should have been, he stopped, split from the rest of himself, still sitting in the car. His mouth was bloody, but none of that was what scared me.

His remaining eye was open, and it was full of the darkness. His face, wet with blood, and the hollowness of his dead dark eye was another image that I knew would stay with me forever.

I looked down at my wristwatch and was unsurprised to see that it was just a little past noon. Chuck was dead again. Just as Leery decided he would be.

'They're here!' Violet called.

Across the other side of the crowd were the two men we'd seen inspecting Bradley's body, pushing their way through, claiming to be police. This time I noticed tiny glinting badges pinned to their chests – the outline of skeletal wings and a ghastly heart. Imperium Mortis. They must have been just behind us – tailing Chuck, primed and ready to clear up after his demise.

This was something that didn't make sense to me – if they were afraid of being discovered, why were they allowing the soldiers to die like this? Why hadn't Leery kept them locked away in his sanatorium until they expired privately? But there was no time to think about that now.

We edged back from the mayhem, desperate to avoid being noticed by the Imperium Mortis associates. My mind was like a cauldron, full to brimming with a potent combination of the visceral images we had witnessed and the information that Chuck had given us. As we slipped away, Detective Jones was just arriving; I spotted her silvery hair and stern features as she shouldered her way through the crowd. Did she also have a list of the soldiers from the sanatorium? Was she keeping tabs on them too? I certainly would if I were in her position.

'We need to leave,' Lois said to me quietly.

Shaken from my reverie, I nodded, and followed her towards Violet, who was already some distance in front.

We had been stunned into silence. As we walked, in no particular direction, I churned it all together, hoping to create a smooth and palatable truth that would be easier to swallow. The soldiers were dead. They had first died in the war. Father had died years ago, and when he died Dr Leery had used magic to bring him back, for a time. The man who'd come back home to us hadn't really been my father at all.

Around us, the lives of everyone else seemed to carry on as normal – unaware of the carnage just a few blocks over. People were buying their groceries from bustling stalls, congregating with friends, even singing. We looped the same bit of street twice, lost in the labyrinthine blocks that seemed to repeat and repeat.

'I'm sorry I doubted you,' Lois said eventually. Her voice was grave. 'What we've seen – it was unnatural. If you're telling me that it's based in magic, that you've experienced magic, then I have to believe that.'

She believed me. It was everything I'd hoped for.

So why did I feel so cold?

21

We stopped at an empty little cafe, settling into chairs at a table by the window. I stuck to my familiar crutch – hot dark coffee.

'We need to find the next soldier,' Violet said. 'And fast. No waiting until tomorrow. I've still got so many questions.'

'First, you need to tell us how you discovered Imperium Mortis,' Lois said, focusing intently on Violet. 'If we're going to stay together, then we need to know.'

Violet looked taken aback by Lois's sudden forthrightness. A taste of her own medicine, I thought. Then she sighed deeply.

'Fine. My father died in the first year of the war. He told us he would be back before Christmas. My mother needed me to start making some money, so I took a job as a maid at this big house in the city of York. The *old* York. I worked for a family called the Adairs, who had recently relocated from Scotland. At the time, I thought it was just because they wanted to escape from Mr Adair's reputation for extramarital affairs . . . But then later I found out the real reason they'd moved was so their son, Lachlan, could join Imperium Mortis.'

'And how exactly did you find that out?' I asked.

'We fell in love,' she said as if it were that simple.

That was the last thing I was expecting her to say. I had to force myself not to laugh or stare at her incredulously.

'Who? You and the son?'

'Yes, me and Lachlan,' she said, and I could tell that I'd offended her. 'Look, I know. I know that it was naïve of me to fall in love with the son of my employer, and there was no way it ever would have worked out. Rich boys don't just marry their maids, do they? But he did love me too.'

I got the impression that it wasn't the first time she'd had to defend their relationship, that their feelings weren't just a fantasy she held in her head.

'So Lachlan told you about Imperium Mortis,' Lois said.

'There's more to it than that.' Violet had loosened a strand of hair from her chignon and was twisting it around her fingers. 'He told me that the only way for us to be together was for me to join Imperium Mortis as well, or else our lives would just be too different. So he recommended me for their mentorship and initiation programme.'

I had suspected that Violet's knowledge of Imperium Mortis had been gathered on a personal level, but I hadn't imagined that it had gone so deep. Given the vitriol she showed when she spoke of them, it seemed as though their values couldn't possibly have aligned sufficiently for her to be actively involved with them ... But, then again, I hadn't accounted for her being head over heels for a member.

'So . . . you were part of Imperium Mortis?'

From the little I knew about the organization, her involvement was nothing good. The people in it were merciless, their obsession was as dangerous as it was cruel, and their magic was only possible through murder . . .

'No.' Violet gave a wry smile. 'I failed the initiation programme. When you sign up, you're sworn to secrecy, but I sent my mother a letter with some money, and I told her I was safe. I didn't want her to worry. The letter was intercepted. That's why I failed. They said I wasn't ruthless enough.'

'And they just let you walk away?' Lois sounded more than a little unconvinced. '"Oh, we've shared with you all the intimate details of our top-secret murder organization, whose members just happen to be able to use magic, but okay, off you go."'

'No.' Violet scowled. 'In Imperium Mortis, either you're initiated, or you die. And I would have been killed if it hadn't been for Lachlan. I'd have ended up as one of their Death Magic experiments.'

'That's horrendous,' I said.

The word didn't seem big enough. I couldn't help but feel a little sorry for Violet. It was clear Imperium Mortis were evil through and through.

And yet . . . Father had trusted them. At least to an extent – or he wouldn't have joined forces with Leery.

'How did you escape?' I asked, trying to distract myself from that thought.

'When Lachlan found out what they were going to do to me, he bought me a ticket on a ship to come here. I honestly don't know how he managed to get me out, or what happened to him after. Hopefully, his money will have protected him. If Ada Leery ever learned he was responsible for letting me go . . .'

She had twisted the loose piece of hair so much that it had become a thin rat's tail. It was as close as she got to the sort of distressed hand-wringing that Mother did when she was feeling overwhelmed. Violet didn't seem like the sort to cry or wail, but that didn't mean that her feelings ran any less deep.

'It was a risk sending me here,' she continued, 'right into the heart of where Ada is setting up the US chapter of Imperium Mortis. But, as an outsider now, I can stop them – and get Lachlan out so we can be together again.'

Are you sure he wants out? I thought, but what I asked instead was 'You're still in love with him, aren't you?'

Violet looked at her hands, linked her fingers together. 'What does it matter how I feel? Ada is here, and she's spreading Imperium Mortis like a sickness. They don't deserve to have magic. Maybe it's futile, but I'm going to spend the rest of my life trying to take it away from them, piece by piece.'

That was the crux of it then. Violet wanted to hurt Imperium Mortis. I had no doubt she'd do her utmost to destroy them if she could, but what chance did a penniless outcast have against an ancient global organization? I was beginning to understand why she needed me.

'If we track down Hugo, will *you* use Death Magic, if it can prolong your life?' Violet asked me now.

'I don't know. I guess I'm just hoping that we'll find a way to undo what's been done,' I said, but I knew that didn't really answer Violet's question.

The only thing I did know for certain was that I wasn't done investigating, that if I only had a few weeks to live, then continuing on the path I'd started to follow didn't seem optional. If there was any hope of finding a way to overcome the curse, then I had to keep going – for my sake, but also for Nick's.

I pushed my empty cup away and stood up, my resolve hardened. 'Vaughan Jenkins,' I said, eager to move the conversation on. Lois and Violet looked at me, confused by the sudden change of topic. 'He's the next soldier on the list. We don't have time to waste.'

22

Vaughan Jenkins was the soldier who had been interviewed in *Disclosed*. As far as we knew, he was homeless and destitute. The only lead we had was the address of a boarding house in the Theater District from Leery's notes. I had stopped thinking of them as patient records because to think of the soldiers as patients was misleading. Dr Leery was no benevolent caregiver; he was a mad scientist, using the magic as a form of experimentation.

I drove us out of the Lower East Side, heading for Midtown West. The Theater District was already glowing even though dusk hadn't yet begun to fall. The electric lights of the billboards created a streaming pathway of illuminations, the Great White Way. The established theatres were at the centre of it all, and around the edges new theatre construction was sprouting up, grasping for a share of the spotlight. Violet's eyes were round and shining with the reflection of the lights; she looked completely in awe. It struck me again what different worlds we'd come from.

The boarding house was a thin slip of a building tucked in behind the main strip. I got the girls to wait in the car while I made my way up a narrow staircase to the front door.

I knocked and waited. Within moments, the door swung open, cast wide in an extravagant gesture performed by a little man with a bulging midriff.

'Are you the landlord here?' I asked.

'I am.' He presented me with a hand to shake that was covered in rings. 'Aloysius Hamilton. I'm afraid we don't have any vacancies right now.'

'Do you know where I can find Vaughan Jenkins?'

Aloysius's face fell, and he looked embarrassed. 'Ah. I'm sorry. Are you a friend of his?' I nodded, and he continued: 'I'm real sorry about what happened to him. I found a tenant to cover his time overseas, and, when he didn't come back, I just assumed he'd died. I kept his belongings for a whole six months after the armistice. I couldn't hold on to his things forever, though. And, as for the room, it's not available. The new tenant has a contract. Legally, there's nothing I can do about that.'

'I understand. But do you know where he's staying now?'

'I heard the Celeste Theater took him in. He trod the boards there a few times, like most of them I get boarding here. They all want to be actors.'

'The Celeste Theater . . .?'

'Where Ninth Avenue meets Forty-third Street. Tell him I am sorry about the book!' Aloysius called after me as I headed back to the car.

'I've got a lead,' I said as I jumped back in, and we followed Aloysius's directions.

The Celeste was small, with four white bulbs that framed the corners of a board where thick letters told us that the company were performing *Macbeth* until Christmas. Compared to the hundreds of gleaming lights all along the district, those four bulbs seemed a forlorn attempt to match the dazzling electric displays of the larger theatres.

The entrance had a moth-eaten red carpet leading into the foyer, and a quiet hush about it. Not exactly a place rolling in trade.

A young woman with a thick blonde braid sat behind a wooden hatch. 'Are you wanting tickets for the show tonight?' Her eyes were a little too eager, bordering on desperate.

'I'm afraid not. We're looking for Vaughan Jenkins,' I said. 'I believe he's staying here?'

'Sure, I can take you to see Vaughan.' The girl ran her hands over the surface of the hatch. 'I'm not really supposed to leave in case a customer comes . . . but I'm sure it'll be fine for five minutes.' She seemed to be accepting the unlikelihood of any ticket sales that afternoon. She disappeared for a moment, and then popped out a side door.

'They call me Ollie,' the ticket seller said, and we how-do-you-do-ed. 'How do you know Vaughan?' she asked, and there was a protective edge to her voice.

I turned to Violet, expecting her to have concocted a story, but she shrugged her shoulders. Not for the first time in our brief friendship, it felt as if she were testing me. Had I picked up enough from her to be able to craft my own lie? Different scenarios chased through my mind, things that I could tell this woman without revealing the truth of the situation . . . and yet they went by so fast I couldn't grab a single one. So I told the truth.

'We're not acquainted yet,' I said, and Violet scrunched her nose up in disappointment. 'Vaughan knew my father in the war.'

'Oh,' said Ollie. She lowered her voice. 'He doesn't much like talking about the war.'

'Does anyone who was involved in it?' Violet said.

'Well, I suppose not,' Ollie said. 'You know he lost his room at the boarding house where he was staying, and they threw away all his belongings? But I convinced my brother to let him stay in the attic here until he gets back on his feet. He's shut himself away up there all day and all night with a second-hand typewriter for the last week. One of the things that landlord got rid of was a stack of his papers, a play he'd been writing. He's awful cut up about having to start from scratch.'

We nodded and made sympathetic noises. Seemingly satisfied that we were friendly enough, Ollie indicated that we should follow her, and she led us to the auditorium, where two actors were running through a scene.

'Oh, full of scorpions is my mind, dear wife!' lamented a grizzled-looking Macbeth with a cigarette between his teeth and bare feet that squeaked on the stage.

I'd heard the line before, but never had it struck such a deep chord inside me. I shivered and hoped that Vaughan would give us the answers we so desperately needed.

23

Ollie led us up a staircase covered in cobwebs to a tiny attic room in the eaves of the building. The flimsy door opened to reveal Vaughan sitting in the corner at a typewriter, his fingers moving with great speed over the keys. He was hunched over, and his lank chestnut hair hung in a great swathe, so long that it almost brushed the paper.

I was surprised to see that, unlike my father, Bradley and Chuck, he had no visible injuries. A golden pocket watch with a distinctive dent at the top near the crown was laid out next to him. It must have had strong sentimental value for him to hold on to it despite his circumstances – I could imagine it might have fetched a good price.

And I noticed right away – he ticked.

Tick. Tick. Tick.

That sound haunted me and transported me. It took me to the alley near the speakeasy, it took me to the stone Peristyle steps, it took me to the front seat of the car, watching my father in the rear-view mirror and wondering how he could possibly fit in at home . . .

'Vaughan,' Ollie called gently. 'You've got visitors.'

Vaughan held his hand up to quieten her, still typing with the other hand. A pained expression crossed his face, as if the process of extricating the words was as agonizing as extricating his organs would be. 'No, no, no, it's gone. The line has gone.' He turned to us, his eyes flaming with fury. 'What do you want?'

I stepped forward. 'Mister Jenkins. My name is Felix Ashe. You knew my father in the war.'

Vaughan raised an eyebrow. 'I knew a lot of men in the war.'

'You were in the sanatorium together,' I continued, giving him a look that I hoped was significant. 'We want to talk to you about Doctor Leery.'

Something cold passed over his face. He turned to Ollie and asked, 'Would you mind giving us some time alone?'

Ollie seemed only slightly offended. She left us to it, and her steps echoed down the staircase.

'You're not with *them*,' Vaughan said, but he didn't seem certain in his judgement.

'No,' Violet said. 'We're not part of Imperium Mortis.'

'Aha!' Vaughan said. 'But you did know who I was talking about!' He jabbed his finger in a gesture of triumph.

'Yes. We know about the magic,' Lois agreed.

Vaughan let out a gleeful laugh. 'Oh, what a relief to be able to speak about it. I'd been starting to wonder if it was all just a terrible hallucination, if I was losing my mind. I haven't dared speak it out loud, and then here you are saying the word *magic* to me as if it's a normal thing to talk about.'

'You're not losing your mind,' I said, although I wasn't entirely sure that was true. 'We know that you died in the war, and that Leery brought you back.'

'Part of me.' Vaughan snorted. 'It's not really like being alive.' His eyes went vacant as he stared at the page in front of him.

'What do you mean?' Lois asked.

'Everything is dull. It's like . . . Imagine being robbed of your senses, the things that make the world feel alive. Yes, I'm here, but I'm not *really* here. I can't feel pain . . . but I can't feel joy either. I can't really feel anything. Can you imagine that?'

I would never tell him, but there was indeed a part of me that *could* imagine that. Fear had made my world shrink, and, at times, joy had seemed like something unattainable, something from an old version of my life. But, unlike Vaughan, I had vowed to change my fate.

'I don't know how I'm supposed to write with feeling when I don't feel anything any more.' Vaughan slammed his hand on the table next to the typewriter. 'It's not going to be finished before . . .'

'Before your time?' Lois asked quietly.

Vaughan sighed. 'At least I know it won't hurt. Not like last time. Do you know, when I signed up, I thought it would give me something to write about? And there are people who have written about it, people who will go on to write about it – will be remembered for it – but that won't be me. Whenever I try, there's something . . . missing.' He gestured around his heart. 'Dead men aren't filled with creative energy. My best hope of leaving behind something that will outlive me is that play I wrote before; I have to try and scrape it together from the recesses of my memory.'

I recognized in him the same desire as in me – to make a mark on this world and leave behind something that would live on.

After a long pause, he asked, 'Why did you come here?'

'We have some questions,' I said. 'About Imperium Mortis. But mostly about Death Magic. Can you tell us how it happened – your second life, I mean?'

'It's a tragedy of errors on my part,' Vaughan said. 'The truth is I had no idea what war would be like. None at all. I was at rock bottom and didn't have a dime, and I heard that the military paid well. It wouldn't be long, I thought, and it would supply me with creative material – about honour and bravery and comradeship. Instead, I found myself surrounded by such death and destruction that imagination can't even touch.'

'How did you meet Leery?' Violet asked.

She was getting more impatient by the minute, her toe tapping, her tone rushing Vaughan on to the inevitable part of his tale, the reason we had come. And yet I didn't feel like I needed to press him onwards; it was a relief that, for once, we had the time. The night was creeping in, but Vaughan wouldn't die until tomorrow.

'In the field hospital, after I was injured going over the top. I was shot three times,' Vaughan said, pointing to his left shoulder, the right side of his chest and then his abdomen. 'They brought us all to be triaged, laid us out in front of the tents, and I was placed in Leery's tent. He performed surgery on me to remove the bullets, and in that twenty-four-hour period I was the only person to survive. The men came into the tent in pieces, bleeding and screaming, and within an hour or two they'd go silent. Twenty-four hours turned into three days, and everyone who came in still died, but I was hanging on. In and out of consciousness, burning up with fever, and Leery came to me each day. He began to ask me how much I wanted to live. I said I'd do anything, and he shared his proposition with me . . . an experimental treatment, to be undertaken after my death.'

I was stunned into silence. Suddenly I didn't want to ask any more questions. The whole time that the war was happening, I had been so wrapped up in my own world and the way that it affected me that I hadn't allowed myself to truly comprehend that every single soldier had made sacrifices that I knew I would have been too fearful to make. I was the sort of person that, upon conscription, would probably have fled and been shot for desertion. I had been in the enviable position where I could close my eyes to it, safe and secure at home.

'When I woke, I'd been moved to a different tent, and I was on my own. I didn't know that I had died. I just knew that I didn't feel anything any more . . . There were four of us, and Leery kept us in a separate tent to hide us, so that we wouldn't be sent back to the front. If the war hadn't ended when it did, we might have been found and made to go fight again, but then the armistice happened.

'Leery forced us to go with him to England, said that we couldn't return to our families as we were, and in truth I don't think we needed much persuading. None of us felt like ourselves, and we were frightened of the way that we'd changed, of the way that we'd returned from death. It was only when we got to the sanatorium that we realized he was part of a whole organization. I think each of us wished that we'd been left to die. We couldn't leave, but he wouldn't kill us, wouldn't end his experiment. The sanatorium was limbo.'

'Why did he eventually let you go then?' I asked. 'Why now, and why are you due to die like this, all in a row?'

Vaughan's mouth drew into an even grimmer line. 'He is murdering us,' he said. 'If you can call killing a dead man murder. He's using our deaths to make a statement.'

'A statement?' My forehead puzzled into a frown. 'What do you mean?'

'All in a row, one by one. It's a warning for his sister, Ada. Hugo Leery has burned all his bridges with Imperium Mortis –'

'Wait,' Violet interrupted, before I had the chance to formulate a question. 'What do you mean? Hugo and Ada are estranged?'

She was ahead of me, her quick mind leaping through the consequences of the information that Vaughan was revealing. Her voice was harsh, and she had this look in her eyes like she wanted to shake him.

'It would seem so. She killed his wife, you see. Quite hard to maintain friendly relations after that.'

Violet shook her head. 'Hugo didn't have a wife.'

Her shock had quickly turned to confusion and then angry doubt. The revelation had completely wrong-footed her. I got the sense that she prided herself on the knowledge she'd acquired. She rather liked being our guide through the world of Death Magic – it made her feel valuable – and now here she was being shown up by somebody who knew something that she had been oblivious to.

'A wife and a daughter,' Vaughan said. 'He led two lives, keeping them secret from each other. But his daughter got sick, and Hugo only told his wife the truth about Imperium Mortis when he thought the magic could save their daughter's life.'

Hearing that felt like Leery and my father had been on parallel tracks – two men leaning into this magic to try and save their children. It wasn't so different. 'What happened to them?'

'The wife was horrified by the truth. She was going to expose them. So Ada killed her.'

'And what of the sick daughter?' I asked, pressing further, my fingers twitching by my side as though they could reach out and pull the information from Vaughan's brain.

'Joy,' Vaughan said, and there was some tenderness in his voice. 'Her name was Joy. I don't know what happened to her. After his wife was killed, Hugo never told us what happened to Joy – if he managed to save her or not. He was wild with grief, and told us he wouldn't rest until he'd seen Imperium Mortis destroyed. He made us promise that, if he let us see our loved ones again, we'd leave a sign for Ada before we died. I can tell you that we all felt like we wanted to die by that point anyway, so a last chance to come home was all the incentive we needed to go along with it.'

That explained the symbols that each of them had painted. They were a warning for Ada that her brother wouldn't rest until Imperium Mortis had been eradicated.

'Then he knocked us out, and we woke up on a boat, each with a slip like this in our pockets.' Vaughan showed us a tattered piece of paper, just like the one Father had. 'And we knew then that he'd done whatever it was he needed to do to bring our lives to an end.'

There was an odd finality to it, knowing that we'd come to the end of the road. Vaughan was going to die, and then there would be no more soldiers from Leery's experiments left.

My teeth ached from clenching my jaw. Hugo Leery had discovered a way to bring the dead back to life, and – more than that – he had the power to control *when* they would die. It was everything that I'd been hoping for since I discovered that Death Magic existed. He had found out how to pinpoint the moment of death, the crossroads with fate, and change it.

My moment, my fate, my time ... it had already been manipulated by Death Magic. It had already been cut short by the curse. Hugo Leery was the only person who could help me to survive it.

My reverie was interrupted by the sound of feet stomping up the stairs, and Ollie shouting, 'Hey! You can't go up there!'

I looked down the stairwell and saw three Imperium Mortis agents taking the stairs at a lick. I noticed the flash of a silver gun in the hands of the leader, pointing ahead. I was torn in half by the fear, a ragged rip inside me.

'They're here.' I was struggling to breathe. I slammed the door shut, but there was no latch to buy us time.

'Quick,' Vaughan said, immediately on his feet. 'Out the fire escape.'

He opened a large window at the back of the attic. There was a short drop down on to a metal platform, with a steep ladder leading down to another platform, and so on until it hit the ground.

Violet scrambled to go first, and I insisted that Lois follow. I have never moved with more urgency in my life, and it was only after landing on the platform that I was struck with the full terror of the height we were at. I imagined losing my footing, the damage that such a fall might do to my body. I took a deep breath to steady myself – surely being frozen in place would lead to a worse outcome.

An Imperium Mortis agent leaned out the window then and called down a sharp greeting. 'Thank you for helping us find him!' Then he slammed the window shut, leaving me to wonder what awful fate we had left Vaughan to.

When the three of us had safely reached the ground, I hugged my arms tightly around me to fight off the chill, but it didn't work. It wasn't the cold of the brisk winter – the chill was *inside* me. *Thank you*, the agent had said.

No. It couldn't be.

But the pieces were slotting into place. I had wondered why the Imperium Mortis agents kept showing up after the men were dead, why they would have allowed them to die in public, risking exposure. Well, that had been Leery's plan all along, and Ada and the agents of Imperium Mortis *hadn't* known where to find the soldiers or when their deaths would happen. They didn't have a list of names and times like I had. No, but they'd heard about my father's death and connected the dots about his association with Leery, and somehow – *When? Where?* – I had caught their attention. *I* was the one they'd been trailing, ever since my father died. And I'd led them right to Bradley, and to Chuck, and now, prematurely, to Vaughan.

'We need to leave,' I said, and we hurried back to the car. 'I think they've been following me since the start. I don't think we're safe at all. We need to find Hugo Leery – now!'

'If Ada hasn't killed him already,' Violet said with a curl of her lip. 'But the best way to find something lost is to start with the last place you left it.'

'The sanatorium,' I replied, my voice sounding hollow.

It was inevitable. There was no possible way I could go back to my old life, let it carry on as normal until Death Magic planned a cataclysmic and fatal accident for me, and for Nick too, eventually. The only way forward was to go deeper into this new world, learning the rules of this odd game with the darkness, and finding a way to break free from its grasp.

'You're serious?' Lois asked in the car. 'You really want to go to England?'

'I don't know what other option I have,' I said. 'Hugo is the only person who can help me. And if I stay here, I'm certain that Imperium Mortis will want to talk to me.'

'He's right. And I'm coming with you,' Violet said without a moment's hesitation, and then she laughed a giddy little laugh, which sounded slightly hysterical. 'If he can be found, we'll find him.'

'That's the gamble,' I said. 'He might be dead already. Or if he is alive, we might not be able to find him. And even if we do, he might not want to help me.'

The doubts were starting to creep in, and fast. It was beginning to dawn on me just what a huge endeavour it would be, to travel to England, and how slim the chances of success were.

'And if I do go, and it's all for nothing . . . I'll have wasted so much of my remaining time.' I looked at Lois again, whose expression was stricken.

'Don't dwell on that,' Violet said sharply. 'You haven't got any other option. If we don't go, then that's just accepting the darkness is going to swallow you up.'

'And Nick,' I said. 'If I accept defeat now, the darkness won't just take me, it'll take him as well, when his eighteenth birthday inevitably dawns. I couldn't bear anything to happen to him, whether I'm around to see it or not. And my mother, without either of us . . .' I didn't want to think about it. Her world would be so very empty.

'Exactly,' Violet said.

She had a strength and conviction that I wished I could tap into and siphon off to keep for myself. Already I was starting to think of all the ways that I could die on an ocean liner crossing the Atlantic.

Lois was watching us both. The caution on her face had turned to determination. 'If you're going, I am too.'

My heart skipped. 'Are you sure?'

'We've come this far together,' Lois said.

The warmth of her words spread through me. We were a team. It was only right that I would go on this journey with her. I squeezed her hand.

Did I imagine the flash of annoyance in Violet's eyes?

'Then it's decided. I'll buy the next available tickets I can,' I said, pushing aside my concerns.

Violet reached into her pocket and pulled out a golden watch, taking a quick glance at the time. I did a double take – the watch had a notch in the metal at the top, by the crown. She seemed to notice me staring and shoved the watch back in her pocket.

'It's not as if he needed it,' she grumbled.

She had stolen it from Vaughan. The thought made me feel a bit sick. I wanted – no, needed – to trust her, and she was making that very difficult.

When I'd dropped both of them off – Violet at the sorry-looking boarding house and Lois at her palatial mansion – I drove home to the realization that I needed to face Father's funeral before I could prepare to travel to England.

I cast my mind back to when Mother told me Father was coming home ... I simply couldn't have imagined the darkness or the horrid sights that I would see in pursuit of the truth.

But I also could never have imagined the way that it would force me to face my fears. In a strange way, I felt more alive than I had done in months, although arguably I had far more to be terrified of. If I had learned anything since I discovered the truth about Death Magic, it was that the frightful things were never going to go away, but in painfully expecting and dreading them I suffered twice. Maybe I would never break the chain of fear that had wound itself tightly around my mind, but I could choose to keep going in spite of it.

The anxiety hadn't gone. It thrummed through me, like an undertow in the sea, at times threatening to drag me down, but I was growing stronger every day I continued to show up, becoming more able to fight against the current and keep going.

It wasn't that fear stopped existing; it was that hope now lived alongside it.

18 NOVEMBER 1920

TWENTY-FOUR DAYS LEFT

24

I helped Nick with his tie, fashioning the black fabric into a knot, pulling it tight and allowing the long end to fall. I felt a deep grief that this was his first funeral. When our brothers died, Nick stayed at the house with Miss Price.

'If you want to leave at any point, you just let me know,' I said.

'That wouldn't be proper, would it?' Concern crossed his face.

'I don't think anyone would mind. People know funerals are difficult.'

'There won't be many people there, though, will there?'

'No,' I said, sorry that my father was being dispatched from this life as if he had barely existed. Mother had deliberately arranged a very small funeral in the hopes of keeping gossip to a minimum. Nick gripped my hand tight.

'All right, buddy. Let's go.' In our matching suits, we looked like a mournful double act.

Mother was in the hallway, wearing a black dress that hung to halfway down her calves. Her eyes were red, the lids swollen. I wrapped my arm around her shoulder, and she sank into me.

'I'm sorry I've been away,' I found myself saying, the guilt from having been absent at such a crucial time nagging at me.

'Don't apologize. I won't have you feeling terrible for living your own life. That's all I've ever wanted for you,' Mother said, giving me a wobbly smile. 'I had a call from the mortician this morning. Somebody tried to break into their property last night, though luckily an employee was working late and stopped them. Probably planning on stealing wedding rings from the dead to pawn. Can you imagine? How ghastly. What sort of person would attempt to *do* such a thing?'

There was a terrible twisting in the pit of my stomach. I had a feeling that it wasn't a case of stealing from the dead, but of something even more sinister. I'd stopped believing in coincidences a while ago, and the timing of this felt more than a little suspicious. I shuddered. Had Imperium Mortis been trying to get to Father's body? Why? Hadn't they already taken everything from him?

When it was time, Harold drove us to the crematorium. Mother chewed at the nails she had so meticulously filed the previous night, while Nick stared straight ahead. In his hands was a small piece of string that he knotted once, twice, three times. We all shivered in our thick black overcoats.

As we arrived at the crematorium, Mother took a sharp breath. There was deliberation behind each movement of her face, as though she were trying to arrange it into an appropriate configuration, the way she always did when we went out in public. She always transformed herself, like an actress. Even I couldn't tell what was going on behind the mask.

I took Nick's hand in mine, pulling the string away and tucking it into his pocket. 'It's going to be fine,' I said, squeezing.

The sunlight was piercing, penetrating the frosty air and causing the crystallized ground to twinkle like my mother's diamond earrings. She led the way past the church and up the little hill where the crematorium, a modern concrete block, perched. Pausing in the doorway, she steadied herself before heading in. I followed, my eyes taking a moment to adjust.

White lilies had been arranged on stands at the end of the rows – there were more flowers than people. The front row of seats had been left empty for us, and in the row behind sat Geoffrey; our family lawyer had taken the next row back with his wife and child; and, finally, there was a stranger in a black suit with a tiny silver pin, whose sharp edges were recognizable at a distance as wings.

A shudder of utter dread crept down my spine. Imperium Mortis had sent somebody. A scream threatened to escape from my throat, but I swallowed it down.

Seeing the depleted gathering, Nick visibly relaxed, his shoulders not quite so bunched up at his ears. Mother lifted her chin proudly. Rising to the challenge, she swept down to the front row.

As I made to follow her, the Imperium Mortis associate put out his hand in front of me.

'Might I have a word with you?'

His face was smooth, and he looked young and scholarly. Mother and Nick had continued walking and the aisle seemed to stretch ahead. They seemed very far away.

'Not now,' I said, eyeing the front row where Mother and Nick now stood together, a little unit.

The man didn't take the hint, his arm still forming a barrier. He rested his other hand on my upper arm. It was overly familiar; I flinched.

A strain of music rose from the organ. The officiant was waiting to begin. I turned and saw the coffin in the entrance hall, carried high on the shoulders of the pallbearers we had to hire for lack of anyone who could carry the coffin.

I had promised Mother and Nick I would be by their side. I pulled away from the man, but he gripped my arm tighter and dragged me into his pew. The coffin began its slow journey to the front. Mother was looking around for me, something between fear and anger flashing through her eyes.

The agent wasn't finished. 'I hope you don't think this awfully disrespectful of me, but there's some property I need to reclaim from your father.'

What could he mean? Did he know that Father had taken the casebook?

'No,' I said, although he hadn't asked a question.

The coffin had reached the front, and the officiant had begun to speak – dry, meaningless words.

The man gripped my jacket sleeve. 'It really is of the greatest urgency. I can't stress that enough,' he hissed. I tore my arm out of his grasp.

As long as we were in public, there was nothing he could do. The mourners, albeit few in number, afforded me protection. The last thing Imperium Mortis wanted was to draw too much attention to themselves. That emboldened me and, allowing the rage to flush its way through my body, I gripped his sleeve right back and yanked him in the direction of the door. We tussled out into the entrance hall and then outside, the cling of the cold air taking my breath away.

'Get out of here,' I spat.

'The property, the thing I need ... it's inside him. It's inside his body.'

Inside his body? He couldn't have meant the casebook then. My forehead knitted itself into a frown.

'How dare you,' I said, my voice rising to match my overflowing temper. 'What were you expecting? That I would halt the proceedings so that you could slice him open in front of us? What is it? What's inside him? And how did it get there?'

'I can't speak of it.' The man stammered as he spoke. I had defied all his expectations with my outburst. He clearly wasn't used to being challenged. His cool authority had dissipated, and he looked at me as if I were a dangerous animal, wary of what I might do next.

'Can't?' I felt my lip curl into a sneer. 'Did Ada Leery say that you can't?'

The blood drained from his face. His hands were shaking. He was frightened of her. Even the mention of her name had spooked him. That was something I could use.

'How do you know that name?'

'You haven't been careful enough,' I said, bluffing, hoping that I had rightly assessed that his fear of the very organization he worked for was powerful enough for me to assert some control over the situation. 'What have you come for?' I asked.

'I . . . I can't . . .'

'Then leave,' I said. 'And don't come back.'

My fingers twitched. I felt if he didn't leave then I might hit him, that was how overwhelming my anger was. He lifted his hands in a gesture of surrender and withdrew.

I turned back to the crematorium, running a hand through my hair, the sweat gathering at my hairline. I slid into a seat at the back, but my mother turned and flashed her eyes at the space next to her where I should have been standing. My cheeks flushed red as I slunk down the centre aisle and took my place.

Awful, agonizing questions invaded my mind.

Should I call it off? Should I ask someone to cut him open? What was inside him?

I started to regret the way I'd spoken to the Imperium Mortis agent. What had felt necessary and righteous in the moment seemed foolhardy when the angry flood began to ebb. Clearly, whatever was inside Father was valuable to Imperium Mortis and presumably connected to Death Magic in some way.

Father's coffin made its slow entry towards the furnace. I knew that once we stepped outside the building, they would turn it on, and Father's body would be swallowed up by the fire.

*

It was only afterwards, in the quiet of the evening, that a thought struck me. Whatever it was that Imperium Mortis had wanted from inside Father's body . . . was it something that I might have needed too?

The thought made my stomach drop. It was too late for those wonderings. Far too late. In my haste and temper, I might have turned a lifeline into ashes.

19 NOVEMBER 1920

TWENTY-THREE DAYS LEFT

25

The following day, I got up early and went to the bank to withdraw as much cash as I could from the allowance Mother released to me every month. When I came out, my wallet was near to bursting. Then I headed to the port, where I was told that we could take a cancellation on an ocean liner that was leaving the following morning. The liner would be able to transport us across the Atlantic in seven or eight days, depending on the wind – not a record-breaking time, but a testament to the incredible progress in engineering nonetheless. The cancellation was for a parlour suite in first class, made up of three connected bedrooms, a private bathroom and a drawing room, and it came to a princely sum that wiped out more than half of the cash I had withdrawn from the bank. The rest of it I exchanged for British pounds. I booked return tickets for us all and hoped that my optimism wasn't misplaced.

When I returned to Pitch House, I rang Lois to let her know that I would be collecting her early the following morning. I had no way of calling Violet, but no doubt she would have already prepared a bag.

Next I knew I needed to have the conversation with Mother, the one that I'd been dreading. Honesty had become unavoidable.

She was in her bedroom, underneath the silk of her coverlet, but not asleep. Oftentimes, she would spend long days in bed, not sleeping but not fully awake either, lost in the world between the two. This wasn't something new – it had been a habit for a long time now. A tiny candle flame flickered on her nightstand, and she was watching it.

'Mother,' I said, and when she lifted her head I noticed that she was cradling one of Father's old shirts.

She pulled herself up to a sitting position, and a little noise caught in her throat. She was stroking the shirt the way she would have stroked Father's cheek, and then she let out a big sigh, one that seemed to go on forever.

'I'm dreadfully confused. I miss him terribly. I've missed him for years. I feel as though he's been dead a very long time. I thought he was never coming home; then, once he was here, all I wanted was him gone again. And now I feel so wracked with guilt.'

'You couldn't have known what was going to happen.' I clambered on to the bed to sit next to her.

'When he came back, it was as if the light inside that made him who he was had gone out,' she continued. 'Do you understand what I mean?'

I understood exactly. I too had felt that some essential part of what made Father himself had been extinguished.

'Felix . . . I found out that your father changed his will,' Mother said. 'Everything has been left to a stranger.'

'A stranger?' When would the shocking revelations stop?

'Wade Griffin,' she said, a small sob escaping her lips. 'I've never heard of him before. I can't understand it.'

I shook my head. Father had left everything ... to someone else? It stung. This was the fortune that my life was payment for. And now he'd taken even that from me.

'Everything?' I couldn't believe it.

Mother bit her lip and nodded. She looked as if she wanted to run away. 'The worst part is ... it's all gone already. He began this process years ago, before he left for the war – he signed away the deeds to the house, drained the accounts. This Wade Griffin owns it all.'

'What? How can that be possible?'

Mother shook her head. 'The household expenses have been coming from a separate account, it seems. One that we've nearly burned through. What if this Wade Griffin shows up here and demands that we leave? Where would we go?'

I felt a little dizzy. None of it was ours. We were nearly broke. Father had left us with nothing ...

Well, not exactly *nothing* ... I was struck by the memory of Father's face sagging with relief as he pressed Leery's journal into my hands, and I promised to crack the code. I had to believe that its contents were valuable, perhaps worth more than my inheritance. I had to believe that the casebook held the answers I was looking for.

I was only scratching the surface in understanding what exactly had happened at the sanatorium in England, and I had no doubt that, if I could just follow the trail, I'd eventually learn all the things that Father wanted to explain to me himself, but couldn't.

It was time. I had to tell Mother.

'I have to go to England.'

Mother frowned. 'What are you talking about?'

I took her hand, and I told her everything I'd discovered so far. All of it.

Mother looked down at our linked hands and ran her thumb over my knuckles. 'I didn't want to believe it was true. That would mean believing that the reason your brothers are gone . . . is this.' She gestured around, at the house, the luxury, the extravagance. 'And now your father has even taken this away from me.' A stream of anger bubbled between the words.

'I know,' I said.

That George, Scott and Luke had been lost forever to Death Magic seemed like the greatest cruelty.

Mother's face was streaked with tears now. 'Sometimes I struggle through the day, and I feel almost normal, but there isn't a single night I don't go to bed and think of them. I'm just a fragment of who I was before. They took some part of me with them.'

'I feel the same,' I said.

When I was one of many, I felt that my brothers' strengths enhanced parts of me. With George, I was bolder. With Luke, I was quicker. With Scott, I was gentler.

'And now you're going to leave me too,' Mother said, her face creasing.

'No,' I said firmly. 'It's not like that. Father was right. Hugo Leery is the only person who might be able to help me survive this. To come back to you – forever.'

'And do you think he will?' Mother asked. 'Help, I mean.'

'I don't know. He tried using his magic to save Father and the others, and then to save his daughter,' I said. 'And when he was faced with the evil at the core of Imperium Mortis, he broke away from it, even though that meant severing ties with his twin sister ... That sounds like someone who understands the cost of this magic. That sounds like someone who might help me.'

'Then you have to go,' she said, resolute and stoic.

The warmth of her love wrapped around me like a cocoon. It was bittersweet, and my eyes prickled with tears that were not wholly sad. I was proud of her being so staunch in her support and her belief in me.

She insisted on helping me pack, filling my valise to bursting, each garment folded with care. She talked me through how she had organized it, looking after me in a way I didn't even know that I needed.

When we were almost finished, Nick appeared at the door to my room. 'You're leaving,' he said. He perched on the edge of my bed, looking for all the world like a baby bird that could be blown away in a strong wind.

'I'm sorry,' I said, exchanging a glance with Mother.

How could I explain to him why without terrifying him? We had protected him from the knowledge of the curse so far. If I was successful in my endeavours, he need never know that his life had ever hung in the balance.

'I'll be back before you know it,' I said.

'What about us?' he asked. His eyes were accusing. In them, I saw the way I looked at our father when he told me he was leaving.

'We'll be fine,' Mother said, pulling Nick on to her lap as if she were going to read him a story. 'Your brother has an important job to do to keep our family safe, and when he comes home it will nearly be Christmas, and we can celebrate.'

Nick looked doubtful. Then he said something so unsettling, I knew it would stay with me for my entire journey. 'I hope you come back safer than Father did.'

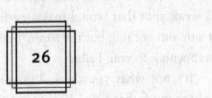

26

There was only one person I could trust to take care of Mother and Nick as well as I could. Geoffrey had continued to stay away from the house, out of respect, but, when I made the call, he arrived within twenty minutes.

'Is she okay?' Geoffrey asked when I opened the door, his forehead creasing.

'We need more security for the house,' I said, thinking of the way the Imperium Mortis agents had been tailing me. Who was to say they weren't lurking outside the perimeter? 'Armed security.'

'Has something happened, Felix?'

I didn't answer him and continued with what I had to say. 'And I need you to promise me that you'll look after Mother and Nick. I've got to go away in the morning for a few weeks . . . to England.'

Geoffrey raised his eyebrows. 'That's quite the trip, young man.'

'Don't try to dissuade me. This is something I have to do. I don't want to leave them right now, but it's . . . time-sensitive.' I cleared my throat.

'"Time-sensitive",' he echoed, his eyes searching my face as if I were a criminal that required careful evaluation for a weak spot that would make me fold and tell the whole truth and nothing but the truth. 'I don't understand what's happening to you, Felix.'

'It's not what you think. I'm going to the sanatorium where my father was,' I said, and then I pressed my lips together, as though that would stop the words from tumbling out. 'I need to go, and I know you're the only person who cares about Mother enough to make sure she's okay. And looking after her means looking after Nick too, do you hear me? You have to be really patient with him and let him talk to you about plants and . . .' I started to choke up, the reality of leaving them sinking in.

Geoffrey's expression softened. 'I give you my word that I'll look after them both while you're gone.'

I did know Mother and Nick were in safe hands with Geoffrey. He might have looked soft, but when the heart is involved, it makes people twice as dangerous.

He put a hand on my shoulder. 'The only thing I will say is that sometimes some things are better left buried.' It was a solid piece of advice, the sort of thing a father might say to a son.

Perhaps some things *are* better left buried, but Death Magic was not one of them. No, Death Magic was a writhing, living darkness that wouldn't stay put beneath the earth.

*

Later that evening, I ran hot water into the large claw-footed tub in my bathroom. The steam rose in elegant curls. As I stripped off my clothes, leaving them folded on the black and white arrow-shaped tiles, I couldn't help but reflect on the fragility of my body. Tracking the soldiers had showed me the damage that could be done to flesh and skin and bone. What awful way would Death Magic claim me if I didn't succeed?

The water surged up the sides as I lowered myself in, splashing over the edge. The heat began to unknot the tightest parts of me. I held my breath, slid down so that my face was submerged.

I had been managing my fear up until that point. I'd been able to tame the most menacing parts of my mind, but – out of nowhere – my thoughts started racing thick and fast.

You're doing to die. You're going to end up overboard, submerged in the freezing-cold water of the Atlantic Ocean. It'll swallow you, suffocate you, and you'll die, flailing and desperate.

I emerged from the bathwater, and the steady sensation of the air filling my lungs cast aside those fears. They felt so real, it was hard not to attribute significance to them. Was it a premonition? Was it a possibility that just such a scenario might unfold on my return journey, which could well line up with my birthday? Was I making a terrible mistake? Was I walking right into the fate that Death Magic had planned for me?

No, no, no.

I wasn't going to go down that route. This was my only chance to break the curse, and I couldn't let it slip through my fingers. It was normal to feel nervous. My brain was just throwing up the scenario in an attempt to prepare me, to protect me, but I didn't have to engage. I didn't have to be a willing participant. Just because the imaginings seemed real in the moment didn't mean they *were* real, didn't mean they *would* happen.

I was becoming more resilient now to the things that my mind was throwing at me. They were almost boring in their predictability . . . And look at everything I had already overcome. Those thoughts were a frightened echo, and I was determined that they would *never* be stronger than me.

27

That night I dreamed of my brothers. I wish I could say it was remarkable and prophetic, a clear sign from them that I was doing the right thing, that they had a message for me before I set off on my journey.

But it was so simple that it felt less like a dream and more like dragging out an old memory from the archives.

We were playing a game of cards – the one where you have to try to get rid of yours before anyone else, and no lies are off-limits in order to make that happen. The real key to winning is spotting who else is lying first and taking your chance to call them out.

That's it really. The four of us sat around, cross-legged on the ground, while Nick gurgled in his bassinet nearby.

It was warm, and I woke up feeling like I wasn't alone.

Maybe that was the remarkable thing.

20 NOVEMBER 1920

TWENTY-TWO DAYS LEFT

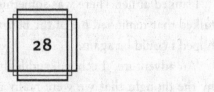

28

I left before anyone was awake so that I didn't have to find the words to say goodbye. That didn't stop me from sneaking a last look at Nick, asleep in his bed, and trying to commit him to memory.

I picked a different car – a cream and black Vauxhall that I hoped Imperium Mortis wouldn't recognize as one that belonged to me. As I left, Simpkins reassured me that Geoffrey Garton had provided him with a revolver, and that he'd spent the night patrolling and seen nothing untoward.

Lois was already waiting outside her house when I arrived, sitting atop her trunk, which was embroidered with her monogram, LB, and had a pink ribbon tied to the handle. She wore a blush-coloured coat with silver buttons all the way to her knees, white gloves, and a little hat that was pinned to her hair at a jaunty angle. She looked the picture of first-class elegance.

'So this is really happening,' I said, helping her to lug her suitcase so it sat side by side with mine in the boat.

'You could almost be forgiven for thinking it were some kind of adventure,' she said.

I smiled at her. There was something in the easy way we talked that reminded me of the person I used to be. That I hoped I could be again.

'An adventure,' I echoed, suddenly feeling all jazzed up by the thought that we were really about to travel to the port and board an ocean liner. A voyage to England – my first trip abroad. There was a wildness to it all that gave the day an air of anticipation and excitement. It tingled through me, a sensation remarkably similar to terror.

When we arrived at Violet's boarding house, I was greeted by the brusque owner. She was a formidable presence with a wide, stocky body and a large bosom. She looked me up and down. 'What do you want?'

'I'm here for Violet,' I said.

'Violet!' the landlady boomed, and Violet appeared, holding a battered case.

I noticed for the first time how strong her arms were, the biceps creating a defined bulge beneath the sleeves of her thin coat. Were these muscles developed during her days as a servant? The dress she wore was dated, worn a bit thin in places, and it dawned on me that perhaps I should have considered her financial situation before expecting her to fit in among the other first-class passengers and assimilate with the crowd. Whatever money Lachlan must have given her for her journey was probably beginning to run out, if it hadn't already. Maybe Lois would be able to lend her a dress or two, for the dinners.

'I can't believe we're really doing this,' Lois said.

There was a sheen to her eyes. Like me, Lois had no experience of travelling outside of America, and so I knew we must have shared feelings on the matter – apprehension, sure, but undeniably excitement too.

'Me neither,' Violet said grimly, looking faintly sick. I imagined she must be feeling very differently – having escaped Imperium Mortis by coming here, she was now returning home.

When we arrived at the harbour, I paid for a valet to take the car down into the hull of the ship and arrange for our cases to be delivered directly to our suite. The ocean liner was enormous and magnificent, striped in black and white, with four grand funnels that reached for the sky. It was a gigantic whale of engineering brilliance, a stylish and impressive creation. It was amazing to consider that this behemoth boasted not just size and power, but speed as well.

I had always wondered what it would be like to cross the Atlantic. The air was full of the smell of the ocean, the sharp, salty tang of the sea being blown in, and everyone was exuding excitement about the prospect of the voyage ahead. A long line of steerage passengers were filing down into the lower bulk of the ship, but a gantry for those of us with tickets to first class provided a smoother entry up a gangway into a higher part of the ship. While Lois took it in her stride, I noticed Violet staring at the extravagance of the passengers with admiration.

After our tickets were inspected, we headed straight up to the promenade deck to take in the glorious view. The three of us stood there together, hands on the railing, and I closed my eyes for just a moment, teetering on the thin line between terror and exhilaration. When the ship finally moved, Lois gripped my hand, her nails creating little half-moon crescents on my skin. We none of us had anybody to seek in the crowd below.

I turned to Lois. 'What did you say to your family?'

'They think I'm staying at yours for intensive tutoring with Geoffrey so I can attend college interviews over the next month,' she said. The smile she gave me didn't reach her eyes. The truth was her father didn't care enough to dig into her absence, as long as it didn't inconvenience him.

My mother and Nick would just be waking up to find me gone. If I looked down, over the railing, I could see the white foam where the water was sliced open for our ship to move through. Lifting my gaze, I took in the view of New York City stretching out – the new architecture competitively reaching for the sky – and felt the distance between my family and me widening. I tried to imagine what it was going to feel like to be an ocean away from them.

Time was ticking, and this journey was a gamble, with the remaining days of my life as the stake.

I became quite light-headed and in need of a sit-down.

'I'm going to our rooms,' I said.

The girls both seemed eager to stay on the promenade deck and take in the sights. As I headed down below, I thought I caught a glimpse of a passenger who was related somehow to the British royal family, and realized that we really were mingling with the uppermost echelons of society, people with even more money than my family, money that went back generations. For the first time in my life, I felt faintly fraudulent. The fortune I'd grown up with was not the product of noble birth *or* hard work – it was the product of lies and Death Magic.

The door to our parlour opened directly on to the large living space, which was decorated in muted creams and caramels, like being inside a jar of toffees. It made me almost anticipate a sugary scent, but all I could smell was fresh paint fumes. Part of the room was set up for relaxation, with a mahogany settee upholstered in a heavy cream-coloured quilted fabric with golden detail in elegant swirls. It sat beneath the windows, which let in natural light reflecting off the draped satin curtains. I went to shut them – as long as I couldn't see the endless expanse of blue sky and ocean, I could pretend we were just guests in a country house, not being propelled across a seemingly infinite expanse of water. That made the light-headed feeling dissipate a little.

I peeked into each of the three bedrooms, which were carbon copies of each other, save for a different piece of art hanging on the wall of each one – while two of these focused on visions of the sea, one of them depicted the skyline of New York. I plumped for that room, thinking that it might make me feel more at home. I carted my valise in and placed it on the chest of drawers at the end of the bed.

When the others eventually joined me, Violet's eyes brightened. 'How much did you pay for this?' she asked.

'Forget about it,' I said.

'I bet it cost more than I'd have made in my lifetime as a maid,' she said archly. 'It's certainly more than I'll ever be able to repay you.'

A knock at the door interrupted us. It was a member of the waitstaff, his stiff-collared shirt as rigid as his voice when, glancing around the suite and seeing only the three of us, he said, 'Good afternoon. May I speak to your parents?'

'It's just us,' I said, feeling a little offended by his condescension. 'I bought and paid for this trip.'

'Ah,' he said, his face turning a little pink. 'I just came to run you through the schedule for mealtimes.'

While he explained the timetable, along with which rooms we had access to as members of first class, I saw Lois grab Violet by the hand, and heard her delicately broaching the subject of what dresses they might wear to afternoon tea. I was relieved that I hadn't had to be the one to say anything and hoped that it signified the start of a growing connection between the two of them.

Later, when Lois and Violet finally emerged from Lois's room, the pair of them had been transformed for afternoon tea. Lois had loaned Violet a dress made from a fine silvery-blue lace that lay over a duck-egg crêpe, and had slotted a jewelled hair slide above Violet's ear. Now Violet looked every inch the lady and would no doubt fit right in as though she were a wealthy British heiress. It was just a small change to make – Violet already had rich, shiny hair and had no problem adopting a haughty expression – but the expensive dress made all the difference, elevating everything about her.

Lois herself was dressed in a sandy-coloured crêpe-de-chine midi dress. It was simple, but somehow its simplicity only made her look more beautiful. She caught me staring, and her face lit up as she gave me a charming smile. I returned it, wishing I could bottle the joyful feeling of being the recipient of a smile like that.

The dining hall was busy, and everyone was dressed to the nines. The room was lit by pointed light bulbs that looked like seeds, captured inside fixtures in the shape of petals that protruded from the wooden panelling. Each of the tables was covered with a white cloth, and decorated with little purple plastic flowers in china vases. Even the carpet was floral.

We were seated at a table by a window overlooking the sea, and I positioned myself with my back to it, eager to continue the illusion that we were in a regular restaurant, and not on a journey that took us further away from home with every moment that passed.

Whatever situation I had been in previously, there were always adults to lead the way, but on this ocean liner I had stepped into a new freedom, and with that came responsibility. For Lois and me, whose family names were well known, there was a pressing need to keep our endeavours quiet, and that meant not standing out or drawing attention to ourselves in any way.

'What are we going to do when we get to England?' Lois asked once we had placed an order for afternoon tea on the recommendation of the young British guy who was waiting on our table.

I looked to Violet for guidance.

'Well, the first thing that you need to know about England is that, compared to America, it's tiny. You can drive pretty much the whole length of the country in a single day, if you really have a mind to,' she said. 'As it is, we'll dock in Southampton, which is at the very bottom, and we want to head to Yorkshire, which is much further north, where Imperium Mortis have always been based. I propose that, when they get your car out of the hull, we drive as far as we can in one go and find somewhere to stay overnight in the Midlands. Then the next day we can drive the second leg before finding a hotel in York. The moors are further north, and that's where the sanatorium was set up, in a converted priory.'

'Have you been there before?' Lois asked.

'No.' Violet shook her head. 'When I was a recruit, we knew that Hugo was based at Saint Anthony's, but not what he was working on, and we certainly weren't allowed to go there. But I know where it is.'

Two metal stands arrived, holding plates with miniature sandwiches, scones with little bowls of thick cream and red jam, and a range of tiny iced delicacies.

'A taste of England,' the waiter said as he placed them down.

'Have you had afternoon tea before?' I asked Violet.

'Not like this,' she replied, tucking in immediately, and her eyes closed for a moment in bliss as she tasted an eclair.

'Do you think Saint Anthony's will still be occupied by Imperium Mortis?' I asked.

'I doubt it,' Violet said. 'Knowing Ada, the first thing she'd do if she thought attention was being drawn to it would be to shut it down completely.'

'How well *do* you really know her, though? Hugo had a secret family that nobody knew about, and Ada was capable of completely severing ties with him – her own twin. She killed his wife. And who knows what happened to his daughter?' A note of hysteria was creeping into my voice. The thought of Ada Leery petrified me.

'Calm down, Felix,' Lois said quietly. Her gaze was steadying, and I immediately felt a shade better.

Violet shrugged. 'Saint Anthony's served a purpose as a sanatorium. With the soldiers all sent away, it wouldn't serve that purpose for them any more. The initiation programme itself operated out of a big country house in York, but the rest of the associates were placed around the country, connected to various universities. That's how they've always operated – through a web of academic connections, harking back to where they originated.'

'That's useful to know,' Lois said as she smeared the thick cream over a scone. 'At the sanatorium, we'll be looking for any kind of clue as to where Hugo went. In the meantime, I think we should focus on decoding as much of the casebook as possible.'

There was a silence.

'Casebook?' Violet asked sharply, and I flinched.

I still hadn't told her about that.

When we'd started out on this journey together, I had wanted to keep something back, had wanted to retain the slim advantage it gave me. Now it seemed cruel that I'd withheld it from her, but that was never my intention.

'One of the things my father left for me was a leather-bound journal. It belonged to Hugo, but it's all in code,' I explained sheepishly. 'I would have told you sooner, but . . .'

But what? *I didn't trust you?* I couldn't say it aloud.

'Let me see it.' Violet was breathless, her cheeks flushed as though she had been running. She flicked a loose strand of hair behind her ear so forcefully it was like a whip. Where another girl might have had hurt splashed across her face, Violet had pure rage. Without meaning to, I had damaged the delicate tapestry of trust we had woven by always being honest with each other.

Secrets are just the quietest kind of lie.

29

We gathered around the glass-topped table in our suite, and I brought out the casebook.

'I should have showed you before,' I said.

Guilt was churning relentlessly in my stomach. I glanced at Lois, and her cheeks were flushed with discomfort.

'I've told you everything about myself,' Violet said in quiet fury. 'Even the parts that are embarrassing and horrible to relive ... and you were hiding this the whole time.'

'I didn't really mean to hide it,' I said, and Violet shot me a disbelieving glare. 'Okay, I mean ... I did keep it to myself deliberately at first, but then after we'd got to know each other, and we were working together, there just never seemed to be the right moment to tell you about it.'

'But you did find the right moment to tell Lois,' Violet said. 'She's known about it all this time, even though I'm the one who taught you everything about Imperium Mortis. You wouldn't be here without me.'

'I'm sorry,' I said.

'Did you think I wouldn't be able to help because I was just a servant before all this? Thought you'd only share it with your more *educated* friend?'

'That's not it at all,' Lois said. 'I'm so sorry you feel that way, Violet, but Felix only showed me because I was so difficult to convince about all of this at first.'

'I don't know how to make this up to you,' I said, hanging my head.

'Let me look at it,' Violet said. 'And tell me what you know about it.'

I handed her the journal, and Violet turned it over in her hands while I explained about substitution ciphers, and how our attempts to crack the code so far had failed. As Violet was flicking through the pages, Lois scrunched up her nose.

'Wait a second,' she said. 'Can I have another look?'

Violet gave her the book, and Lois performed the same action again – a fast shuffle through the pages. She let out a triumphant sound.

'What?' I asked. Whatever Lois was seeing, I wasn't seeing it.

'Look,' Lois said. She bent the cover back and the pages seemed to pop out at the centre of the spine. She grabbed the corner of one and peeled it, revealing a hidden double page on the inside.

I looked at her in awe – I would never have spotted that, but of course she did. There was nothing Lois loved more than a book.

We didn't need to crack a code to understand what the hidden page revealed – it was an intricate diagram of the human body, and inside ... It looked like the face of a watch, but there were wires and places marked in the spine, in the organs ...

'It seems as though Doctor Leery was planning something that would physically go *inside* the soldiers,' said Violet. 'I guess we would have to decode the notes to fully understand how it works, but ...'

It was a grotesque idea, though I couldn't deny that it aligned with everything I had learned about Hugo Leery. He was searching for greater control over the magic, to create ever more powerful objects ... so he had blended his skill set: his knowledge of the human body, his proficiency with clockwork, his dexterity in surgery, his power over Death Magic.

'Leery was doing something very wrong in that sanatorium,' Lois said with finality.

It seemed as though she were still wrestling with the impossibility of it all, but couldn't ignore the physical evidence.

'Whether there's a supernatural element to it or not, at the very least there's evidence here that he was planning to conduct experimental vivisection.' Her face twisted in horror.

The magic Hugo Leery used was a cruel thing, born out of blood and horror and murder, and my father had been reduced to one of his experiments. I shuddered.

'You said there had to be a keyword,' Violet said. 'Have you tried Joy?'

Joy. That was his daughter's name. How could we have forgotten?

I ran out of the room to source some paper and a pen. I wrote out three sets of alphabets – the J substitution, the O substitution, the Y substitution. And then, as I applied it to the code, a sinister message began to appear in my writing.

THESE BEING THE NOTES OF EXPERIMENTAL METHODS FOR THE CONTROL OF DEATH MAGIC

'You did it!' Lois exclaimed. Pride shifted across Violet's face.

'It will take days to decode,' I said, flicking through the pages. 'No, weeks.'

'Well, the one thing we have right now is plenty of time,' Violet said, and she was right. How else would we spend our journey time?

We began immediately. Violet sat with the three alphabets, Lois read out a letter, which Violet would substitute, and I transcribed. For every page we completed, we took turns to read aloud what we had decoded. It was a slow and laborious process, but that was the best way we could think of working through it.

*

The days of our journey passed in much that way – meals in the dining hall, walks along the promenade deck, and long afternoons and evenings spent with the casebook, unravelling the threads of Hugo Leery's work.

Most of it took the form of a diary, but some of it was incredibly technical, and other parts were borderline nonsensical notes.

The casebook began with a grim depiction of the field hospital, matching Vaughan's account of the horrifying existence the soldiers were subjected to. It was inhuman. The more we read about the realities of the war, the sicker I felt. Then came the moment in the diary when Hugo started to consider the possibility of using the magic. His words were almost giddy with the thrill of it. He described the field hospital as humming with the magical energy he needed. The sheer scale of the death and trauma that was occurring made him feel as though he were in the perfect situation to be a conduit for it.

He depicted the magic as like catching the tail of a tiger. In the moment of death, sometimes it was possible to pinch his fingers around something intangible, tear a thread of it away. It was described a little like how Mother said it had happened for Father in the factory. I became more certain than ever that the magic was what I had seen when George died – the midnight wisp that dissipated into the air.

Leery wrote about the way that this essence could be welded to an object. He felt his connection to the magic growing throughout the war, and that was where his idea was born. Only somebody as connected as he was would be able to *decide* what the magic could do, and *control* where it went. He wrote extensively, obsessively, about capturing the essence of the magic in clockwork, so that it might affect the time that somebody had on earth. Time.

Clockwork. It certainly appealed to the sense of irony that flowed through the Death Magic I'd heard of.

Clockwork. That was the Death Magic object at the heart of all his work.

Leery had a notion that it was only through blending the magic with the clockwork and human biology that he would be able to do this most extraordinary thing – bring someone back from the dead.

He'd created a clockwork device for each of the soldiers and placed it inside them.

Was it just that his sheer genius had worked out the exact requirements of the magic? Was the magic responding to his fervour and being guided by him? Or was the magic more sentient than that, with its own reasons for giving Leery what he wanted?

I didn't know.

But it did work. And, as always, not without a cost. In the immediate aftermath of peacetime, Hugo's entries focused on a huge regret: his deep sorrow at the limited lives the four men led. They were still dead, he believed, even though they might move and walk and talk. They were dead in some indefinable way, a way that truly mattered. He took care of them in his sanatorium, lamenting that they knew too much and could never be sent home.

Then the entries stopped for a while. When they resumed, he wrote about his daughter, Joy. She was sixteen years old, and she was dying. It was consumption, the doctors said, ravaging her lungs.

The thought of using the magic was throwaway at first, the notes about how it might work. Leery was deeply aware of the necessity to mitigate the adverse effects of the magic if he used it on Joy, and that was where the idea came to use his technique *before* she passed away. The soldiers were only so terribly affected because he had brought them back from the dead. But with Joy it wasn't too late. He began to speculate that by operating on her while she was still alive she would be able to hold on to who she was.

We shuddered as we read it.

'If he could do that to you, would you want him to?' Lois asked. 'Is that what you're hoping for?'

'No,' I said, finally giving voice to the thoughts that had been consuming me. 'I don't think so. The cost just seems so great. The soldiers told us it wasn't really like being alive. Vaughan said he couldn't feel anything at all, no sensation, no emotion, nothing. It's not just being numb for a day or a week or a month . . . A lifetime of nothingness? Is that worth the trade?'

I was filled with disappointment. A part of me had hoped that, when we cracked the casebook, there would be an obvious way to break the curse. Father must have hoped the same thing, stealing it from Leery and bringing it across the ocean for me.

'But he doesn't say if it worked on Joy. He might have been able to stop the side effects. He seemed pretty confident.'

'There's always a cost,' Violet said. 'There always has been. For every positive action, there's a negative reaction.'

I had heard her say that before, but this time it seemed to truly sink in, so that I knew it right to my core. There wasn't going to be a magic solution that I could use that didn't have a consequence.

'I'm not looking for more magic,' I said. 'I know how terrible it is. What I am looking for is a way to break free of what's already been done. I want to know if I can sever Death Magic's hold over me. I want to know if I can get back control of my own life.'

'I think this might be harder than we thought,' Lois said, and she bit her lip.

'It's too late to turn back now,' Violet said.

They were both right. There was only one path in front of me, and I could choose to keep going, even though I was stumbling into the darkness, or I could curl up at the side of the road and admit defeat. But the tiny spark of hope that I'd been nurturing wasn't extinguished yet. Without it, I would have been utterly lost.

My hope was sustaining me – I couldn't afford to let it die.

27 NOVEMBER 1920

FIFTEEN DAYS LEFT

30

Throughout the voyage, we had been suspended in-between worlds, it seemed. Every day had a repetitive quality, following the rhythms and routines of the ship ... and yet I couldn't feel as though my time had been wasted because Lois and I were closer than ever, and we'd learned more than we could have hoped from cracking the casebook.

When we disembarked, it felt odd to be back on land, and I realized I had grown used to the gentle sway that had accompanied every movement. I was struck with wonder that we had travelled across the ocean to arrive in this place. I'd never dared dream it would be possible for me to accomplish a journey like this – and yet I was setting foot on land so far from home that the very idea was dizzying.

'We're here,' I whispered under my breath, and Lois squeezed my hand.

'Can you believe it?' she whispered back.

I shook my head and laughed. It was the lightest I'd felt in some time – travel was something that I'd always longed to do, and I'd managed it. I hadn't let fear stop me. And yet remembering that there were only two weeks until my birthday felt as if we had suddenly hurtled into the final stretch of the days I had left . . . and that was like a stone in the pit of my stomach.

The car was unloaded from the hull of the ship, and we began the long and exhausting drive north. After stopping for gas and lunch, we kept going until my eyes were beginning to glaze over with tiredness and my leg was aching from its position on the gas pedal. We stopped overnight at a cosy inn somewhere near Nottingham and filled up on the meat pie included with the price of the room, but I couldn't relax. I found myself thinking, over and over again, about the hours that were being lost forever.

The following morning, we continued, but by this point conversation between us had run dry, and there was a rising irritation in us all.

Eventually, we entered the county of Yorkshire, and then the air seemed fresher and the hills seemed greener than I had ever seen, and I marvelled as we passed field and farm. Violet appeared more comfortable in her skin the closer we got to her home ground, and, when we arrived in York, she was able to direct me to a hotel in the centre of town. We found a place to park the car and walked the rest of the way through the haphazard streets. As we stumbled along on the uneven cobbles, the buildings on either side slanted in towards us. It was as if they were leaning in to share secrets.

'I feel as though we've stepped back in time,' Lois said, her head whipping round as she tried to take it all in.

I felt equally awed by the architecture – it may not have been neat or organized, but the exposed beams and the black-and-white contrast of the half-timbered walls held centuries of experience.

'There's nowhere quite like this place.' Violet sounded proud.

'Well, it's nothing like New York City, that's for sure,' I said. 'It's quite extraordinary.'

Our hotel was called the Ouse Side, named for the way it perched along the bank of the River Ouse. It looked as though it had been plucked from the pages of a fairy tale – wide and squat, with rows of windows set into dark brick, and ivy that crawled all over.

When we entered, there was a reserved, quietly spoken manner to the people in the foyer, from the guests reclining on couches and the staff at the reception desk alike. I asked for three rooms, covering the single-occupancy charge for the sake of giving everyone their privacy – after so long travelling together, we were all feeling slightly frayed and in need of some space. The porter took us to the first floor.

'Not our largest rooms,' he said apologetically. 'And not right next to each other, but our best at such short notice.'

As we had been travelling since the early hours of the morning, we all planned to get a rest throughout the afternoon, fill up on a substantial evening meal and then head out to the countryside to take our first look at the sanatorium with the blanket of night as our cover.

From the window of my room, I could see the Minster, a masterpiece of architecture whose tower seemed to be trying to touch heaven. A bubble of longing for home blew up inside me. I found myself wishing I could make a telephone call, just to hear Mother's voice, as comforting as wrapping myself up in my old bathrobe. All I wanted was to know that she and Nick were coping, were safe. Imperium Mortis knew too much about me, and the people close to me, for me not to worry about them. But for that very reason I couldn't risk a call.

Somehow I had managed to plough through the days of travelling by focusing on my purpose and immersing myself in the heavy work of decoding the casebook. Now, though, I couldn't stop thinking about how I felt when Father left us. It didn't matter when he told me he was going for the best possible reasons – what mattered was being left. The thought that Nick might be feeling equally abandoned was painful to me.

I sank on to the bed, so tired of beds that weren't my own, and attempted to push away the feeling. I closed my eyes and floated in the space between waking and sleeping for a while, until hunger began to gnaw in the pit of my belly, and a look at my watch prompted me to get ready to head downstairs for dinner.

The dining hall of the hotel was all glamour and delight, with a menu that spoke of indulgence, and tablecloths that whispered the secrets of many rendezvous between lovers. Violet was already seated at a table at the far left of the room, sequestered in a private corner. Her long dark hair swished down her back, and, when she turned to me, I was struck by the intensity of her gaze.

I sat opposite her, and we ordered drinks while we waited for Lois. When I asked the waiter to put it on my tab, Violet pressed her lips together, as if trying to hold something in. She failed, blurting out, 'Is there no end to your money?'

'Of course there's an end,' I said bitterly, thinking of Wade Griffin. The end was sooner than I'd imagined.

I changed the subject swiftly. 'Did I ever tell you about the Collection?'

'No,' Violet said with a wry grin. 'Go on.'

'It's full of rare, unusual items. My father started it, and I've spent many years learning what makes an object valuable or unique.'

'It's pretty horrifying,' Lois said, making me jump as she took the seat next to mine. 'Some of the items are grotesque.'

'Father used to look for things that purported to be magical, but everything was fraudulent ...' I explained to Violet. 'That's how he first unearthed Imperium Mortis. He was looking for ... like-minded people.'

'That's something that I've been wondering about,' said Lois. 'How like-minded do you think they were?'

I sensed her nervousness in asking the question. I knew what she was getting at – the things we'd uncovered about Imperium Mortis suggested they were truly evil. How involved had Father been? Was it only Leery he had grown close to, or had he been a fully established member?

I paused. It was something I had been thinking about a lot too. 'I thought I knew my father. I grew up hearing about his legacy, about this fortune that he'd created for us as a family, but that wasn't the whole story, was it? He didn't earn it. He lied to me my whole life. Even though he knew about the curse, he hid it from me. And you ask about the end of the money? Well, before we left, I found out that he gave his fortune, the house, everything ... to somebody else, even though it's my life that's being held ransom for that money. So I can't answer your question. I don't know what his involvement was with Imperium Mortis. I don't know why he did anything, because it turns out I didn't know him at all.'

My face had gone all red and hot. Sweat gathered on my top lip. There were tears in my eyes, and it felt like the sludgy sensation of embarrassment was pumping through my veins instead of blood. I needed to get out of there. I stood up so quickly I almost knocked my chair over, pushing my way past other hotel guests in my rush to get out and clear my head.

I ended up just walking along the riverside, with no direction. I tried to appreciate how far I had come, soak in the beauty of the city's cobbled streets and historic architecture, but it was enough just to remember to breathe, breathe, breathe. The lingering thought that my heart might just burst in my chest resurfaced after having been dormant for so long.

Regurgitating all that bitterness about my father had left me feeling shaky – I hadn't even realized it was there inside me. I'd allowed myself to grow so hopeful about an escape from Death Magic that I'd also allowed myself to push aside the cruel memory that it was all Father's fault in the first place. I tried to walk fast, faster than the fear, until I heard the clatter of shoes behind me.

Lois caught up with me, a little out of breath. 'I'm sorry, Felix. I didn't mean to upset you. I was just thinking out loud.'

'It's just so overwhelming,' I said. 'My life has been ripped completely out of my control.' My temples were throbbing with the beginnings of a headache.

'You *are* taking control,' she said. 'You've come so far. Remember what you were like just a few months ago? You were frightened of everything.'

'I'm still frightened,' I admitted. My stomach lurched.

'Yes, but you're also resilient, and you're not letting it stop you.'

I let out a dry laugh. 'I don't know that that's true. All I can think about is how the choices I'm making might kill me. What if my death is something completely unavoidable that I'm walking into right now, getting closer to it minute by minute?'

'You are walking closer to it,' Lois said with a shrug. 'And not because of the curse, but because we all are. None of us escape death in the end. None of us are promised a long life. It's what we do with the time we have that matters.'

She had a knack for articulating things that struck deep inside me, as if I'd swallowed a pin.

'At least I'm trying – is that what you're saying?' I asked.

'I suppose I'm saying that if you're going to die anyway, which you are eventually because we all are, then you want there to be something more to this time than fear and misery.'

'So don't worry?' I raised an eyebrow at her. 'Oh gee, I wish I'd tried that one.'

She gave a cynical laugh. 'I know it's not that simple. I'm not helping much, am I?'

'You are,' I said, and realized I meant it. 'It's better than feeling like I'm alone.'

She took my hand in hers and squeezed it tight. 'You're not alone, Felix,' she said, and for one dizzy, glorious moment I truly thought she was going to kiss me, and my stomach was doing somersaults as I anticipated what it might be like . . .

But then she dropped my hand, and dropped her eyes at the same time, and I wondered if I had messed it up somehow, if I was supposed to be the one who did the kissing. But how was I to know if she wanted me to?

If it had been the right moment, the moment had gone.

And yet that didn't seem in the spirit of the words that had passed between us, and I wanted her to know that I meant every word, and appreciated her attempts to understand me, to reach me, even when I probably seemed like an unfathomable conundrum to her.

It was time to be as brave as she thought I was.

'I'd like to kiss you,' I said.

A little smile flickered into life across her lips. 'I'd like it if you did,' she said.

With a combination of relief and anticipation flooding through me, I dipped my face towards hers until our lips touched gently. I closed my eyes, and wrapped my arm around her waist, and my hand fell naturally into the dip of her back as if it belonged there.

Her lips were soft, and her breath was warm and sweet, and I knew that this kiss, at least, had been worth persevering through the fear for.

31

When twilight had bathed all of Yorkshire in its shade, the three of us set off to find St Anthony's. The built-up town fell away as I drove, immersing us in nature as the headlights of the car lit up a host of creatures I had never seen before – a pheasant shooting into the underbrush; a fox with reflective eyes; an owl crossing the sky. The hills tumbled over and over, dark and stark and so unlike home. I almost had to catch my breath with the wonderment that flooded through me.

When we reached the crest of one of those hills, Violet pointed out the window. 'There!' she said.

I nearly slammed the brakes on to see what she had spotted. At the peak of the hill, there was the murky outline of a short, squat building. I pulled the car over into a passing place and turned the engine off.

'You wouldn't know it was there unless you were looking,' Violet said.

'It's smaller than I imagined,' I said.

'At least it looks deserted,' Lois added. 'No lights on.'

'Right then,' I said, bracing myself.

We got out of the car and began to tread the worn track that weaved towards St Anthony's. It was an old priory building, made from pale grey stone blocks with rounded edges. It looked more like a cottage than a hospital. When I had tried to imagine where Father was, in those two long years after the war ended, it had always been grand, modern, and filled with specialist nurses and doctors in freshly pressed uniforms. I couldn't have been more wrong. Calling it a 'sanatorium' had been generous, to say the least – Imperium Mortis really had been pulling the wool over our eyes for years.

We traipsed over the uneven ground, Violet leading the way with a battered flashlight. When she turned it on, I noticed engraved letters on the handle – LA. Lachlan must have given it to her to help her escape. I followed the bobbing light, and Lois brought up the rear, one hand on my shoulder to steady herself.

The door to the priory had been stove in, and it hung like a broken arm. When we entered, the smell was overpowering and rancid. The air inside was as frigid as it had been outside, the stone like blocks of ice. Violet's flashlight flitted around like a paintbrush, and, in the glimpses it revealed as we moved from room to room, I could see that Imperium Mortis had completely trashed the place. Furniture had been tipped over, curtains pulled down and discarded in corners of the living quarters, and in the kitchen the source of the putrid smell revealed itself when the beam of light landed on a garbage can that had been emptied all over the floor.

Upstairs, there was a long room that would have served as a dormitory in its previous life as a priory, but had since become the makeshift ward for the soldiers. No, not a ward, I corrected myself. They were never truly patients while they stayed at St Anthony's. They'd been more like prisoners serving a sentence. Hugo Leery might have found killing them unpalatable, but he wouldn't let them go home either. Not until it suited him.

The four beds had been stripped, the cabinets by their side pulled out and ransacked. In one corner, there was a metal gurney, separated from the rest of the room by a dividing screen. If there had been anything of note, it was long gone. I found myself feeling thankful for my father's foresight in pilfering the documents he had; I wondered if Hugo had ever discovered who took them.

A door at the end of the room revealed a single-occupancy bedroom, no doubt belonging to Hugo, which had also been turned inside out.

There was nothing that gave any indication as to where Hugo might have gone. My heart sank. I didn't know what I had been expecting, but it wasn't *nothing*.

It was the end of the road. There were no more threads to pull at. I cursed and threw a kick into the stone of the wall, the rage and disappointment flooding through me. I felt Lois flinch away from me. Violet's face was made of shadows, but I could tell that she wasn't impressed by my outburst.

'What now?' I asked, my voice a pained roar. 'What are we even doing here?'

The disappointment carried a physical weight to it. I felt as if I were being crushed beneath it, my ribcage splintering, my breath hard to catch. My days were numbered, and I had wasted the ones I'd spent coming all this way.

Lois's hand slipped into mine. 'It's not over,' she said. 'We just need to think this through, work out what our next move is. Right, Violet?'

Violet shone the light on us, just as Lois released my hand. I wondered if Violet noticed how close we were standing together, if she could sense that something had shifted in our dynamic.

'Right,' she said. 'We just need to come up with a new strategy, maybe try the place where they were training initiates.'

'See? Not a dead end. But let's go back to the hotel,' Lois said as soothingly as she could.

I steadied myself against the gale of disappointment that was knocking me around. They were right; it wasn't over. Already I could see that they were chasing ahead mentally, no doubt starting to develop their plans and schemes. As for me, though, I wasn't ready to move on from St Anthony's. I had spent so many years trying to picture where my father was, trying to shut down the way I felt about having been left behind.

As we walked back through the room that the soldiers had once shared, I couldn't help but look at the beds. Which one of them had my father rested in? How had he and Bradley, Chuck and Vaughan filled their days here? It must have felt endless.

When our journey had led us to St Anthony's, it had seemed destined. There was a neatness to it that appealed to part of me that was ready to say goodbye. In the room where he languished, all I had left was a profound sorrow at what had been taken from my little family. I hugged my arms around me, thinking of Nick and Mother, an ocean away.

'Come on,' Lois said, her words a gentle tug out of my reverie.

As we came to the front door, as we were mere moments away from leaving, I noticed something that I hadn't seen before. Attached to the back of the door, at waist height, there was a thin metal box with a hooked catch to open its lid.

'What's that?' I said, pointing.

Violet strode over to the door and ran her hand over the top of the object. 'A letter-catcher.'

It was the sort of thing that you wouldn't spot unless it just happened to catch your eye. It was unobtrusive, and if the door had been at just a slightly different angle, then it would have been concealed. Imperium Mortis could well have neglected to check it when they came to tear the place apart. I tried to temper the rising excitement inside me.

I unhooked the catch at the top of the box and lifted the lid. Inside, there were several pieces of mail, which I took out and sifted through. Violet held the flashlight as I appraised my findings, my fingers shaking. The one that immediately caught my attention was a white envelope addressed to Dr H. Leery, in a looping feminine hand. It was stamped with the face of the King gazing somewhere into the distance, a regal lion reclining beside his likeness.

I tore into the envelope, unable to stop trembling and making rather a hash of the job, ripping it up in three segments instead of one smooth flap. Lois and Violet seemed to melt away, and so did my surroundings – all my attention narrowed down to the letter, which came into sharp focus in the beam of the flashlight as I slid it out.

Dear Papa, I read, and an audible gasp came out of me, seemingly of its own volition. His daughter. Joy. I began to read aloud for Lois and Violet, tracing her cursive script which danced beneath my fingertips.

Dear Papa,

I write to you from the Wellness Centre. Aunt Elizabeth has had me admitted here, for my own welfare she says, although I rather feel it is for her own comfort. She will not believe me when I talk about magic. She has refused to accept what I have told her about your truth, about what happened to Mama, about how I came to survive the sickness. Even when I showed her the healing wound on my chest, she refused to contemplate that there is more to this world. It is easier for her to believe I am mad.

Papa, I know that you sent me to Aunt Elizabeth to be safe, but she has decided that my nerves are shredded, that I am not of sound mind. She brought me here and said that she and Cousin Peter would visit, but they don't. I do not wish to stay here any longer. They treat me well, and it is something like a spa in many ways, but I don't want to be peaceful when Mama is dead. They say I am free to leave, but how can I do that when

I am in the middle of nowhere, with nowhere to go? Come and get me, Papa. Come and bring me back to stay with you.

 There is something wrong with me. It is a chill deep down in my bones, an eternal coldness. You said to be aware that it might be different with me, that I wouldn't be dead the way the soldiers are . . . Well, it is different, but not in the way we hoped. There is no feeling, no sensation . . . There is a new sense instead . . . I can't explain. But there is no fear. I want to be with you, even if that is dangerous.

 Papa, you saved me. I am alive and I want to use this life. Let me help you. Come and get me.

Your loving daughter,
Joy

'When is the letter dated?' Lois asked, her voice imbued with the urgency I was also feeling.

'Last week,' I said, feeling a little dizzy from the discovery.

The despondency that had seemed all-encompassing just a few moments before had evaporated. I could almost touch the optimism that Lois and Violet had retained; it was tangible again.

It really wasn't over.

32

On our return to the hotel, we sat on velvet-topped bar stools and drank soda while we worked out our plan in low, hushed voices. I struggled to suppress my anguish that our search was spilling over into another day, one I wouldn't see again. We decided I would go to the Wellness Centre the next morning, under the name of Cousin Peter, pretending to be a visitor for Joy. It was a risky move, sure, but it seemed unlikely that the real Cousin Peter would have made an appearance in the time since the letter was sent.

'The key to making this sort of thing work is confidence,' Violet said. 'You just have to act so sure that you should be there that the idea of them questioning it is absurd.' She put her straw between her teeth and took a sip of soda.

'Should I try and do a British accent?' I asked, giving it a go.

Violet winced. 'Absolutely not. How are they supposed to know her cousin isn't from America? Just act natural. Anything they ask you, tell them the nearest possible truth so you have less to remember, but, if you're doing it right, they won't ask you anything. Ideally, what you want to do is ask *them* questions, and keep them busy talking so they don't have a chance to turn the tables on you.'

Lois was thoughtful and quiet while we planned. I couldn't tell what was running through her mind. I wondered if she was starting to regret coming, if she felt it was a useless endeavour, despite everything she had said indicating the opposite. It was difficult for me to believe that she could really care about me enough, could really think I was worth it. That said more about me than her, though.

'How will you play it with Joy, when you get inside?' Violet asked.

'Well, if I get the chance to speak to her alone, I'll just be honest with her. It's not as though we have to convince her that Death Magic is real. I want to know what she means by it being different for her. Leery's casebook seemed to suggest that he thought putting the magic inside somebody who was alive might have a different effect. I think that's what she's referring to.'

'Tell her that he's gone,' Violet said, sounding like a military officer barking out orders. 'Tell her that he didn't get her letter because he's not at Saint Anthony's any more. Find out if she knows where else he might be, where he would go.'

'You don't think Imperium Mortis have taken him?' I asked.

'Definitely not,' she said. 'The stunt with the death of the soldiers was too coordinated. No, I think he planned every part of this, and he's in hiding somewhere. If they had him, they wouldn't have been ransacking Saint Anthony's. They wouldn't have needed to search for information. If Ada wants someone to talk, they talk. Now let's discuss interrogation techniques,' she said as calmly as if she'd suggested we get a cup of tea.

'I'm going to turn in for the night,' Lois said, suppressing a yawn. She slid down off her stool and started to slope off in the direction of the elevator. 'Goodnight.'

'Sleep well,' I said with a smile, but she didn't smile back.

Violet turned to me and clasped her hands together, a gesture that seemed to say *let's get to business*. But I'd had enough for one evening, and I wanted to check whether Lois was okay.

'I'm going to head to bed too,' I said. 'We don't need to go over it any more. You can trust me. I won't mess it up.'

Violet pursed her lips and flexed her fingers as if she were struggling to physically relinquish control of the situation. 'Okay,' she said finally, sounding a little strangled. 'Okay.'

She seemed to have lost her edge – perhaps being back in the place she had run from was unsettling her. Surely Lachlan's house, the place where she'd worked for his family, was nearby. It must have been very strange for her. Despite my sympathy for Violet, Lois was my priority.

'I'll set off first thing in the morning,' I said, and left her alone at the bar, with only my and Lois's half-empty glasses of soda for company. But instead of going straight to my room, I went to Lois's. I had the distinct impression that something had been bothering her. I knocked on the door and, when she opened it, saw she had already begun the process of removing her make-up. She was bare-faced and her hair was scraped back from her forehead by a band. Without her usual powder and lipstick and mascara, her face seemed softer.

'I'm sorry to disturb you,' I said, 'but you seemed a little distant downstairs, and I was wondering if there was something wrong?'

Lois looked both ways down the corridor. 'Come in,' she said.

Once I was inside her room, I didn't know what to do with myself. Lois plonked herself down on the quilt. The only place to sit was next to her on the edge of the bed, but I was worried that that might be improper, so I hovered awkwardly instead.

'I don't mind if you want to sit down,' she said. I did, trying to leave a respectful distance between us. 'It's not as if anyone knows us here.'

It still felt strange sitting next to her on the bed, even if the people who would consider it damaging to her reputation were on the other side of the ocean.

'Did something upset you tonight?' I asked.

Lois gave a small nod and looked at me carefully. 'Don't you think it's strange the way Violet talks about Imperium Mortis? She always sounds like she's impressed by them.'

'When she told me about the initiation programme, she made it sound a bit like a cult,' I said. 'I guess some of that conditioning takes a while to shake.'

'I guess,' Lois said, but she didn't sound convinced.

'She's intense,' I agreed. 'But she lost everything because of them. I think sometimes she just struggles to channel the passion she feels in a way that's –' I struggled for the right word – 'healthy.'

'Maybe . . . It's just the way she was focusing on confidence and strategy and interrogation,' Lois said. 'It's a bit creepy. Do you know what I mean?'

'She's just trying to help,' I said. 'She learned things from Imperium Mortis that are useful. I think we need to accept we're a bit in over our heads here and use what we've got. They don't play by the rules, and we need to be adaptable.'

'Just . . . don't forget that Joy is a person,' Lois said. 'A girl. One who, a few months ago, had never even heard of Death Magic. And now her mother is dead and her father's missing, and whether they treat her kindly or not she's effectively been locked away in the Wellness Centre because the person that was supposed to look after her decided she's lost her mind. Maybe you do need confidence and strategy and interrogation, but I think the strongest thing you've got in your favour is compassion. You know, what I was struck most by in that letter was the fact that she wasn't being listened to. If you just listen to her, you probably won't have to rely on all of Violet's tricks.'

When she had finished, her eyes were sparkling. She seemed effervescent and optimistic, and reminded me of a bubbling glass of champagne. Empathy and kindness seemed to come so naturally to Lois.

'It's what you did for me, even before you believed what I was telling you,' I said. 'Listening, I mean.'

Lois smiled, but only for the briefest of moments. It made me wish that I could always make her smile. 'Do you want to know the truth?' She looked at her hands linked in her lap. 'Sometimes I think I focus so much on what everyone else is saying and doing, and what they might be thinking, because it's easier than asking the difficult questions of myself. It's easier to look outwards than work out how I feel or why I'm feeling it.'

'How do you feel?' I asked, and her eyes met mine.

She opened her mouth as if the answer were already on the tip of her tongue. She paused, and I recognized in her eyes the same internal debate I'd had so often.

'I feel like . . . if we don't find a way to undo the curse, I don't want to be left with a list of things I wish I'd said to you.'

'So say them,' I said, my heart jumping up as if it could burst out of my chest and into her hands.

She looked at me, and her gaze was filled with fondness. 'You're the only person who ever looked at me and saw me and believed in me.'

I thought of our long late-night conversations, remembered telling her I thought she could do anything she put her mind to.

'Of course I believe in you. I know you'll do all the things you set your mind to,' I said.

'Well, you're the only person who thinks that,' she replied. I knew she was dwelling on the disinterest of her father and brother. As far as they were concerned, she would tire of the idea of college eventually, then find a suitable son-in-law for her father, and that would be that.

'I'm sorry that I hurt you by pushing you away. It was a kind of self-preservation, but that was a mistake,' I said. 'If I've learned anything from all of this, it's that I wouldn't have wanted to do any of it alone.'

'No more wasting time.' There was a strength in her tone that seemed unshakable. 'When all of this is over, I want us to do this properly.'

'This?' I didn't dare assume what she meant, even though my hope was spilling over.

'Us. Courting.'

'I want that too,' I said, and, when she leaned in and kissed me, I could almost forget that we had anything to fear at all.

29 NOVEMBER 1920

THIRTEEN DAYS LEFT

33

I drove north with the sunrise, and the roads became thinner and more winding, with the kind of hill crests that gave me a swooping sensation in my belly – or maybe I was just driving too fast.

A sign for the Wellness Centre pointed me towards a long, broad gravel drive that led up to a country house painted white, with a white door whose knocker was so shiny it looked as though it had been polished that very morning. In front of the house, neat rows of flower beds were arranged in perfect lines, with sharp borders cut into the grass. In summer, they were no doubt riotous with colour, but now the empty beds were blanketed with a thin layer of frost. The gardens then cascaded down to the right of the house, and every blade of grass seemed to have been cut with precision. If only it were as easy here to tame a mind. I'd check in without a second thought if that were the case.

When I knocked on the front door, I was greeted by a woman wearing a navy blue blazer and a smile that would have been perfect were it not for the smudge of red lipstick on her front tooth. It made me lick my own teeth, as if doing so would wipe it away for her.

'I'm here to visit Joy Leery,' I said with cheery firmness, remembering Violet's direction to be confident. 'I'm her cousin, Peter.'

'Of course.' She took me to a polished wooden counter with a book for signing in atop it. I glanced over the other visitors' names – and was relieved to see that none of them was for Joy.

'Has she been well?' I asked, remembering Violet's guidance to keep focused on asking questions so that there was no opportunity for me to be asked any myself.

'Fairly well. As far as I understand it, the doctors have put her on a mild sedative to keep her calm.'

I winced internally. Joy had ended up in the Wellness Centre not because she needed treatment, but because she had naïvely trusted that people would take her at her word, even though she'd discovered something as unbelievable as magic. Instead of believing her, her aunt had brought her to this place, and they'd sedated her.

'Excellent,' I said, plastering on my most charming smile.

'Now I'm sure you understand that we don't allow guests to have visitors in their rooms. Should we set you up in the games room?'

'Perhaps we might do a circuit of the gardens,' I replied, thinking that our conversation would be afforded more privacy outside.

She peered out the window. 'It's a bit chilly.'

'Oh, it's not so bad once you get moving,' I said, briskly swinging my arms by way of demonstration. The smile on my face was beginning to feel a bit forced. I must have convinced her, though, as she asked me to wait. I sat down on a wicker settee facing a framed painting on the wall – it was recognizable as a Yorkshire landscape, and yet it was a brighter version; the hills still rolled, but they were painted in happy greens that banished the wild and moody atmosphere that I had quickly grown to love about this county.

The woman soon returned with Joy, reminding her to button up her coat as they entered the room. Joy had a pretty heart-shaped face framed by red corkscrew curls, and wide eyes that got even wider when she saw me, and definitely assessed that I was not Cousin Peter. She looked younger than her sixteen years, more vulnerable and naïve than I'd been expecting. That made me nervous. My whole body tensed up. The success of this endeavour was reliant on Joy being curious enough, or brave enough, to accompany the boy impersonating her cousin on a walk around the gardens. Perhaps I'd have to rely on her being foolish enough.

'Joy,' I said, before she had the opportunity to express her wariness, 'it is so good to see you looking well. I have news from your father.'

That appeared to pique her interest sufficiently. She cocked one eyebrow, but seemed to be willing to play along.

'Let's go for a walk, and you can tell me everything,' she said, pulling on a pair of knitted gloves.

'Take your time,' the woman said. 'I checked your schedule, and you're not due to see the doctor until after lunch.'

'We'll be back well before then,' I said, giving what I hoped was a reassuring smile. There was a cagey look in Joy's eyes, and yet it was unpractised, as if being wary were a new skill she had only just begun to learn.

We stepped outside together, our breath creating pale curls in the air and our feet crunching on the gravel.

'Who are you?' she asked as soon as we were out of earshot. 'Are you . . . with them?'

She obviously hadn't managed to develop any sort of subtlety yet. At least we weren't going to dance around, performing a charade.

We walked side by side, past rows of evergreen bushes with tapered tops like ice creams in a cone. 'No, I'm not part of Imperium Mortis,' I replied. 'I'm trying to understand what it all means, just like you are.'

She stopped, closing her eyes briefly. 'You don't know how good it feels to hear somebody say that.' She sounded on the brink of tears. 'When somebody tells you you're deluded enough times, you almost start to believe them.'

I was quick to reassure her. 'You're not deluded,' I said. 'I've learned just as many unbelievable things as you these past few weeks.'

'You said you had news from my papa,' Joy said. 'I wrote to him. Is he coming for me? Are you working for him?'

I quickly explained everything – my own death sentence from the magic, how I had come to track down her father, how I'd found her letter to him.

'He never got it,' I said. 'I think he's gone into hiding. Do you have any idea where he might be?'

Joy thought about it. 'If he's not at the sanatorium, there's only one other place he would go. But I'm not going to tell you.' There was a glint in her eyes, the seed of something shrewd beginning to take root and develop. 'If you can get me out of here, though, I'll take you.'

'Get you out of here?'

'Papa sent me to my mama's sister to keep me safe, but I don't care about being safe,' she said. 'I care about putting a stop to Ada. I'm not frightened.'

'Is that . . . because of the magic?' I asked.

Joy lowered her eyes. Her feet dashed the tiny stones on the pathway. I remembered what Lois said, about her not being listened to, and so, even though my instinct was to rush in with another question, I let the silence fill the space between us instead. She would speak eventually – I was sure of it. I just had to let her know I was listening.

'I was dying,' she whispered at long last. 'The doctors had tried everything, and Mama said we'd do all the things I wanted to do, for as long as I could. She let me keep a little grey kitten I found, and that was the only thing that gave me any joy. Papa had been staying at Saint Anthony's ever since he got back from the war, but he used to visit every week. One afternoon, when I'd gone up to bed, he came to my room and started to tell me about the magic. It sounded like something from a fairy tale. He said that he might be able to save me.'

She traced a line from her breastbone down to her stomach. The incision line. 'When he put the clockwork inside me, he said I'd live to be a hundred.'

I shivered.

'He did warn me about what it had done to the soldiers. That they couldn't feel anything when they woke up. But he said he thought that, because I was still alive, it would be different. And it was different, but not how he expected.'

'How is it different?' I couldn't imagine the way that Death Magic worked any more than I could predict my own future.

'All of my feelings are gone. Just like what happened to the soldiers he saved from the war. There's maybe a tiny remnant left, but there's something else instead, like a new sense. I didn't know what it meant at first.' She took a deep breath and looked me square in the eye. 'It's like being able to feel death.'

'Feel death?' I started to become aware of an uncomfortable prickling at the back of my neck.

'I can feel it pulsing. Say when I'm close to someone.' She stopped walking and gazed intently at me. 'If I tuned in to you, then I could feel how much time you have left. It's like a piece of string between my fingertips, and I can trace it along, see how far it goes. When I get to the end, I can feel the pulsing, and I can tell when it is – when you're going to die – down to the minute.'

262

If Joy could tell me the exact moment of my death, then it would confirm, once and for all, the claim that Death Magic had over me. A combination of dread and excitement danced in my chest. 'Will you?' I croaked. Faced with this, my voice had gone into hiding somewhere, like a timid mouse.

'Will I what?'

'Will you tell me when I'm going to die?'

'When you've got me out of here.'

Joy set her jaw defiantly as if she were testing her ability to negotiate. She needn't have worried. She was the only connection I had to her father, who was the only person in the world with the skills to free me from Death Magic. Of course I was going to help her get away.

'Okay,' I said, and I stuck my hand out so we could shake on it, but she tucked hers into her pocket.

'No, I don't want to touch you. I'll be able to feel it.' She shuddered.

I wondered what it was really like to be able to sense death. From the look on her face, it wasn't pleasant.

'Why do you want to know?' she asked. 'What difference does knowing make? I can't change it. Believe me when I say that you don't want my papa to do this to you.'

'That's what the soldiers said too. It's not that I want your papa to implant that clockwork inside me,' I said.

'What is it that you want then?' She looked at me despairingly as if she couldn't fathom me out at all.

What was it that I wanted? The more information I'd gathered, the more certain I was that I didn't want to use the clockwork myself. I just needed to know if there was any way to break the grip that Death Magic had over me, to free myself from it, once and for all . . .

'I don't know what can be done to save me now, but I'm hopeful, in a way that I wasn't for a dreadfully long time.'

'If anyone knows what can be done, it's Papa,' Joy said after a long pause.

'So let's go,' I said. 'I'm parked over by the entrance. We just need to head back to the car as if there's nothing unusual about what we're doing.'

'If you're sure. They won't notice I'm gone until lunch,' she said. 'I'm allowed to go anywhere in the grounds. We're supposedly allowed to leave whenever we want, but they rely on the Centre being in the middle of nowhere to be enough of an incentive to stay put. There's nowhere to run to.'

'Just keep your pace steady so we don't look suspicious,' I said, thinking my plan out loud. 'And when we get to the car, you get in the back and duck your head down, so if anybody sees me driving away, they won't realize you're in the car.'

We turned and started heading back in the direction we had come, maintaining the same casual pace. I had the twin sensations of dread and excitement wrapping around each other inside me, but I had to keep my steps even and my expression neutral, just in case anybody spotted us and raised the alarm. The grounds were empty, the cold weather acting in our favour.

'Get in,' I hissed, and in one swift movement Joy opened the back door of the car and slid across the seat, keeping her head low. My heart started thumping as I got in the front seat and turned on the ignition. If we got caught, then how would I be able to explain myself? The police would be called . . . and I couldn't spend my last days in a police cell an ocean away from home.

I reversed the car so I could turn around, and then I drove as nonchalantly as I could down the driveway, with my fingers crossed atop the steering wheel. It was only when I'd managed to get on to the main road again without raising any suspicions that I put my foot down on the gas pedal, keen to put as much distance between us and the Wellness Centre as possible.

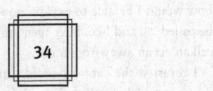

34

I couldn't wait any longer. I had to know my fate. When we arrived back at the hotel, I walked Joy through to the sitting room for guests, which was thankfully empty, sparing us the impropriety of heading to my room.

'How do we do this?' I asked her as I cast off my winter coat and sat in a plaid armchair by the crackling fire. Impatience coursed through me.

'Are you sure you want to know?' Joy asked, sitting in the chair opposite me, keeping her voice to a low hush, despite the fact we were alone.

'Yes. I need to know,' I said, although now that the moment had arrived, the resolute determination I'd felt earlier was waning slightly. Was doubt creeping in? There was something about it that seemed so final. The confirmation I had been seeking all this time – were these really my last thirteen days on earth?

'I've never done it so deliberately before,' Joy said warily. 'Well, if you're really sure . . . give me your hands.'

I held them out to her, palms up. Instead of taking them, she grabbed my wrists, digging her thumbs deep into the flesh so the blue ribbons spooling up from my hands started to bulge out from the skin, the pressure building. When she released them, the veins had a segment of pale emptiness until the blue rushed back through. She held her thumbs back in place and closed her eyes. I listened to the beating of my own heart. We stayed like that for an age. My breath slowed in rhythm with hers. Suddenly she pulled away from me as if she had touched fire, and as I opened my eyes, hers snapped open too.

'I don't understand it,' she said tremulously. 'There are two. Two threads, two pulses. I don't know how to explain it any better than that, but it's as if you have two timelines.' Joy looked dizzy, her head wobbling on top of her neck, her eyes glazed over. She rubbed her eyes, forcing them to focus.

'Two threads,' I said. A lightning flash of clarity struck me, leaving me feeling shaky and dizzy. 'Because Death Magic has interfered.'

'You're right,' she said. 'It's like there's your original life, the time that you were always meant to have, and the other, which says when Death Magic is going to claim you. But I can't separate them,' she said. 'They're both tangled up. I don't know. I honestly don't know.' She sounded a little panicky, as if she were concerned about my reaction, as if she thought that I might lose my temper with her for not fulfilling her side of the agreement.

My heart started to beat faster. I sank further into the armchair, crushing dizziness sweeping over me and pressing me down. I covered my eyes with my hands, let my fingertips press just enough to turn my vision into a field of jumping white spots. Joy placed a hand on my shoulder, and the sensation pulled me back from my spiral of unease.

'I've had a thought,' she said. 'I can't say for sure, but what if the reason the threads are so tangled is because it isn't over yet? What if it means that it's not decided, that there is actually a way for you to undo what's been done?'

My hands had dropped into my lap, and I noticed that they were clasped together as if in prayer. The hope fluttered down from Joy's words, and I allowed it to land on me like a baby bird with sharp little feet that dug into me.

'If my papa can help you, he will,' she said. There was an earnestness in her expression and a softness in her voice when she spoke about him. 'I can't promise I'll be able to find him, but there's only one place I can think of that he would go to hide. And if he's there, he'll help you.'

I couldn't marry up all the different versions of Hugo Leery that existed in my mind. Joy made him sound like a hero. In her eyes, he had saved her; he had saved the soldiers. This version of Hugo was filled with altruism, would do whatever he could to help his fellow man.

It could not have been a more different image than the picture that Violet painted. Her version had been a leader in an organization where ruthlessness was the prized trait, where death was not just a fact of life, it was a way of life. Murder and manipulation and magic.

Was it possible that he could be both these people at once, a mass of contradictions? And which of these versions had my father partnered with?

There was one thing, I supposed, that would have made all the difference. Everyone I had spoken to reflected on the war with an awful sort of haunted look in their eyes. Could it be that Leery's experiences in France had changed him so fundamentally that he could no longer stomach the work of Imperium Mortis? There had been enough chaos and bloodshed for all our lives; it was an abomination the like of which had never been seen before. Would surely never be seen again. And it seemed as if the way he had tried to use his magic since the war was for the extension of life, not the extinguishing of it.

Was Leery seeking redemption?

'I have to tell you, I'm frightened to meet with him. After everything I've heard about what he's done . . .'

Joy looked as if she had a bad taste in her mouth. 'He told me everything, even the really horrible parts. I know he hasn't been a good person. He kept it a secret from Mama and me because he didn't want us to hate him for it, and when Mama found out, her reaction was all his worst fears come true. She couldn't look at him; she spat in his face; and she swore that she'd make sure the whole world knew the awful things he'd done. So that's why Ada killed her. She could never risk their secrets being revealed.'

'And what about you?' I asked. 'How are you able to forgive him for what he's done?'

'I'm not sure I can,' she said, her voice wobbling with emotion. 'But I believe he's trying to find a way to stop Ada and Imperium Mortis, and he's committed to eradicating the magic now. He's trying to do the right thing. Does that erase the evil things he's done? Of course not. But just because I don't think bad deeds cancel out good ones, doesn't mean I believe he's completely irredeemable. And he and Ada were just children when they were initiated. I have to wonder . . . just how much choice has he had in any of this?'

I remembered what Violet had told me about the initiation programme in its current form. I doubted it was any less brutal when Ada and Hugo were children, and I couldn't imagine how it would affect a person to be brought up in the world of Imperium Mortis, feeling the power of the darkness from such a young age.

'What makes you so sure he'll help me?' I asked. 'He hasn't exactly got a reputation for being charitable.'

'I think that regret can be paralysing, or it can be galvanizing,' she said. 'For Papa, it's been the latter, and you can't underestimate the sheer weight of the remorse he's feeling. If you tell him how the magic has affected your life, I think he'd want to do anything he can to undo it.'

Joy seemed utterly convinced by her father's change of heart. I so badly wanted to believe that it might be true. He was my only hope.

'Where do you think we'll find him?'

'My guess is that he's hiding in our family cottage in Cumbria. It's where we used to go for a precious week every summer.' Her eyes misted over. 'Papa told me it was a secret place that Imperium Mortis didn't know about.'

'How long would it take us to drive there?' I asked.

'Maybe three or four hours?'

'I think we should set off today then,' I said.

Time, the matter of time, was ever present in my thoughts, demanding to be acknowledged.

'I'll go tell the girls to pack.'

'The girls?' Joy asked.

'I probably should have told you . . . I'm not here on my own,' I said. 'Lois and Violet are friends of mine. You can trust them. They want the same things that we do.' I steered clear of mentioning that she didn't really have any other options; I'm sure that was already abundantly clear to her. 'I'll be back soon.'

I headed up the stairs to Lois's room – she was in there with Violet, anxiously awaiting my return. When I explained what I'd done – that I had brought Joy out of the Wellness Centre – Lois's eyes went all wide and concerned, and I could tell that she thought I had been reckless. But it was Violet's reaction that unnerved me. She let out a great laugh and looked delighted.

'Excellent!' she said, clapping her hands together. 'Now we have leverage.'

'Leverage?' I asked. 'What do you mean?'

'Now we have a way of making Leery do whatever we want,' Violet said slowly, as if I were stupid. 'We have his beloved daughter!'

'No,' I said. Even knowing how dangerous Leery was, that didn't sit right with me. 'We're not using her as a pawn. This isn't a game. I promised her that we would help her.'

'We *are* helping her,' Violet snapped. 'But we don't have to let Leery know that right away. We need to be smart about this.'

I felt as if a crack had formed between us, like the splitting of an eggshell against the side of a bowl – not a clean break, but a messy, fragmented one. Violet and I had been on this journey together because it was mutually beneficial. In that moment, though, I realized that our goals might no longer be aligned.

'Remind me: what is it that you want from him?' I asked.

Violet looked at me coldly. 'I want to know where Ada is now, and I want to know how to bring her down.'

'Okay. You say you want to put a stop to Imperium Mortis. Well, that's what Hugo wants too. That's seemingly been his whole plan, and Joy wants to join him. You can't see him as an adversary, or her as a tool to be used. They want to achieve the same thing that you do.'

'Enough,' Lois said as Violet looked about to jump in. 'You both have questions, and Hugo Leery is the only person who can answer them. We need to get packed and reach him as soon as we can. The Wellness Centre must have realized that Joy is gone by now, and they'll be trying to find some way of tracking where your car went.'

'You're right,' I said, and Violet nodded in agreement, though she still looked angry. Not for the first time, I was filled with gratitude for Lois. It was good to know that she was there for me.

Lois and I were deeply connected by our past together and by our hopes for a shared future. But now I could tell that Violet was always going to put Violet first. Once I outlived my usefulness, she'd shrug me off like an old coat that had never fit well in the first place. I pressed my lips together, holding the information close to my chest like a winning hand in a game of cards.

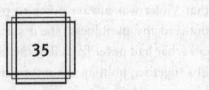

35

Leery's cottage was cradled by two snow-dusted mountain peaks that seemed to touch the sky. There was nothing but empty countryside for miles around, and we had to abandon the car to walk the final stretch of the way. The cottage sat on a small mound, overlooking a lake that was shaped like a comma. It was made of grey stone, with a tall chimney that puffed out signs of life.

'Papa!' Joy cried as we approached.

We spied a man carrying firewood into the house, by way of its duck-egg-blue front door. His ashy blond hair was speckled through with great streaks of white, he had thick grey stubble that covered his square jawline, and his eyes were a piercing blue that stood out even at a distance. When he saw us approach, he froze as if we were pointing a gun at him. He dropped his firewood and took a few steps closer to us. Then he recognized Joy, and he started shaking his head in disbelief, although he couldn't disguise his delight. He started to run, his arms wide, and Joy sprang towards him. His gloved hands squeezed tight around her back, and she almost seemed to disappear into his embrace.

'What are you doing here, my love?' I overheard him mumble into her hair. 'I told you, you need to forget that I ever existed. It's the only way for you to have a semblance of a life you can choose.'

Joy immediately started filling him in on her story, and when she told him what her aunt had done, his expression changed to one of horror.

'She sent you to an asylum?' he said, his mouth contorted. 'She was meant to keep you safe . . .'

'I know. But in any case I want to be with you, Papa,' Joy said. 'I want us to do this together –'

'Who are you?' Hugo interrupted his daughter as he caught sight of us properly for the first time. He pulled away from her and squared up to us, as if preparing to fight. He was broad, and, even through his many layers, his physical fitness and strength were apparent in the way he moved.

'My name's Felix Ashe,' I said. 'I'm Alfred's son.'

'I'm sorry for your loss,' was the gruff reply. Hugo wouldn't meet my eye.

'And this is Lois and Violet.' I gestured at them. Lois bobbed her head deferentially, but Violet's face was tense, a muscle in her cheek twitching.

'They helped me come to you,' Joy said.

'You trust them, my love?' Hugo asked, and Joy nodded. Something seemed to ease in Hugo. 'Come inside,' he said, beckoning for us to follow him.

The tip of my nose had gone numb, and my ears were aching, so entering the cottage was a welcome respite from the cold. It was very simple on the inside – a far cry from the extravagance I'd been used to all my life. A fire roared in the grate. There was the smell of something hearty cooking on the stove, bubbling away in a saucepan. Hugo gestured to a small round table surrounded by three spindle-back chairs. Not enough for all of us. Violet gestured for us to take one each, and then stood by the door, leaning her back against the stone wall.

'What brings you here?' Hugo asked, not letting us out of his sight as he filled a kettle with water.

'We decoded your casebook. You might have already guessed, but my father stole it so I would be able to trace it all back. To you.'

Hugo placed the kettle on the stove and cleared his throat. He rubbed his hands over his eyes. 'Your father was a good man.'

'Thank you,' I said, though I was no longer sure if I agreed with this.

'Why did you do it?' I asked. 'How could you experiment on them like that?'

Hugo sighed. 'The first time I saw someone die, I was thirteen years old. The first time I killed someone to make magic, I was fifteen.' He looked at Joy. 'These truths about me are unpleasant. These are the things that drove your mama away.'

Joy gazed at him mournfully. 'I know,' she said, taking his hand.

'When I was in France, on the front lines, I saw death and destruction differently. Boys no older than you,' he said, pointing at me, 'dying in my hospital, crying for their mothers, and I couldn't save them. I started to think that maybe the whole point of my existence was to use what I'd learned about the magic for good. I knew I wouldn't have to kill anyone to make it because the air was already so potent and full of essence . . .'

He closed his eyes, and his hands clutched at the air, as if they were sensing something we couldn't see, plucking something out of nothing.

'Once I'd made up my mind, I knew my device could only ever be clockwork. That's what I used to do when I was younger – take apart clocks, learn to fix their mechanisms. With Death Magic, you've got to work with the essence, give it your intention. If you have the intention when you're crafting, you can direct how it works, you see, but you have to be really strong. And I wasn't strong enough to mitigate the side effects. I never have been. The truth of the matter is that Death Magic is a force for evil. It always has been, and I think it always will be. I keep thinking it's going to be different.' His voice cracked as he looked at Joy sweeping a red curl behind her ear. 'But it's never different. Now I just want it all to end.'

'And what about those four soldiers?' I asked. Leery might have had noble intentions, but that didn't change what he'd done to my father, or to any of them. The one thing those poor men all had in common had been their misery and distress. 'You kept them trapped in your sanatorium for years!'

Hugo started growing defensive. 'I kept them alive. I looked after them. Perhaps it started as an experiment, but I grew to care for them. You can't understand it. You can't possibly know what we all went through . . .' He trailed off, and I got the distinct impression that he was done talking. I regretted my accusatory tone and looked over at Lois for reassurance, but she wouldn't meet my eye.

Hugo cleared his throat. 'You're welcome to stay tonight, but in the morning I think it's best if you leave.'

He began busying himself, making tea, counting out cups that didn't match from the cupboard. I was struck then by how very ordinary he was. This man, who I had mythologized on our journey and had wrestled to understand, was just a man. A man with cups that didn't match. He was flawed and damaged, and he had built his entire life around a force for evil, just to end up with a pile of regrets and a desperate desire for redemption. His hair was turning white and his eyes were framed with wrinkles – he wasn't some immortal being, and his life was just as fragile as ours.

The kettle on the stove started to whistle, startling us all. When he had given us all tea, he went outside to continue chopping firewood.

Hugo Leery was my only hope, and I didn't have long to convince him to help me.

'You need to tell him,' Joy said, once her father had left the room. 'You need to let him know about the curse and what's at stake for you.'

'I don't think he wants to talk to me.'

'She's right,' Lois said. 'You at least need to tell him. We've come all this way.'

Where Lois was firm but gentle, Violet's demeanour emanated frustration with me. She nodded sharply in agreement, frowning at me, her arms folded across her chest. I steeled myself against the cold and against the fear that my hopes were unfounded, and went outside to find Leery.

The thunk of the axe and Hugo's heavy breathing were the only sounds disturbing the quiet.

'I'm going to die in thirteen days' time,' I said. There was no use in being evasive about it. He turned towards me, the axe swinging by his side. My lip wobbled. 'It's Death Magic. A curse. My father ... he thought you could help me. He trusted you.'

Hugo winced. 'He was wrong to.'

'He thought you'd be able to save me.' The desperation was leaking out of me. 'Is there anything you can do? I don't want to be like Joy. I don't want you to put Death Magic inside me. I just want to know if what's done can be broken.'

Hugo paused. His face was lined and sorrowful.

'Your father told me about you and your brothers. About how the magic came to be wound around you. So I'll tell you what I told him – his wallet would need to be destroyed and you must cast off any gifts from the magic, rid yourself of it completely. If you're still benefitting from the magic, you'll never be free of its influence.'

'You told Father this?'

Hugo sighed deeply. 'I did. But . . . it was too late.'

'Too late? What do you mean, too late?'

'He had already lost possession of the wallet.'

Fear rippled through me like thunder rumbling through a cloud. It was so loud and so strong, I thought I might collapse to the ground with the weight of it.

'He . . . he didn't have his wallet any more?'

'No,' Hugo said. He pinched the bridge of his nose. 'My sister persuaded him to entrust it to her before he left for the front.'

My stomach curled up inside me. It was hopeless then. I had learned enough about Ada to know that appeals for mercy would be useless. 'I . . . I'll never get it back.'

'No, you won't.'

Hugo looked thoughtful, gazing off into the distance over my shoulder. 'But perhaps . . .' he began. 'Your father could see the essence . . . Some part of it is passed down through the generations, but it only seems to spark into Death Magic ability when you see somebody die at a young age.'

I shivered, thought of Father watching his own father die, burned to death in the accident at the factory in Brooklyn, then myself watching George twitch on the spearheads of the fence. 'What are you saying?'

'I'm asking if you can see it too.'

I pressed my lips into a thin, tight line. He meant using the magic myself, entering a deal with the darkness all of my own.

'I saw it once,' I said.

Hugo looked weary. 'Well then, you might want to learn how to channel it, how to use it for yourself. Nobody can make that decision for you,' he said. 'But the cost on your soul would be great.'

My father had succumbed to the song of the darkness and struggled against it for the rest of his life, like a sailor dragged down into a watery grave by the tentacles of a sea monster. Now I was tempted by the notion that I could try and control Death Magic myself.

Was it in my blood, this predisposition to fall under its spell?

My options were dwindling, the paths open to me were narrowing down, and there seemed to be an inevitability drawing me ever closer to the darkness.

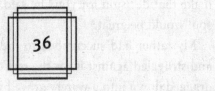

36

Joy had given me hope. I had two timelines. Hugo had given me options. I had two pathways open to me.

They had both given me *possibilities*. Either I attempted to destroy the wallet, if I could find it, and rid myself of its benefits ... or I opened myself up to the idea of entering into a new pact with the magic, learned how to control it myself.

That evening, we gathered around the fireplace while Hugo dished out a thick stew. In hushed tones, I recounted most of the details of our conversation, but I couldn't bring myself to tell Lois and the others that I could see the essence, and that I could try to learn to craft and use Death Magic. That was one of those things which, once uttered aloud, would change the way they saw me forever.

Hugo finished spooning the stew into bowls. 'You'll leave as soon as it gets light,' he said. 'I'm sorry that you've come all this way and I'm no use to you.'

'I've got to ask,' Lois said, carefully watching Hugo. 'What made you send the soldiers home? What were you trying to achieve?'

Hugo grimaced. 'When Joy got sick, my wife, Rose, was running herself into the ground, and I was trying to take good care of the soldiers, and Ada was in charge of recruitment – talking about going to America, to start looking for suitable candidates there ... and it all felt untenable. Too much. I couldn't keep the two parts of my life separate any more. I told Rose about it all, about the hope I had of making Joy well again. She couldn't forgive me when she learned what I am, what I've done.' He brusquely wiped a tear from his eye before it could drip.

'Papa,' Joy said, and her lip began to wobble.

'Rose was hysterical. She showed up at the house where Ada was training the recruits and started threatening to reveal the deaths we were responsible for. Ada shot her. Immediately. Didn't give me a chance to make it right.' He was weeping freely by this point, clutching Joy's hand as he spoke.

'It wasn't your fault,' Joy said.

'What happened to Ada?' Violet said.

'She had dedicated her entire life to Imperium Mortis,' Hugo said. 'So when she discovered that I had been living a double life, she couldn't comprehend it at all. She has never had the desire for family. She's always had this insatiable need to prove herself instead. After she killed Rose, she told me she was leaving for America to set up the US faction.'

'Did any part of you want to go with her?'

'No,' he said, shaking his head resolutely. 'The day Ada killed Rose, she killed the largest part of me. That's what

Ada can't understand – I don't think she's ever loved anyone. She seemed to think that I'd still want to be part of the future of Imperium Mortis eventually. I was happy to let her believe that so she'd leave, and I could make sure that Joy was safe with Rose's sister. That's when I decided I was going to bring down the organization once and for all – destroy everything they represent. The soldiers said they wanted to die, so we formed the idea of using their deaths to expose Imperium Mortis in New York.'

I thought of the eerie symbols they had painted at the scenes of their deaths.

'And that was your plan?' Violet said, an odd hostility rising in her voice. 'That was it? It doesn't exactly seem foolproof.'

Hugo tensed. 'I suppose I hoped that people like you, people with real, personal experience of the way this magic is wrong, would be dedicated to unveiling the truth and putting a stop to what Ada has planned.'

Violet opened her mouth to retort, but before she could there was an almighty crash as the door burst open, slamming against the wall and nearly jumping out of its hinges with the force. Lois and Joy screamed, and I leaped to my feet as a tall young man with sandy hair marched through the doorway, a shiny Imperium Mortis badge on his lapel and a revolver in his hand. Before I had a chance to react, a gunshot cracked through the air, and Hugo Leery screamed and grasped his leg. Blood began to spurt from the hole in his knee, and he made an awful sound of pain as he fell to the ground.

The room erupted into chaos – Joy ran to her father and clung to him, sobbing; Lois was screaming and had backed up into the corner of the room; Violet was holding the door open and looked as if she were about to make a run for it.

And me? All I could do was stand there, gaping, useless.

Then the man threw something to the ground that made a clattering as it fell and instantly began hissing. My vision immediately began to swim, and I bent over, coughing uncontrollably. The shooter backed out the door . . . and appeared to mutter something to Violet. It looked like she was following him. But that couldn't be right.

Smoke continued to fill the room, and when I breathed, it filled my lungs, and everything became confused and dizzy. A dark edge seemed to be closing in on me, and I knew that I was losing consciousness. I tried to crawl over to Lois, where she had slumped in the corner, her eyes closing.

I tried to hold on, but I couldn't.

Everything went dark, as if I'd been plunged into midnight, with no stars to light my way.

30 NOVEMBER 1920

TWELVE DAYS LEFT

37

I was in a room I had never seen before. I was stretched out, still fully dressed, on harsh white sheets, the bed built into a wooden wall. The air was stale, and the only window was circular and bolted shut. Groggily, I pulled myself off the bed and stumbled over to the window. It felt as if the floor were shifting beneath my feet, rocking uneasily. When I peered out the window, one glance confirmed my suspicions – I was at sea.

The door to the cabin was locked from the outside. I tried bashing on it and calling for help, but there was no response. What had I expected? My head was throbbing, and I was so, so thirsty. How had I ended up here? And how long had I been under?

Trying to extract the last thing I remembered was like performing surgery on my mind. We had been in the cottage, and Hugo Leery had been talking about stopping Ada … and then … and then …

The images came flooding back in strange fragments. Lois's terrified face. Hugo's shattered knee, the blood spurting. Joy's devastated wailing. And Violet ... Violet had been by the door.

An awful realization began creeping in. Violet had left with the Imperium Mortis associate as he gassed us into unconsciousness. Had she been working with him all this time?

I brought his face to mind – the youthful college-boy look of him, the fringe of sandy hair. There was only one person it could be, I was sure of it.

Lachlan Adair.

I groaned aloud. The information was shifting and twisting as I tried to grasp hold of it and wrestle it into some sort of sense. What did I really know about Violet? She had failed her Imperium Mortis initiation. She was in love with Lachlan Adair, who had been successful where she had failed and had saved her life. What she wanted more than anything was to find Hugo and Ada Leery and destroy what they had created.

Violet's guidance before I went to see Joy, teaching me how to lie to and manipulate others, started to echo in my mind: *Tell them the nearest possible truth*.

Which parts were true and which parts were not? Just how stupid had I been to trust her?

Trapped and alone in that cabin, I had too much time to stew over my thoughts. I picked apart and overanalysed every exchange I'd had with Violet, looking desperately for what I'd missed. She was a flawless liar; there had never been a moment when I'd doubted her.

The betrayal that I felt was a wound the like of which I had never experienced. I was still alive, which I supposed was something to be thankful for – and yet I had no idea what their intentions were for me, or what had happened to Lois and Joy. Or, I supposed, to Leery.

That thought sent fresh ripples of panic through me. If something terrible had happened to Lois, it was my fault for getting her involved and dragging her along with me on this ill-advised venture. My heart ached with fear for her life. She had to be alive, or I would never forgive myself. Maybe she was on this boat too, in another cabin. I closed my eyes and tried to bring her face to mind, but all I could see was the way she had wilted in the corner of the cottage, losing consciousness and surrounded by the gas.

And what about Joy? She couldn't be dead – she had the clockwork inside her. She was artificially sustained by the magic until she was a hundred years old. Surely the only way to kill her would be to take it out, and that would be a messy business. No, they'd had to act quickly – and, besides, I was sure Ada would want to study her brother's most impressive experiment yet.

How long had I been unconscious? Where were they taking me? And what could I do about it? Nothing, I knew bitterly. Absolutely nothing.

The powerlessness filled me with an overwhelming white-hot rage, and I yelled in frustration and bashed on the cabin door again until my fists started to turn red and sore. I had no sense of time, trapped in the cabin like a creature in a cage, and eventually I sank down by the door, overwhelmed with sorrow.

I just needed to breathe.

Sitting there on the floor of the cabin, my back up against the door, I let a steady stream of air in and out. My thoughts started to slow down, make more sense. I figured I was being taken back to America. That was where Ada had based herself now, with her plans to expand and find new recruits for Imperium Mortis – like the one who had showed up at my father's funeral. All I could do was wait and hope that Lois was in another cabin, safe and unharmed.

*

When, hours later, there was finally a noise at the door, I jolted up and scrambled away. A key scratched in the latch, and there was a click as the door unlocked. It was him – the young man who had gassed us at Leery's cottage.

'Don't try anything,' he barked. His voice was rich and his accent Scottish. 'I'm bringing you some food and water.'

I held my hands up in submission. The thirst was making my throat feel like sandpaper, no doubt partly thanks to the gas. And what was the use in trying to tackle him or wrestle my way out the door? We were on a boat; there was nowhere to run.

Kicking the door shut behind him, he came into the room and proffered a plate that held two slices of bread with a few pieces of cheese and ham, and a water jug. I snatched them out of his hands and gulped directly from the jug, slurping as if I'd never had a drink before. Even though the water was warm and tasted sort of stale, it was the most refreshing drink I'd ever had.

'The gas does that,' he said, confirming what I'd suspected.

When I had finished, I wiped my mouth with the back of my sleeve, my manners discarded. They were no use to me in the situation I found myself in.

'You're Lachlan Adair, aren't you?' I asked.

He smirked by way of response. He was handsome, but he had a cruel mouth and eyes the same green as a cat's. It was an infuriating face, and it made the anger bubble back up inside me.

'Tell Violet that I want to speak to her,' I said. 'Tell her it's the least she can do.'

'Oh, is it?' he said, and then he leaned a little closer to me and lowered his voice to a whisper. 'I think you'll find that you're in no position to be making demands. I've got a bullet with your name on it, and Violet is the only reason it hasn't gone straight through your skull already. Do you understand?'

His breath was hot and sour, and I flinched away from him, refusing to give him the satisfaction of an answer.

'I said, *do you understand*?' He delivered a deft kick to my ribs. The pain reverberated through my body, new waves intensifying with every breath I struggled to catch.

'I understand,' I choked out.

He smirked, then left me gasping on the floor. There was the sound of the lock clunking back into place, and then I was alone again.

I was alone again for a very long time, and the sky grew dark through the porthole window.

38

The key scraped in the lock, and the door's metallic latch shifted open. Violet stepped into the cabin. The tears that sprang to my eyes surprised me, and I wiped them away with an angry hand, not wanting to give her the satisfaction of seeing me cry.

'Finally,' I said. 'Were you too ashamed to face me?'

'Not at all,' she said, bristling and shutting the door with a click behind her. 'I just thought you needed a bit of time to cool off. You sounded like a wild animal howling and scrabbling at the door the way you were.'

I had spent hours thinking about what I would say to her when she finally came to me. I had so many questions, but the most pressing burst out of me without warning: 'Where's Lois? What have you done with her?'

'She's in another cabin like this one,' Violet said, and the relief was so refreshing, it was like plunging into a lake, being submerged in the cool water.

'If you've hurt her –'

'I haven't hurt her,' Violet said with a sigh, interrupting me. 'And you don't need to waste our time making threats. You have no power here.'

'And what about Joy? Is she safe too?'

'Joy is very important collateral,' Violet said. 'Or hadn't you worked that out? I thought you were reasonably intelligent. Do you really not understand what's going on here?'

'How am I supposed to understand what's going on when you've lied to me from the very beginning? You expect me to be able to decipher what you had planned this whole time, when I don't even have the first clue what's true about you?'

'Most of what I told you was true,' Violet said nonchalantly, flicking her dark hair over her shoulder and twisting the ends together. 'The only bit I left out was that I stayed in touch with Lachlan. We sent letters and telegrams, and I knew that if I wanted us to be together I was going to have to find a way to become more ruthless and then prove myself to Ada. I knew I could be stronger, and I knew I could do better – if it meant I could be with Lachlan, then I'd make it happen.'

'What about your mother? What happened to her?'

'Nothing. She thinks I'm dead,' Violet said. 'It's safer for her that way, and it will prove to Ada that I've got the resolve it takes to dedicate myself to Imperium Mortis. Lachlan and I are going to give Ada Leery everything she wants.'

'And what exactly is that?'

Violet gave a small smile. 'She wants Hugo to implant clockwork inside her. She wants to live forever.'

'So you never wanted to destroy Imperium Mortis,' I spat.

'No,' she said simply. 'I want to join them. I want to earn my place. When we first met, I knew you were going to be useful. The things your father left for you: they were the trail to lead us back to Hugo. I really was trying to track down Imperium Mortis in America, but all I had were newspaper articles and telegrams from Lachlan with updates, but they took so long to arrive I was always on the back foot. And, of course, your money didn't hurt. It's been like having my own personal benefactor.'

Her pride was so brazen, her eyes shone with it.

'And if I'd told you what I really wanted, right at the beginning, would you have trusted me? Your father was dead. You were horrified by Death Magic. Once I'd committed to it, I couldn't tell you the truth without making you doubt me.'

I had trusted this girl, shared my deepest fears with her, defended her to Lois, and relied on her companionship . . . But it turned out I hadn't known her at all. Even though most of her story had been true, a crucial piece had shifted, like knocking through a wall in a home, only to find the house crashing down around you.

A sickly feeling crawled beneath my skin, sending ripples of nausea through me.

'If I'm no longer useful to you, and you're so ruthless, then why am I still alive?'

'I have a proposition for you,' Violet said. Although she smiled, I couldn't help but see it as a sly grin and wondered what machinations lay behind it. 'You could join the initiate programme.' Excitement rippled through her voice. Every word she said seemed imbued with electricity – they fizzed and sparked.

I frowned. 'What do you mean?'

'Imagine it: you could join us. Become part of Imperium Mortis.'

I gave a harsh bark of laughter. 'You've got to be kidding.'

But she seemed earnest and a little thrilled. 'Look, Felix, let me be honest with you. I never envisioned a scenario where I would care what happened to you. You were expendable. But that's not how I feel now ... I've never had a friend listen to me the way you did. Never in my life. I want to help you, to repay you for everything you've done for me. I didn't expect to care about you, but I do. We're friends, aren't we?'

I snorted in disbelief. '*Friends?* Friends don't do this to each other,' I said, gesturing around the cabin. 'You're stealing my last days.'

She shook her head. 'I'm giving you a chance to live beyond your countdown. When we dock, we're going straight to Ada, and I want to be able to ask her to save you. The only way she'd ever consider that would be for me to offer you as an initiate. Won't you let me do that for you?'

I pretended to consider this. It felt sensible to play along. 'What about Lois?'

'Her too, of course. She's smart. And I know how you feel about her. You can't think I'm blind to that. I know you wouldn't even consider joining us if anything happened to her.'

'Am I that transparent?'

'Unfortunately for you, yes,' Violet said. 'That's one of the first things I'm going to have to drum out of you if you're going to be successful in the programme. But we have time on this journey for me to teach you the things you'll need to know.'

'And what if I don't agree to it?'

'You won't get out of this alive unless you do,' she said matter-of-factly. And wasn't that the awful truth that underpinned it all? Either I embraced a life inside Imperium Mortis, where I might be released from the curse, but had to dedicate my life to the darkness . . . or the knowledge I had would be the death of me. I knew too much, and I was not going to be allowed to walk away from the things I had uncovered. I realized that they wouldn't even have to dispose of me; they'd only need to wait the few remaining days until my birthday, when Death Magic would claim me anyway.

Death Magic had me in its grip, whichever way I looked at it.

'All right,' I said. 'I'll do it.'

She smiled, and it was the most terrifying thing I'd ever seen.

*

The next day, and every day during the rest of our journey, Violet came to my cabin to prepare me for my initiation into Imperium Mortis. She brought me written tests – thought experiments, ethical paradoxes between two moral imperatives, philosophical and psychological disputes on the use of magic – and questioned me on my answers. I tied myself in knots as she interrogated me, I struggled to make sense of the complex debates she challenged me to, and – even though I tried my best – I was failing every step of the way.

My heart might not be brutal and cruel the way Imperium Mortis wanted it to be, but I needed to do better. Success in the initiation programme was my only hope of survival. I had to be convincing enough to buy myself some time to think, and try to defeat my curse – for Nick, as well as my own self-preservation. I knew that Lachlan wouldn't hesitate to kill me if he was ordered to, and I couldn't rely on Violet's sympathy for me – she needed to prove she was ruthless if she wanted to have any hope of regaining her position within Imperium Mortis. If that meant murdering me, then I was certain she would see it through.

It was more than just a question of my own life and death, though. It was about what I was willing to do in order to live. I knew that, if I became an initiate, at some point they would ask me to kill somebody. I didn't know whether I had that in me; perhaps I wouldn't know, until the moment arrived, what I was truly capable of.

At night, I felt the darkness whisper to me, and had dreams about the things that I would be able to do if I allowed myself to attempt to harness its power. Was this what Hugo Leery had meant by working with the essence? It had been following me, looking over my shoulder, all my life. Was this the person I really was underneath everything?

9 DECEMBER 1920

THREE DAYS LEFT

39

The long days passed in a haze that made me wonder how secure my grip on reality was. I felt enormously physically and mentally weakened. The bread had grown drier by the day, and eventually the ham and cheese stopped accompanying it. Violet grew happier with my responses to her initiation materials, some of which involved making judgements on the value of lives; in scenarios she presented, I had to decide who deserved to be saved and who should be utilized for the creation of magic. The fact that it became easier to answer her – save that one, kill that one – left me wondering if I was fundamentally susceptible to the darkness, or whether there was some logic to the way that Imperium Mortis operated ... As I say, my grip on reality had begun to loosen.

When it came to Violet, she still seemed to think that she was doing me a favour, but the friendship we had built was tarnished by her betrayal, even as she sought an opportunity to save my life.

On the surface, at least, I was presenting as a diligent student, eager and ready to be handed over to Ada as a willing initiate, begging for a way to be released from the curse. Beneath that, I was screaming internally. My thoughts kept turning to Lois – wondering what she'd been told about me studying for initiation, what she thought of me … Was she playing along too? Did she know me well enough to understand that my heart hadn't changed?

When I wasn't trying to get my head around the initiation materials or thinking about Lois, I couldn't get my family out of my mind. How were the pair of them coping? I hoped they were faring well in my absence. I hoped that I'd have the chance to be reunited with them; my heart ached at the thought of never seeing them again.

*

When the boat finally docked, Violet came to my cabin to release me, or so I thought. Instead, she looped a rope around my hands, tying them behind my back and incapacitating me, although I knew that I wouldn't stand a chance against Lachlan's deadly aim even if I did try to escape. She led me up on to the deck so that for the first time I could see we were on a large ship, no doubt belonging to one of Imperium Mortis's wealthiest benefactors. Not as powerful and impressive as the liner that had taken us to England, but it had still achieved the journey at quite a pace, even if the time had felt interminable for me. The sky was clear, and the salt in the air was refreshing.

The New York skyline was a welcome sight. It felt like a lifetime since I'd left, even if in reality it had only been a matter of weeks. Nick wasn't far away. If only there were some way to contact him and Mother, let them know that I was surviving, that they were my reason for going on.

Lachlan brought Lois and Joy up on to the deck, their hands similarly tied. Seeing Lois again, dishevelled but unharmed, was an incredible relief, and it took all of my resolve not to run to her. My hands twitched behind my back, the impulse trying to turn into motion. There were dark bags under her eyes that I had never seen before, and she looked as if she had lost weight around her face; her cheeks were pinched. She bravely tried to smile at me.

When we finally docked at a quiet quay, we got off the boat, and Lachlan directed the three of us to the back of a coach-style motor vehicle driven by an Imperium Mortis recruit, silver badge shining. Joy, Lois and I sat on the floor with our backs up against the unsanded plywood, as if we were nothing more than boxes of produce to be delivered.

'What happened to my car?' I asked, the indignation in my voice undermined by the way it wobbled. My nerves were getting the better of me, and although I wanted to be strong and show no sign of the fear and doubt I felt, my voice betrayed me.

'Call it a gift to Imperium Mortis,' Lachlan said. He snorted and slammed the doors, plunging us into darkness that was only broken by a crack where the doors were fastened.

'It's so good to see you,' I whispered to Lois. 'Are you okay?'

'I'll survive,' she said. She shuffled a little closer to me and rested her head on my shoulder. 'We're together. When we get there, we have to watch and listen and work out what to do next.'

'Did you agree to be an initiate too? Have they been training you as well?' I asked, and she nodded sharply.

'We just need to go along with it for now,' she said. She turned to Joy. 'Have they spoken to you about an initiation?'

Joy shuddered. 'No. I don't even want to imagine what Ada has planned for me.'

A few moments later, Lachlan returned with Leery. He could barely walk without Lachlan to support him, his leg bandaged up. He winced with every movement. Joy whimpered at the sight of him. She tucked her legs up so that her chin could rest on her knees. Hugo shifted nearer to her and said something I couldn't quite hear in a low, soothing tone.

The vehicle set off, and we bumped around like fruit bruising on its way to the grocery store. We fell into a sullen silence. I wished that there were something I could say or do. It began to feel as though we were on our way to an execution.

After an hour of driving, the vehicle finally came to a halt. Lachlan opened the doors and helped us to our feet and out into the sunlight. We all blinked as our eyes adjusted. He released the bindings from me and Lois, and I used the moment to reach for her, managing to squeeze her little finger. Leery and Joy remained bound, like prisoners.

Before us was a great Georgian mansion made from elegant white brick, with a balustrade balcony across the top floor and twin chimneys on either side of an impressively large round window. It was utterly isolated. We were greeted at the door by a young woman dressed all in black whose hair was scraped back off her face.

'You must be Lachlan. Ada got your telegram, and she's expecting you,' she said, eyeing his badge and then us.

We must have looked horrendous – nervous, gaunt, sweating despite the cold. She snapped her fingers, and another initiate, who appeared to be in his late twenties, jumped to attention and herded us on the other side.

'Follow me.'

40

The front doors of the mansion led into a great hall which stretched up the full height of the building – there was a set of stairs both to the left and the right of us that led to two great walkways on the second floor and then repeated the pattern on the third floor. A magnificent chandelier draped down in an elegant column, like a drop earring. The American chapter seemed to be thriving. We were led out of the great hall, and the female initiate knocked on a door.

'Send them in,' a crisp voice called.

The initiates gestured for us to enter the room while they waited outside. Inside, everything was decorated in deep jewel tones – emerald curtains, a sapphire rug, a blood-red ruby chair by the fireplace. The woman sitting in the chair, eyes narrowed, was Ada Leery, the director of Imperium Mortis. And I'd seen her before.

I had seen her impersonating a member of the police force. She had interviewed me after Father died, appeared like a grim omen in New York City following the deaths of Bradley and Chuck, and now I could see the ways in which her appearance echoed Hugo's. The ash-blonde hair, striped through with white, the arctic blue eyes. My courage withered like a summer plant left to fend for itself in the winter months.

Ada Leery was 'Detective Jones'. They were one and the same. No doubt she had been involved with removing the evidence that might have led to the exposure and downfall of Imperium Mortis.

'Hugo,' Ada said, getting up and drawing close to her brother. 'I didn't appreciate your little stunt with the soldiers. It was dreadfully messy cleaning up after you.'

Hugo spat on the floor.

Ada sighed. 'We might have shared a womb, but you have become a dreadful liability.'

She went back towards her desk and picked up a little golden bell from the table next to it. When it rang out, the initiates entered.

'Wade, take my brother and my niece to the basement,' Ada said.

Recognition zipped through me. *Wade.* An unusual name. Where had I heard it before? I cast about in my mind for the source of the familiarity and caught hold of Mother's voice – the conversation we'd had before I left.

'*I found out that your father changed his will. Everything has been left to a stranger.*'

'*A stranger?*'

'*Wade Griffin. I've never heard of him before. I can't understand it.*'

This Wade had long black hair that was swept across his forehead, green eyes and high cheekbones. Was he the same

Wade, the one who owned my home, the one who had my fortune sitting in his account? Had Father chosen someone from Imperium Mortis as his successor?

Ada's barked instructions continued. 'Lock them in and stand guard. Pearl, continue to bar this door. I do not want to be disturbed.'

The initiates led Hugo and Joy away. There was a wrench inside me when they were out of sight, as I realized I might never see them alive again.

'Well then, Lachlan.' Her voice was like the crunch of ice underfoot. 'Welcome back. You were successful in fulfilling my request it seems.'

Lachlan seemed excited. 'It's good to be back, Director Leery. As you can see, I've done everything that you asked of me in delivering your brother and his daughter. But I wouldn't have been able to do it without my accomplices. I'd like to make a recommendation that these three are brought into the initiate programme.'

Accomplices? I didn't want to be an accomplice to this. It was odd to hear him speak of me that way, and ever odder to hear some humility coming from his lips.

'I require no introduction for these young people. I have made it my business to know everything about them,' Ada said, and even my teeth felt cold. It was beginning to sink in that she had been ahead of me at every turn. 'What I do wish to hear, Violet, is how you came to escape your own execution?'

Violet licked her lips. She was nervous. I remembered what she had told me about Ada – *If Ada wants someone to talk, they talk.* I wondered what sort of magic object might compel someone to tell the truth against their will, and what the cost of that might be. If that was even what she was using – her own force of will felt frightening enough.

I could see Violet's mind turning, deciding whether to lie or not. 'Lachlan helped me to escape,' she said.

'I know,' Ada said, and Violet blinked at her in surprise. 'But thank you for not attempting to patronize me with a lie.'

Violet steadied herself. 'I have dedicated myself to improving to the standards you require, and I'm here to show you that I have attained the levels of ruthlessness that are necessary for success in Imperium Mortis,' she said, channelling the boldness I had long admired in her. 'Despite being estranged from the organization, I managed to learn about Hugo's traitorous actions. I was able to gather the resources necessary to deduce the truth about the soldiers and their time in Saint Anthony's, and I was able to track down your niece, who led us to her father. Now I've brought them to you so that you can see that I'm willing to do whatever it takes.'

It sounded like an answer to a college interview question, the sort that Lois had been seeking help for from Geoffrey. I wondered how long it had taken Violet to rehearse exactly what she was going to say.

'I see,' Ada said.

Her eyes ran over them both, and there was a heavy silence as we waited for her to reach a verdict.

'I must admit that I'm impressed by your dedication and tenacity. If you want to enter this organization, you must be willing to commit your entire life to it. Understand this – I have lived my life in the shadow of a brother who is less dedicated, less passionate and less faithful, always having to try ten times harder, always having to work for longer, strive more, just to be treated the same ... I got to where I am today by being ruthless and by being indefatigable in striving for my aim.'

Ada returned to her chair and ran a perfectly manicured nail across her lips. 'I know what I'm going to do with you two,' she said. 'Tomorrow morning, you will take part in a trial.'

Lachlan's expression was inscrutable, but I could see a flash of excitement in Violet's eyes. I got the distinct impression that she considered this to be a triumph of sorts.

Ada called for an initiate to take Lachlan and Violet for 'preparation', whatever that might mean. I had no idea what an Imperium Mortis trial would look like, but I was certain that Violet and Lachlan were going to be put through some kind of test, and I was sure that Violet would do whatever it took to succeed. As she left, I tried to catch her eye, but she stared ahead so intensely it was as if I had become invisible to her.

'Felix Ashe.' Ada's cool gaze ran over me. 'You have been as resilient as I would have expected Alfred's son to be. I must also thank you for bringing this impressive young lady to my attention.'

I had brought Lois into this, and whatever happened to us next was my fault.

'I'm still so delighted that Alfred managed to find us,' Ada continued. The way she said his name – with such fondness – it was as if they'd been the best of friends. And yet ... there was no sign of grief at his passing. 'He has been a very generous benefactor over the years.'

My mouth went dry. 'Benefactor?' I croaked.

My heart cracked. I loved my father, and I had hoped – no, trusted – that all along he'd been trying to muddle his way through this twisted world in order to save me and Nick. And now ... now it seemed that he'd been more tangled up with Imperium Mortis than I'd dared to believe. He'd given of his fortune willingly, to fund their endeavours, and for years he'd kept them a secret from me.

She smiled a wolfish smile, all teeth. 'Why, we wouldn't have this new faction without him,' she said, lifting her arms to indicate the extravagance of the house. 'It must be a relief to know that his fortune hasn't gone to waste, seeing as you're the one who really has to pay for it.'

He'd been sucked into the darkness and swallowed whole.

'What a legacy,' I said, my voice sounding hopeless and small.

In fact, I'd never *felt* so hopeless or small in my entire life. Tears beginning to well in my eyes, I looked at Lois. Her expression was so sympathetic, I thought it might break me.

'I never felt that your father reached his true potential. When one of our scouts first got wind of him through the collecting circles, I knew I had to meet him in person. It didn't take much to get him to trust me – he was so desperate for someone else to believe in Death Magic and what he'd experienced. The truth is he could have been such a skilled practitioner if he had just applied himself. He didn't know what he was doing when he first experimented with it. How could he? But once you've had a taste of magic, there's no going back. So, when I first told him about Hugo's notion of defeating death, he couldn't get to the front fast enough.'

'He wanted to save me,' I said. 'I'm going to die in three days because of Death Magic.'

Ada smirked knowingly. 'On your eighteenth birthday, on the stroke of the hour you were born, just like your brothers.'

Mother had always made a fuss about the fact I was born at midnight. She said it was good luck. I'm not sure where she got that idea from. It sure didn't feel like luck.

'Unless . . .' Ada said, drawing out the word.

'Unless?' I asked, my voice hoarse.

This was what I'd hoped for – that Imperium Mortis could break the curse. But I wasn't sure I could take any more illusion of hope.

'Well, I would need to destroy your father's wallet,' Ada said, pretending to think about it. 'Which would be an awful shame, seeing as it was a gift. A gift that has been incredibly valuable, as I'm sure you can appreciate,' she said, fixing me with a penetrating stare.

The feeling of being cornered and trapped was rising within me. Ada looked as if she were thinking deeply, her eyes narrowed.

'Your father might not have reached his full potential . . . but that doesn't mean you can't.'

'In that case, will you consider me for initiation?' My voice came out pleading.

Lois stiffened up next to me. I didn't want to look at her face. Just imagining the disappointment on it was enough.

'Yes,' Ada said. 'I will consider you for initiation. Both of you.' She smiled benevolently at Lois, as if she were bestowing a gift.

'And what if I've decided I don't want to be initiated?' Lois asked.

Ada chuckled. 'We have a saying here. Once you've entered the world of Imperium Mortis, you are initiated, or you die. The choice is yours.'

Initiation or death. For the longest time, I'd wanted so badly just to survive that I hadn't considered what the cost to my soul might be. Now it was all I could think about.

41

Ada ordered the initiate called Pearl to set us up in attic rooms and introduce us to the routines of the Imperium Mortis house. Pearl took us the back route, up a winding stone staircase that led right up into the eaves. In a previous life, the attic rooms would have been for servants to reside in, out of sight and out of mind. It brought to mind our team of staff at Pitch House, and I found that I missed the comfort of being able to rely on Miss Price or Mr Reed to keep the wheels of my life turning. Thinking of our staff reminded me of home, and once again the great wrench of homesickness threatened to overwhelm me.

'We all share rooms,' explained Pearl in a more clipped version of Violet's British accent as she walked us down the corridor.

Each room we passed was furnished simply and held two or three Imperium Mortis recruits, sitting on beds, cross-legged, reading, or sitting at desks writing. The corridor made me think of college dormitories, almost letting me forget the sinister undertone to this place – each one of these students was here to defend and learn about a dark magic practice. They burbled with excitement and whispered to each other as we passed – clearly our arrival had piqued their interest.

Now Lois and I were becoming part of their number.

'I've been on my own since I lost my last room-mate, so you can share with me,' Pearl said to Lois. I wondered what had happened to this room-mate, and decided I didn't want to ask. Pearl opened the door and showed Lois her new bed. Lois perched on the edge of it, and ran her fingers through her uncombed hair, whose honey-coloured sheen had darkened since we hadn't been able to bathe on the boat journey. She fidgeted self-consciously on the bed.

'There's a spare bed going in Wade's room too,' Pearl added, as if I were an afterthought. 'It's that one.' She pointed at a door across the corridor.

Wade. With any luck, I'd get the opportunity to speak to him alone. My nerves jangled at the thought. What could he tell me about Father? I went over and peered inside the room. It was a mirror of Pearl's, two beds beneath a slanted roof – one made up with a quilt, the other empty. So this was where Wade lived. I'd have to ask him how exactly he came to be the beneficiary of my fortune.

'How long have you been here?' I heard Lois ask.

'Just a month,' Pearl said. 'I was already in training back in England, but Ada selected a handful of us to come and start this new branch with her.' Her face beamed with the honour.

Everything had a surreal feel to it. It was as if I'd walked into a dream world and been swallowed up by a new and different reality. I drifted back into Pearl and Lois's room, not wanting to be left alone with my thoughts.

'I suppose you don't have much in the way of belongings,' Pearl said. She looked us both up and down, taking in our dishevelled clothing. 'Let me fetch you some towels and uniforms, and then you can freshen up. I'm on kitchen duty tonight, so you can help me out with the cooking.'

The way she spoke of the routines of the house reminded me again of the predictably comforting rhythm of boarding school. It was easy to forget that we weren't here by choice and the real reason for the existence of this place. She left us alone in the room, and I sank on to the bed next to Lois, feeling as if my legs might give way beneath me.

'Back in the office, was that a bluff?' Lois asked, her voice as cool as steel. 'Or do you really believe you could use Death Magic?'

I hesitated for a moment before replying. 'It wasn't a bluff.'

She recoiled from me.

'I haven't ever done it before,' I blurted, trying to reach for her hand, worried that she might draw the wrong conclusions.

Lois was breathing heavily, and her eyes were wary. She was frightened of me. 'I see. So what is your plan here?'

'I haven't got a plan,' I said. 'I thought that was obvious. At the very best, I only have three days to live, Lois, unless I cooperate with Ada. This is the end of the road.'

'But you know where it's going to take you,' Lois said.

I knew what she was thinking. At the centre of Imperium Mortis was a rotten core. Their magic only existed through death. Either way, I was doomed.

*

When Pearl returned with towels and two matching sets of the uniform every recruit wore, she showed us the bathrooms down the corridor that we could use to finally wash away the grime of the journey. I combed my hair over and dressed from head to toe in the sharply pressed black suit. When I inspected myself in the mirror, I realized I no longer looked like me – I was gaunt, my skin was sallow, and the suit made me indistinguishable from the rest of the recruits.

What would Father think if he could see me now? What would Nick? Mother? Geoffrey?

I left the bathroom and headed back to join Lois and Pearl in their room. Lois looked like she belonged there – her uniform was elegant and could have been tailor-made for her. Her skin and hair had regained their brightness, but the impact of the journey was written in the tiredness of her eyes. When she spotted me, she seemed just as taken aback by my appearance.

We had been transformed into initiates.

'You ready for kitchen duty?' Pearl asked.

'I'm not sure how much help I'll be,' I said. 'I've not had any experience cooking.'

'You can peel potatoes, can't you?'

I winced with embarrassment. 'Well ... I'm sure I'll figure it out.'

Pearl raised an eyebrow. 'I see. Well, no matter what our background, there's a rota of duties for the upkeep of this place. We have to do chores for a few hours every day, and the rest of the time we spend preparing.'

'Preparing for what?' I asked.

'For initiation,' she said, incredulous. 'You don't know anything, do you?'

'We're lucky that you're here to run us through the basics,' Lois said in a perfect pretence of gratitude.

Pearl smirked, pleased. 'You are indeed. There are people here who would eat you alive if they realized how little you know. I'll take you through what you need to know and give you a quick tour of the house. Think of me as your guide.' She cleared her throat. 'But then we have got to get to the kitchens.'

'Willing hands,' Lois said.

She was doing a good job of creating the illusion of enthusiasm, but I knew better. She was gathering information, assimilating, and no doubt coming up with a plan.

'There's four layers to initiation,' Pearl said, leading us back down the stone stairs. 'They've been the same from the very start of Imperium Mortis, but since Ada advanced to director she's made it a much more structured programme. I suppose it's like a syllabus. It takes years now, like going through university. So the first level is psych testing.'

I found myself nodding, thinking of the hours Violet spent on the boat taking me through various moral quandaries and the magical paradoxes.

Seeing my slight show of confidence, Pearl snorted. 'That's the easiest part. Most people do their tests while they're being scouted. It's meant to be a way to tell if somebody's a good fit or not, before they've even heard the name "Imperium Mortis".'

'Then what?' Lois asked.

'Well, most people don't pass, and they just carry on their lives and never learn about magic. But if you do pass, then you're in, and you start training in craft.'

'Craft?' I couldn't help but interrupt. It sounded so incongruous. Somehow I doubted we'd all be sitting around doing embroidery.

'Yes, craft. You've got to be talented at making stuff,' Pearl said. 'Whether that's as an artist or in something more technical. It's the future of Death Magic, Ada says; custom-built items that she can manipulate the way she wants to.'

Like Hugo and his clockwork.

Pearl stopped on a small landing halfway down the circling stone steps and took us through a door that led to a long hallway decorated with mosaic tiles in grey and blue. 'All the rooms off here are the makers' rooms.' She opened the nearest one, revealing a pair of recruits, heads bent over a woodworking table that had been positioned in the centre of the room. Wood shavings littered the floor.

'Get out of here, Pearl!' one of them yelled.

Pearl closed the door. 'People can be a little protective over their making. A lot of them don't pass the final test to be an associate, so they need to make sure they at least have a skill unique and specialized enough for them to be a maker instead of support staff.'

Lois and I exchanged a confused glance. 'What do support staff do?' Lois asked.

Pearl rolled her eyes. 'They're often scouts for potential magic practitioners. They source benefactors . . .'

'They clean up the mess,' I said, thinking of the uniformed recruits who had appeared when the soldiers died.

'Exactly.'

Pearl showed us into a few more rooms – a shining steel laboratory complete with bubbling flasks; a half-complete library stuffed with dozens of boxes of books that hadn't made their way on to the shelves; a tailoring boutique where two initiates were hunched over a sewing machine; and finally a film studio replete with great lengths of film tape in canisters. I'd never seen anything like it, and I was filled with awe. I kept having to remind myself that this was no ordinary school. Everything crafted here had a sinister undertone – if the initiates wanted to turn their creations into magic, then they would become murderers.

'So what happens next?' Lois asked. 'Once we've settled on a craft, I mean.'

'Eventually, you have a trial. Ada brings you something she's imbued with Death Magic, and you use the item. It helps her to discover what its effects are. It's not an exact science.'

'So . . . you're like the subject of an experiment?' Lois couldn't stop the distaste from dripping off her tongue.

'You could look at it like that,' Pearl said. 'But there are benefits. How many other people get to use magic? And Ada always tries to make sure the object is something that matches your interest or your skills. Some people have ended up with these incredible powers. There was a girl in York who passed her trial and literally stopped ageing. She's going to look like she's twenty forever.'

'There's always a cost, though,' I reminded her.

Pearl shrugged. 'When do you ever get anything for nothing in this world?'

For the first time she sounded defeated, and I began to wonder how she had ever become involved with the organization in the first place, what had led her to accept this darkness. The question buzzed on the tip of my tongue, but I waited just a moment too long, and Pearl pressed on.

'The final stage is an attempt at Death Magic itself. You take the life of another, and if you can see – or, better yet, harness – the essence, then you are apprenticed to Ada herself and learn how to use it. It's quite rare that that happens.'

'What level are you at?' Lois asked.

'Oh, I'm still in craft training,' Pearl said. 'I'm making moving pictures. It's cutting-edge technology, but Ada thinks it's going to be big. And if it is, Ada has this notion that if we could find a way to infuse the reels with Death Magic then we'd have an impact on a huge scale. We could influence the whole country.'

It sounded nightmarish to me, but Pearl was shining with conviction. The psych testing had obviously done an excellent job in selecting her to join the organization. There was part of me that could see how the power of Death Magic – the things it offered – could be tempting, seductive. Yet it also inspired a profound revulsion in me. The magic was a darkness – a malevolent living thing skulking beneath the consciousness of people going about their day-to-day lives. It got under the skin of those individuals who were susceptible to it, whether through nature or through conditioning, and everyone else was none the wiser.

Pearl took us on a meandering route to the kitchens, pointing out the dining hall and the games rooms on the way. 'We tend to get pretty competitive,' she said with a grin. I didn't doubt it for a second.

When we got to the kitchens, two recruits who looked a few years older than us were seasoning slabs of ham ready to be roasted. Pearl set Lois and me to work right away with paring knives and potatoes, and I couldn't help but eavesdrop on the conversation being held between the boys prepping the meat.

'. . . trial tomorrow,' one of them was saying. 'And we're all going to watch.'

'Yeah, I heard that.'

'There's a reason they usually happen behind closed doors. Trialling new magic, you never know if someone's going to get hurt. What if the negative effect is something really horrific?'

'Close your eyes.'

'Can't close your ears if they're screaming, though, can you?'

Lois and I kept our heads down. Even after everything, I found myself caring what happened to Violet. I didn't want to care – I really didn't – and I tried to squash the part of me that hoped she might change, might become the version of herself who would use her tenacity and bravery for good instead of evil.

42

The evening meal was served in the great hall, which was arranged with two long tables. The recruits trickled into their seats in dribs and drabs, grabbed greedily from the platters in the centre of the table and stuffed their faces, all in an atmosphere of convivial jollity that belied their common motivation. I counted eighteen in total, although Pearl had said that dinner was a casual affair and sometimes makers wouldn't descend into the hall to eat until later in the night if they'd been captivated by an element of their project. It was easy to see these recruits as human, as potential friends, and forget that they were future murderers.

Lachlan and Violet were nowhere to be seen.

Neither was Wade. If I just had the opportunity to speak to him, maybe I could find out a bit more about his connection to Father, discover why he'd been chosen as sole inheritor of our estate. Was it just a way of funnelling more money into Imperium Mortis?

Yet my new room-mate remained elusive, even as the hour grew late. I eventually retired to our room, squeezing Lois's hand when we said goodnight, and then I spent half an hour struggling with sheets to make up my bed.

I had just clambered in under the covers and closed my eyes when the door opened. Wade came in, looking exhausted. His face was drawn, and a muscle near his eye was quivering. He caught me staring.

'I'm real tired, so you'll have to forgive me if I'm not throwing you a welcome party.'

He closed the door and turned the lock, before lying down on his own bed. He rubbed the bridge of his nose, as if loosening a knot, and when he next spoke it was in a hushed rumble. 'Though I have to say, when I imagined us meeting, it wasn't like this.'

'You imagined us meeting?' I was surprised that he'd given me any thought at all.

'Yeah. I thought it would be pretty unavoidable once the will was executed.'

'I don't know that I'll live long enough to see that happen,' I said, my throat tightening, so that my voice sounded as if it were being squeezed.

'It's all due to be finalized tomorrow, or so I've been told. Unless your mother's lawyers have found a last-minute loophole.' He looked at me now, hard. 'Why are you here, Felix?'

'I don't want to die,' I said simply, knowing the truth of it. 'Ever since I found out about Death Magic and the curse on my life, I've been trying to find a way to stop it. I've been following the path that Father left for me. And eventually it's led me here. To you. The man who's stolen my fortune – my *brother's* fortune.'

Wade made a little strangled noise. 'I'm sorry. I wish I'd been able to get to you first, but you've seen for yourself what this place is like.'

I had – it was intense, regimented, and everyone was watching each other.

'I'm assuming Alfred – your father – didn't tell you anything about our work together?'

My head started to swim as though I were being dangled upside down and the blood was rushing to it. My heart pounded in my chest and tears pricked my eyes. I shook my head. What work together?

'He couldn't,' I said.

'No. Of course he couldn't after he came back, but it goes back a lot further than that.' Wade ran his fingers through his hair, leaving it standing upright in places where it should have been smooth. It gave him the harried look of a mathematical genius trying to solve a complex equation.

'So I have to take a risk here,' he went on. 'I have to assume that, whatever I say, you're not going to rat me out to Ada.'

I tried to look calm, persuasive. 'You can trust me.'

Wade snorted. 'No, I can't. You can't trust anyone under this roof – that's lesson number one.' His eyes bored into me, as if he were trying to appraise the value of my soul. 'Now that you know about this world, do you really want to be a part of it?'

It seemed like he was testing me. Asking me why I was truly here. 'I don't think I have a choice.'

It was true, but the admission felt heavy. My options had been whittled away, one by one. It didn't matter whether I wanted to be part of Imperium Mortis – the alternative was death.

Wade fell silent, chewing at the corner of his thumbnail.

'Would you tell me about Father? About how you knew each other, and why he left you everything?' I asked, my voice wobbling.

Wade's expression softened. 'You don't know anything about me, do you?'

I frowned. Of course I didn't know anything about him – we'd only just met. I had heard his name only once before today, as the cuckoo in the nest of the fortune that I was about to pay for with my life.

'When I was seven years old, my dad died in your father's factory.' A muscle twitched in Wade's jaw – a tiny movement that stood in place of a full expression of grief and distress and an incomparable pain. 'Right in front of me. And your father.'

I gave a sharp intake of breath. 'Then did you also see . . .?'

Wade nodded sharply, and I respected his reluctance to say any more. I knew, first-hand, what it felt like to see someone you loved take their last breath. I knew, first-hand, what it felt like to see that wisp of midnight essence escape. What I couldn't imagine was how it felt to see someone capture that essence and know that it wasn't a figment of your imagination.

'Your father and I . . . we had both seen something that we didn't understand. He took me home to my mother, and from

329

that day onwards he provided for me in every way. He bought us a new apartment; he paid for private schooling for me . . . I had everything I could wish for growing up. Except . . .'

'Except your dad.'

Wade's face pulled into a tight smile, matching dimples like tiny creases ironed into his face. 'We only really talked about it when I was older . . . What we'd seen and what it meant. The wallet. The fortune. Your brother George. Then Luke and Scott. And then he found Imperium Mortis, and we were trying to save you and Nick.'

The years of Wade's life, running parallel to mine. I let out a steady stream of breath from between my lips. We had always been connected, well before this business with the will.

'At first, your father was just so relieved to have found Imperium Mortis. He would do anything to ingratiate himself with them. By the time he realized the truth about the murders being committed in the name of the organization, it was too late. He knew too much.'

'You are initiated, or you die,' I said, echoing Ada.

'Exactly. I hoped that he might have prepared you. We were going to start taking down Imperium Mortis from the inside out, found our own secret society dedicated to the eradication of the use of Death Magic – try to burn it out of the soul of the world. He wanted you to be part of it.' Wade gave a small laugh. 'We were going to call it the Ignis Society.'

Ignis. I remembered the Latin word from my lessons with Geoffrey. *Fire*. Because they were going to burn it all down. In memory of his own father. In memory of mine.

'I didn't know,' I said. What else could I say?

Wade nodded. 'Ada told him she knew a way he could save you and your brother . . . and she asked for the wallet in return for that information.'

I swallowed hard. 'But Hugo Leery told me the wallet would need to be destroyed in order to save us.'

So Ada had tricked him into handing it over. My father had only given it away to learn how to save us; he *hadn't* wished to fund this empire built on murder. It was presented as his only option.

'I know,' Wade said. 'Ada told your father that he needed to rid his family of the gifts of Death Magic.'

'Hugo said that too. So Ada told him half the truth.'

'Exactly. I think Ada was hoping he'd promise the money to Imperium Mortis, but he made me the beneficiary of every bit of the fortune he gained from Death Magic – the house, the Collection, the accounts.'

Wade looked a little nervous at this admission, but he needn't have worried. The idea that I might still be freed from the curse was the greatest news he could have given me. My life was worth more to me than Father's fortune. And it was worth more to Father too.

'And then Ada sent him to find Hugo at the front, said that he'd discovered a way to defeat death with Death Magic. Your father couldn't get there fast enough. I promised him that I'd keep an eye on your family, from a distance, let you live in the house undisturbed.'

The truth was complex. My father was flawed and had been haunted by the consequences of his entanglement with Death Magic, but he loved me, and he'd been trying his best to remedy his mistakes. And the whole time Nick and I had been at the centre. I began to cry, the relief and exhaustion pushing me over the edge. My father was long gone now, but he had loved me and tried to save me ... And just knowing that brought me a strange peace.

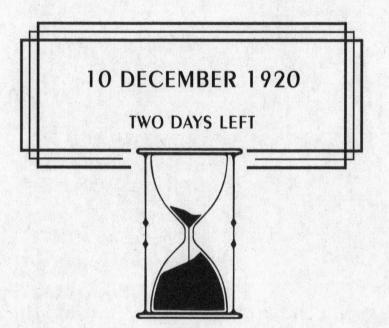

10 DECEMBER 1920

TWO DAYS LEFT

43

The next morning, the attic corridor was full of recruits rushing to get ready for the day, each one of them bursting with contagious excitement. The word 'trial' was on everybody's lips. Lois and I went down the stone staircase together with Pearl and Wade, swept away in the current of the crowd. The recruits were gathering on the walkways overlooking the great hall, leaning over the bannisters like an audience at the theatre. I desperately wanted to be able to tell Lois about the conversation that I'd had with Wade the night before, but I couldn't envisage a moment of privacy or the opportunity to take her to one side.

Below the walkways, the show was just beginning. Two initiates who looked well suited to being used for tasks that required brute force brought Violet into the hall. She looked lit up from within, an eager and determined energy radiating from her.

Lachlan was marched in with similar performance, and the pair of them were seated facing each other. They grinned at each other. The recruits began whispering among themselves, speculating on what might happen next.

'Usually, trials take place in private,' Pearl muttered by way of explanation, trying too hard to remain composed and self-possessed. She wasn't fooling me. She spoke too quickly and too eagerly. She was excited. 'We've never been given the chance to see one before.'

Wade's voice was a low rumble. 'And people who've done one don't like to talk about it.'

There was a carnival feel to the morning, although a tremor of uncertainty ran through the hall. We had become a single entity, united in terrible anticipation. When Ada appeared, we all tensed, stood a little taller, held our breath. She wore a fantastic, many-pocketed coat in a deep burgundy. It swept along the ground like a bridal train as she walked.

'When you commit to Imperium Mortis, you forsake all others,' Ada said. Her voice was as clear as a bell ringing out through the great hall. 'You see before you two initiates who are eager to demonstrate this for you today. They are about to prove to you their commitment to our cause by undertaking their trial publicly.'

Lachlan gave Violet's hand a quick, secret squeeze, the way I'd often done to Lois. I knew what that squeeze meant. It meant *we can do this as long as we're together*.

'She's using them to make a statement,' Pearl said in a low, hushed voice. 'There was a lot of gossip when Violet disappeared, and then we found out Lachlan had been sent on a mission.'

Ada reached into a pocket and produced a white box. She flipped the lid open, revealing something small and shiny.

'Lachlan, your trial begins,' she declared.

'What is that?' Lois squinted and leaned a little further over the bannister.

We all watched as Ada presented the contents to Lachlan, and he plucked the shiny object from inside. It appeared to be some sort of small metal box that fit inside the palm of his hand. Lachlan inspected it closely, and the rest of us waited with bated breath. There was a clicking sound as Lachlan brushed his thumb across the top of the metal, and a tiny flame appeared, flickering near his thumb. The object was a lighter – except we all knew it wasn't just any lighter. Ada had imbued it with the essence, and that meant there was a dark magic ebbing through it.

Lachlan oozed confidence. He lifted the lighter above his head to show us the flame, and that was when the magic revealed itself. The flame grew bigger, spread down the lighter and across his hand, creating a glove of fire. Lachlan's mouth fell open – but not in pain. He looked in a delighted state of shock, and he stared at his hand as though he couldn't believe what he was seeing. He laughed a little and moved his fingers to watch the flames dance.

He had the ability to manipulate this fire as though it were an extension of himself. He was able to make it leap from one hand to the other, feeling out the possibilities of the power he had been granted. The recruits all along the walkways oohed and aahed as if they were watching a performer at the circus. Lachlan pointed his hand and lit one of the oil lamps along the wall. He clenched his fist and created a ball of fire that he was able to aim towards the nearest window, which shattered in a shower of glass.

'Enough,' Ada said, seeming to tire of the display.

Lachlan snapped the lighter shut, and the fire disappeared instantly, as if it had never existed. That was when everyone simultaneously remembered that every instance of Death Magic has a cost.

Lachlan began to scream. His hands were horrifically burned. The air was pungent with the smell of his singed flesh. Violet twitched, as if suppressing the urge to run to him. All her excitement and the smug smile had gone, replaced by a humbled grimace. One of the recruits along a walkway vomited; below us, one of the bulky recruits who had marched Lachlan in went to fetch a bucket of cold water. Lachlan was guided back to a chair and plunged his hands in the bucket, crying with the pain. I averted my gaze, staring down at my shoes, trying to remember to just keep breathing.

I felt a hand at the small of my back. Lois's touch was grounding, and I tried to focus on pulling myself away from the spiral of panic. It was a gentle steering back to calm. My smoother breaths were interrupted by a sharp jab in my ribs from Pearl, directing my attention back to the unfolding of Violet's trial.

'And for Violet,' Ada said, presenting her with a second box.

Violet opened it, pulling out a small glass disc. Under Ada's instruction, Violet placed two fingers around her eye, pulling down the bottom lid, and dropped the disc on to her eye. Geoffrey had mentioned to me once the development of these lenses, intended for those who wore glasses, but said that they were too heavy, too uncomfortable. Violet winced. I flinched as she blinked several times, adjusting to the presence of the glass on her eye.

Where Lachlan's trial had been dramatic for those of us watching, it was impossible to tell what was happening to Violet. She stumbled forward, like a baby deer learning to use its legs on uneven forest ground. It wasn't clear what the effects were – perhaps it hadn't worked? Ada drew close to her, and they spoke in low tones. The hall was silent, except for when Lachlan let out a moan of discomfort. Soon the recruits all along the walkways began to mutter and murmur among themselves, wondering what was going on.

Ada clapped her hands, and the low hum of chatter stopped immediately, but there was the distinct feeling that everyone was bursting to discuss what was happening below.

'I want to thank you for your attention,' Ada said, addressing us all, a fierce smile on her lips.

Violet still seemed dizzy and lost. What was happening to her?

'I want to remind you why we are all here. There is a powerful force in this world, one that requires sacrifice in order to bestow us with extraordinary gifts. As your leader, I am offering you the opportunity to be part of the betterment of humanity. It is only through our research and experimentation with Death Magic that we will be able to find a way to finally harness it. But there are people who would stamp us out of existence like cockroaches if they could. It has always been the way – people fear science, fear what they do not understand.'

The initiates seemed all fired up, as if they were part of something necessary and righteous, despite being forced to face the cruelty of it. There were whispers and nudges and smiles.

'This journey requires your complete commitment,' Ada was saying, her hands in the air like a conductor. 'We survive only if we are willing to sacrifice. For the final part of today's trial, I wish to address the concerns I have regarding these initiates' loyalty. They have proved deeply committed to each other – and to Imperium Mortis. Now we shall see which commitment is stronger.'

Ada reached into her striking coat, and from an inside pocket, next to her heart, she pulled out a revolver.

'Death Magic only erupts from the body in the case of extreme emotion,' she said. 'That is why it has always been traditional to ask our initiates to take a life for their final test. It is also the witnessing of death that can spark your ability to see the essence, if the potential runs in your blood. I'm afraid that I must have either you, Lachlan, or you, Violet, but not both. Imperium Mortis must come first in everything.'

There was a heavy silence as everyone in the room tried to understand what Ada was saying. It was a harsh ultimatum, but the intention behind it was clear. One must kill the other. The noise of my thundering heart was so loud I thought everyone would be able to hear it. Next to me, Lois had her hand over her mouth and was shaking her head in disbelief.

Down below the walkways, Lachlan and Violet were both visibly distressed. Ada arranged for them to stand opposite each other, at a distance of twenty paces, and placed the revolver in-between them at an equal distance. Lachlan's hands were raw and dripping with the water from the bucket. Violet was unsteady on her feet.

Ada began to count down.

'Five.'

Violet stared at Lachlan.

'Four.'

Lachlan's hands were shaking.

'Three.'

Violet's mouth moved, but no sound came out.

'Two.'

There was a collective breath in.

'One.'

Lachlan moved first. He flung himself towards the revolver, but Violet was swift and nimble. She dashed, slid to the ground, and kicked out her legs, swinging them into Lachlan and tripping him. He crashed to the ground with a heavy thud, his injured hands outstretched to break his fall. The sound that came from him was animal.

Violet groped around for the revolver, missed, cursed, tried again. With the gun finally in her hands, she aimed and shot into the ground, missing Lachlan by several inches. It was as though she had no perception of distance and had lost all balance. How could she do it? It was horrifying to watch – this was somebody that she professed to love. I knew she was ruthless, but I wouldn't have thought her capable of this. The shock was numbing – I felt as if I were watching from somewhere outside my body.

She shot again, and this time she hit Lachlan in the shoulder. He yelped, straining to look at her in disbelief and scrambling away. The next bullet entered his gut, and there were gasps of horror from the spectators. My own mouth hung open as I sucked in the air. She really was going to kill him.

Another gunshot cracked through the air, and Lachlan clutched at his throat. Blood began to spurt from the hole in his neck, and he made an awful gurgling sound as he squirmed on the floor. I tried to look away, but found I couldn't. I hadn't liked the man – not even close – but this was an awful end for anyone.

Violet was weeping. Tears streamed down her cheeks, and she gave an ugly wail.

Then I saw it – the essence.

It was as beautiful and horrifying as it had been all those years ago, released from George on those spiked railings. Deep midnight, exhaled with a dying breath. It shimmered and glistened as it twisted through the air.

Ada moved swiftly, striding towards Lachlan, and pinching her finger and thumb together, as if she were threading a needle. She seemed to be able to pluck a fragment of the vapour, turn it into something tangible.

Her face was in a trance of concentration. A shudder went through me.

With one hand, Ada wove the essence around her finger, and with the other she plucked a tiny bottle, no bigger than my little finger, from her pocket, pulling the cork out with her teeth. She manipulated the essence, feeding it into the open mouth of the bottle before stoppering it shut. When it was safely trapped inside, she called out, 'Are any of you able to see the contents of this bottle? The very essence of Death Magic?'

All the recruits were silent.

My arm twitched at my side.

'Don't,' Lois whispered under her breath.

What Lois couldn't understand was how lonely it had felt, living with the memory of seeing my brother die, the way his body moved, the way the indescribably beautiful and horrifying haze had coiled from his mouth. So lonely, like being trapped inside my own mind.

I raised my hand.

A smile took its time creeping across Ada's lips. 'Come with me.'

44

The eyes of every Imperium Mortis recruit were on me as I traipsed down the staircase. I passed Lachlan's body, crumpled on the floor, the pools of blood spread out beneath him. Violet's face was drained of all colour. The eye that was cradled by the lens had turned a horrid black, and I realized that it had been eaten up by the darkness, the payment for whatever gift it had bestowed upon her.

I couldn't look up at Lois – I didn't want to see the disappointment in her face. All I knew was that a steady calm had made its way through my veins, despite the horror. Seeing the essence again had filled me with a sense of fulfilment somehow, as if this was always going to happen. How could I ever explain that to Lois, who was no doubt still desperately searching for a way for us to escape from this place?

I was struck by a sorrowful pang as I realized that the reason I had not seen the essence when Bradley and Chuck died was because they'd already lost it the first time they died. No wonder they couldn't feel anything. I thought again of Father and wondered what terrible fate had befallen Vaughan.

Ada had led me into a drawing room, where everything had a sickly yellow hue. She pinched the bridge of her nose as if she had a headache. She saw me looking and gave a tight smile. 'It takes a lot of energy to collect the essence.' She tilted the bottle to the light, showed me the way that it moved inside, like a living creature. Now her smile widened.

'So, Felix. You have the gift.'

I remained silent. I wasn't sure I would exactly describe all this as 'a gift'.

'The last time I met a recruit who could see the essence, he was sent to the Western Front like all the other young men his age and died there in the winter of 1915.' Her voice was full of bitterness. 'Such a waste. We are rare, and we have a responsibility to nurture this skill we have. My father had it too, but never learned how to harness it properly.'

Rare. The word glowed like a coal, warmed a part of me that had turned cold – the buried desire for significance. Wasn't that what the Collection had always been about? Making an impact on the world, being important, knowing that I *mattered*?

'You will train with me,' Ada stated as if it were a fact. 'You will learn how to work with the essence.'

I began to imagine a new collection of objects, infused with magic by my own hand. I saw myself wandering corridors filled with my magical creations. What would that kind of legacy feel like? That I was even considering it filled me with horror. This wasn't me. It was a vision of a dark shadow-self. I tried to shake it off.

'Consider this a gift from me to you,' Ada said, holding the vial out to me. 'Keep it safe.' I reached out and took it. I hadn't expected it to feel so warm, so alive.

'Thank you,' I said, but I wasn't sure that I felt grateful. My stomach turned over inside me. I was holding the last living bit of Lachlan – if you could really call it that.

'Think of all the wonderful things we can achieve with your potential.'

'You need to destroy the wallet,' I said, finding my voice. It sounded strange and detached, as though it belonged to somebody else. 'If you don't, I'll be dead in just two days' time. And I won't be much use to you then.'

Ada let out a cruel bark of a laugh. 'Indeed. However, don't mistake my excitement at your talents for trust. I would expect something in return, some indication of your loyalty. I have been considering this. Tomorrow evening, I will be undergoing a procedure. My brother Hugo is going to embed the clockwork within me. We have collected it from all the soldiers – except your father. Or we could always use the clockwork from Joy.'

Ada smiled as if that notion pleased her. *Where are Joy and her father now?* I wondered.

'Once my brother has fulfilled his purpose, you will execute him.'

'What?' I shuddered, appalled. 'No. I can't.'

Ada's self-satisfied smile returned. 'It's the price of entry to Imperium Mortis, no more, no less. You knew this.'

'But you already know that I can see the essence. I don't need to be tested again.'

'Perhaps. But what I don't know is whether you have the stomach for this life. Your father certainly didn't,' she said with a sigh. 'It was always, always about you. And now here you are . . . Think of all the time you've already wasted.' She fixed me with one of her steel-cold stares.

'This is the deal, Felix. Certain death – or a life of magic, creation and power. It's your choice.'

*

After Ada had dismissed me from the drawing room, I paced through the corridors of the mansion like a ghost. I was clearly considered to be trusted enough to roam the halls freely, though that thought in itself wasn't much comfort. What was I becoming?

I also knew that the moment I told Lois about Ada's ultimatum, she would ask me what I intended to do. I couldn't face her until I had an answer.

All this time I had been looking for a way to defeat the curse, and here it was. Ada would destroy the wallet, release me from my bonds – and yet I would enter another sort of bondage. My life would be committed to Imperium Mortis. I tried to imagine what it might be like: years in this house, dedicated to training, the temptation of finding a way to manipulate the darkness and bend it to my will, the way Ada did . . .

I would have more time, and maybe in that time Wade and Lois and I could find a way out. But I would always have to live with the knowledge that my hands were stained with blood, that I had become a murderer for the privilege of continuing my own life.

Was the cure worse than the disease itself?

But the alternative was to face death. And I didn't want to die. I really didn't. I was scared. And, by accepting my death, I was accepting death for Nick too. Nick, who I loved so fiercely, and whose life was also owed to the darkness. If I died without bringing an end to the curse, then it would come for him eventually.

I had to make a choice, not just for myself but for him too.

Joy had told me that I had two timelines. I felt they must rest on this decision, but both of them required me to run into the open arms of the darkness.

'There you are. I've been looking all through the house for you.'

Lois's voice snapped me out of my reverie. I turned to look at her, and saw her face was lined with concern.

It was time to decide.

11 DECEMBER 1920

TWENTY-FOUR HOURS LEFT

11 DECEMBER 1920

TWENTY-FOUR HOURS LEFT

45

That night I lay in bed, restless. The room was quiet and full of the silent machinations of my mind. Wade was sleeping. Even in sleep, he wore a tense expression. My watch informed me that my birthday was creeping ever closer, moment by moment. I had less than a day. Would this be my last night on earth?

I thought I imagined the gentle rapping at first, but it became more insistent. I frowned. Was this yet another test of Ada's of some kind? Or could it be Lois?

I clambered off the bed and opened the door – and was shocked to discover Violet. She had her arms wrapped around her body as though her organs might spill out if she let go. One of her eyes was the same bright green I knew so well, but the other was dead, trapped behind the glass of the lens.

'Can I come in?'

'What are you doing here?' I hissed. I was furious with her – and terrified of her.

'Please?' I'd never heard her so forlorn. 'I'm here to help you, while I still can.'

Help me? I needed all the help I could get.

I moved back from the door to let her through, but placed my finger over my lips in warning. 'Wade's asleep,' I whispered.

'Thank you for giving me a chance,' she said.

'Well, you got what you wanted,' I said. 'You proved yourself.'

The words were cruel, and they left a bitter taste in my mouth. I could have what I wanted too if I were willing to pay the price.

Violet stared at me, hard. 'I didn't get everything I wanted.'

'No, I suppose not.'

She didn't say anything, just looked at the floor. But I couldn't let it lie.

'I thought you loved Lachlan. How could you do that to him?'

'Love feels different when you're staring death in the face,' she replied bitterly. 'Would you let Lois put a bullet in your head?'

'Neither of us are capable of doing that to the other. I have no doubt that we would have both faced the consequences of it at Ada's hands. You didn't even hesitate,' I said.

'If I didn't do it, I knew he was going to kill me,' she said. She gestured at the dead eye that I had been so desperately trying to avoid looking at. 'I could see inside his head. He was prepared to do it. It was me or him.'

'Wait,' I said, struck with the horror of what it meant if Violet could read minds. 'Can you see what I'm thinking?'

'I'm trying not to.'

My thoughts were the darkest part of me, my greatest shame and my ultimate weakness. I did not want someone else to be able to see inside my head, least of all Violet. I tried, unsuccessfully, to rid myself of them, but all I could see in my mind's eye was the determination on Violet's face as she tried to aim the revolver, despite the loss of her depth perception.

'Stop. I don't want to see it. I know what I did. And I saw all sorts of things in his head that I wish I never knew. He was thinking about a girl, a recruit that he met at the York house after I'd left, and that, if he'd realized how easy it was going to be to fall for someone new, he would never have helped me escape in the first place.' Her eyes were filling up with tears. 'I suppose he was a good fit for Imperium Mortis through and through. Self-preservation was all he cared about.'

'You can talk,' I said, bristling at the reminder of her betrayal.

'Look, Felix, that's why I'm here,' she said, the determined look I recognized resurfacing. 'You were nothing but supportive to me. I wouldn't be here without you. I meant what I said to you on the boat – without you, I would have been completely lost. I've made my choices now. I thought Imperium Mortis was where I belonged, and everything I get from here is what I deserve. But you're good, Felix. I want to help you.'

I snorted. Wade snuffled in his sleep.

'You want to help me?'

'I don't know what your plan is, but I do know that unless that wallet is destroyed then you'll die tomorrow. I don't want that.'

'Ada offered me a deal. Maybe I don't need your help any more.'

'I know she did. Maybe I'm wrong about you. Maybe, when it comes to it, you will kill Leery today, and maybe you'll be perfectly happy as an initiate of Imperium Mortis. But . . . I've seen where she keeps the wallet.'

I stared at her incredulously, and she stared back at me, dead eye glinting in the moonlight. She'd seen it in her mind, I realized.

'It's in a safe in her bedroom, and I can tell you the code. Just . . . in case you wanted options.'

I gawped. 'But . . .'

Violet placed her hand on mine and said, 'There's no way it can be traced back to me. She doesn't know the extent of what I can see or how the magic works for me, and I have no intention of telling her.'

'Violet, I . . .'

All my words dissipated. Even though she'd hurt me and used me and betrayed me, after everything we'd been through together, I could see a tiny glimmer of the person that she could have been if her life hadn't been so hard. We'd shared moments of understanding that hadn't been lies. I wished that life hadn't turned her into such a cruel and desperate person.

'I feel the same,' she said, even though I hadn't spoken a word out loud.

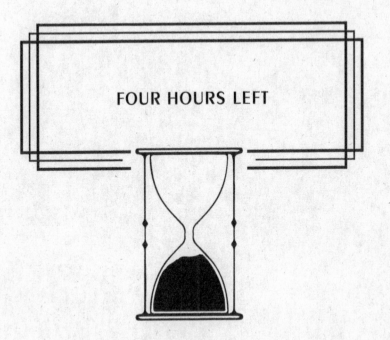

FOUR HOURS LEFT

46

Throughout the early evening, the preparation for Ada's procedure began in earnest. It seemed that every recruit had a job. Several large canisters of numbing gas were rolled down the hallway on the first floor to one of the makers' rooms which was to become a makeshift operating theatre. I overheard two recruits lamenting their terrible fortune at being ordered to clean and disinfect the clockwork that had been retrieved from the bodies of the soldiers. Four initiates were selected to flank Leery and Joy.

These were not the only sets of preparations being undertaken.

I was beginning to grow antsy as the clock continued to tick. I was running out of time.

Ada came to let me know that she would not expect me to perform my part until after she had been roused from the gas. 'I was there when he came into the world, and I want to be there when he is taken out of it,' she said, a grim reflection on her brother.

I wished for a second that I had the ability Violet had been given, the ability to rummage around inside Ada Leery's head and understand the way she worked.

'Don't worry.' Ada winked at me. 'It will all be done long before midnight.'

Again, I felt a strange sense of predestination, as if this were the way it was always meant to be.

Two timelines. I was hovering on the precipice between them. It all came down to the next few hours and if they unfolded the way that I hoped.

Whatever happened, the only certainty was that midnight would strike.

*

Pearl and I were the first to arrive at the operating room. The gurney was in the centre, made up like a bed with a pillow for Ada to rest her head on when she arrived. Next to it was a little table topped with a metal tray holding a selection of tools of the surgeon's trade. I didn't want to imagine the purpose of any of them, designed as they were for use on the human body.

It was unsettlingly quiet. And then I heard the ticking sound. Somewhere in this room, the clockwork was ready and waiting to be placed into its new home. Which piece of clockwork, and from which soldier, had they chosen? I couldn't bear to think of that. My stomach heaved.

Pearl handed me a revolver. The gun was heavier than I expected – I'd never held one before – and she noticed my unease, showing me how to grip it, and where to squeeze when the time came. Ada's orders were that I was to aim at Joy.

Pearl took her own gun out of a holster at her waist. I couldn't stop my surprise from showing. 'You didn't think Ada was going to rely just on you, did you?' she said scornfully.

Our conversation was interrupted by the arrival of Hugo Leery and Joy, each escorted between two initiates. Pearl lifted her revolver immediately, training her gun on Joy. Joy let out a whimper, terror all over her face. Leery was grim and stoic.

'That won't be necessary,' he said to Pearl. 'I know what my duty is here, and I have no intention of putting my daughter in harm's way. I will do what I must do.'

'Orders are orders,' Pearl said, and she nudged me in the ribs.

I lifted my gun and tried to prevent my emotions from leaking out across my face. Joy looked shocked and frightened, and all I wanted to do was tell her that I was sorry, that I would never hurt her.

When Ada finally arrived, dressed in a white smock, everyone stood up a little straighter. Even as a patient, she commanded the utmost respect.

'Well then, brother,' she said, 'this is to be your greatest achievement.'

Hugo breathed in slowly and deeply. It seemed to be taking every fibre of his being to remain composed. But Joy's life was at stake, and he knew it.

'Lie down,' he said, gesturing towards the gurney. The two men who were guarding him also pulled out guns and trained them on Leery.

Ada climbed on to the gurney and lay flat. Hugo hooked up a face mask to one of the canisters, and she put it on. One of the initiates peered over Hugo's shoulder as he turned the dial on the gas – no doubt to make sure he didn't take advantage of the situation and administer a lethal dose. The gas hissed noisily, and the mask on Ada's face began to cloud. Her eyes slowly shut as she was sent deeper and deeper into an artificial sleep. Soon she was as flat and still as a corpse.

My mind was racing – was everything going to plan? My palms began to sweat, making it difficult to hold on to the revolver. If something had gone wrong, I wouldn't know about it until it was too late.

My heart *thud-thud-thudd*ed and my mouth went completely dry. Hugo pulled on latex gloves. The ticking continued, a reminder of the way that time was running out – but for who? Me or Ada?

The waiting was unbearable.

I raised my eyes to the ceiling and hoped against hope.

Still, when the door burst open and the cacophony began, I gasped. The scale of the intervention was one thing to imagine and another to see. I looked into the corridor and saw it was teeming with police throwing open doors, tackling initiates to the ground. It was really happening – Imperium Mortis were being dismantled . . . all while their director, Ada Leery, was unconscious on an operating table, blissfully unaware that her dreams of immortality were slipping further and further away.

Hugo raised his hands in surrender immediately and barked at Joy to do the same, but the other initiates simply looked at each other, desperate for the guidance their leader would have provided.

I needed to move. I didn't want to hurt anyone – or get hurt myself – but if all of this was going to give me the opportunity to save my own life, and Nick's, then I needed to get out of there. To all intents and purposes, though, I would look exactly like an Imperium Mortis agent, dressed in their uniform, wielding a weapon, and I didn't have time to waste getting arrested. As an officer approached me with a set of cuffs, I propelled myself into action. I discarded the revolver, knowing that I would never be able to use it, and instead knocked one of the gas canisters over, so that the officer crashed into it and fell to the ground.

I had to get out of there. Without a backwards glance, I shot down the corridor, faster than I'd ever moved before. All around me there were sounds of chaos.

And in the centre of it all was Robert Flatt, that journalist from *Disclosed*, his mouth agape as if he couldn't believe his eyes or his luck. As he raised his camera, I lifted my arm to cover my face and dashed past him as quickly as I could.

At the end of the hallway, standing in the place where we'd seen Violet kill Lachlan, Wade was waiting with a car key. 'Best of luck,' he said as he pressed it into my hand. 'I hope this isn't the last time we cross paths.'

'I hope so too,' I said.

Lois was already waiting for me in the car that Wade had parked up for us. It was a little two-seater, the sort of car that drew no attention.

'Did you get it?' I asked, breathless, climbing into the driver's seat.

'Yes,' she said. 'Now get moving!'

The engine thrummed to life, and I allowed hope to whisper that we had managed it, we had made it.

'You're not going anywhere!' came the brusque shout of a police officer appearing at the front doors. He was all muscle, and his hands looked as though they could squeeze the life out of a person in seconds. My heart was in my mouth. He started to sprint towards us, and I caught a glimpse of the gun flashing at his hip.

I committed to pressing my foot to the floor. Lois let out a little shriek of fear as we accelerated away. The car rumbled and growled, and I felt as though I were riding an unleashed beast, all too aware that if I lost control then the ensuing crash would be fatal. I gritted my teeth.

A gunshot cracked through the air as the grand Georgian mansion shrank behind us, swallowed up by the dark. I pushed aside the images of the people we were leaving behind – Joy and Leery and Wade and Violet. It wasn't possible to release them all. It had to be enough that Lois and I were free. We had escaped, like the heroes of myth and legend that had wrestled their way out from the depths of the underworld.

ONE HOUR LEFT

47

Wade had told us the route that we needed to take to get back on to familiar roads, and the bright lights of New York at night-time glittered against the darkness. I drove like a fiend, stopping only to grab some gas and a box of matches from a station en route.

Our plan had gone without a hitch. Throughout this whole experience, there was one thing that I had learned about Ada Leery. What terrified her was the exposure and dismantling of Imperium Mortis. If I wanted to live beyond midnight, free from the shackles of Death Magic and Ada's grasp, then I had to reveal them to the world.

Armed with Violet's information, Lois had snuck into Ada's bedroom and stolen the wallet from the safe. Wade had gone to the door and let in the police reinforcements we had contacted in secret the night before – supervised by Sergeant Brady, whose direct line had been waiting in my wallet all along for me to come to this realization. And not just the Long Island police: a detective from the New York Police Department too, who had been searching for the fraudulent Officer Jones after a series of reports following the very public death of Chuck; and Robert Flatt, the journalist from *Disclosed* magazine, ready to collect the evidence of what he'd long suspected – that something very, very wrong had happened to those four soldiers who returned from England in November. The combination of the press and the police would surely be everything we needed to bring Imperium Mortis into the daylight, where they would no longer be able to thrive and grow.

But I still had one task left to perform to try and secure my freedom – I had to make sure the wallet was destroyed once and for all.

*

By the time we arrived at Pitch House, there was an hour left before midnight. The house was all locked up, and the windows were dark. Not even a candle was lit in the window that I knew belonged to Mother's room. My heart ached. I was almost home.

But it wasn't finished yet. I couldn't rest.

Lois reached for my hand to ground me, and I found her touch gave me the reassurance I needed. She handed me the wallet, and seeing it again snatched the breath right out of me. Father's old wallet, with the initials AA embossed in the leather. It was battered and worn, just as I remembered. It had been his most prized possession.

This wallet had begun it all. In the aftermath of an awful tragedy, it had been permeated with magic. Without it, my life could never have been so charmed or so cursed.

We placed the wallet at the foot of my brothers' memorial stones. It seemed as fitting a place as any. I doused it with the gas.

'Are you ready?' Lois asked, handing me the box of matches.

'As I'll ever be,' I said, taking a match out and striking it. The match lit with a hiss, and I tossed it on top of the wallet. It burst alight, and we watched the flames devour it, a hideous-smelling smoke rising up.

Nothing happened. It looked like any other wallet when it burned.

I expected to feel different somehow. I had at least expected to see something different – but what? A great howling of spirits? Some kind of dramatic burst of essence?

A sinister dread plucked at my insides. Was it over?

'Do you want to go in and wake them?' Lois asked, slipping her hand into mine.

'No,' I said.

If I was going to die, then it was imminent. I felt sure it would be a bad death, and I didn't want Mother and Nick to witness it. I remembered all of them – George's awful twitching on the spearheads; Father's brains exposed from the gunshot; the crack of Bradley's head on the stone step; Chuck's detached torso. I would rather my family were able to remember me the way I had been, not the way the darkness took me. *If* it took me.

'When midnight strikes, will you turn away? I don't want you to look at me. You have to promise me.'

'I promise,' Lois said, taking my face in her hands. 'But until then, I'm going to look at you for every second. Just in case.'

We walked hand in hand across the lawn, beneath the twinkling sky. I wished that we had more time. I wished that I'd been braver. Lois was worth being brave for.

I turned to kiss her, maybe for the last time ... and then there was the loud and thunderous noise of an explosion.

Lois screamed, and I turned to see the servants' quarters of Pitch House lit up in a glorious and terrifying eruption of flames. Another crashing boom followed, and there was a great shattering of glass – and flames began to lick at the wing holding the Collection. Then another explosion, then another, until each corner of the house was aflame.

Among the chaos, we saw a car speed out from behind the house, vanishing down the drive.

Lois's eyes were wide and terrified. 'Imperium Mortis. They followed us!'

I shook my head. 'Impossible. They must have had someone here all along.'

We began racing towards the house. Ada had obviously prepared for this scenario, equipped a recruit with what they needed to destroy me if I tried to make a run for it.

I had brought the wrath of Imperium Mortis down on my family while they were sleeping. For once, the panic flooding me had a very real and tangible cause. Mother and Nick were inside the house. If they had survived the blast, then they might be trapped by the flames. I couldn't bear it. The household staff had begun to stream out, but Mother and Nick were nowhere to be seen.

They're going to die, and it will be all my fault.

But once we reached the door, which was belching great plumes of black smoke, I found I was flailing, completely and utterly stuck in the paralysis of my own mind. Fear had me pinned to the spot.

'What do I do?' I turned to Lois desperately. 'Lois, what do I do?'

She looked desperate too. 'Even if someone did manage to call for firefighters, they won't get here in time.' She reached for my wrist, tapping my watch. 'It's almost midnight, Felix.'

I knew what she was saying. If we hadn't broken the curse, then this was almost certainly how I would have died. And even if we had, there was a good chance this would kill me anyway.

Then I thought of Mother trapped upstairs. Of Nick curled up in his bed.

They needed me.

The decorative glass panel of the door was shattered. I carefully reached inside and turned the key to unlock it. And then I entered my home and ran towards the flames.

The house was full of roaring thunder. I immediately felt the sensation of heat on my skin, the temperature rising by the second. I raced up the great central staircase, though I had to pause to hack out great lungfuls of smoke. Fire crackled down the corridor to my left, and somewhere somebody was screaming. I hoped it was just my imagination – that all our staff had got out okay.

I raced towards Nick's room, and the heat rose with me as I took the next flight of stairs on to the familiar landing.

'Nick!' I called. 'Mother!'

The only response was the crackling of the fire, and around the edges of the door frame the flickering of an orange glow. I reached for the doorknob and immediately let out an awful yelp from the burn of it. It was brass – it held the heat.

I ripped off the arm of my shirt and wrapped it around my fist. Using the fabric as a protective layer, I gritted my teeth and turned the handle. Just as I began to feel it burn through, the door shifted open, and the blaze of heat from inside hit my face in a wave.

Thick, choking smoke poured into my lungs, and I flung myself to the ground to avoid its rising plumes. I could barely see; the stinging of the hot air was making my eyes stream, and I tried to keep myself low to the ground to stop myself from inhaling too much smoke, but the floor felt like hot coals.

I could make out the shape of my mother on Nick's bed, but Nick was nowhere to be seen.

'Mother!' I tried to call, but it came out in a spluttering cough.

She didn't move. Flames were licking away at the side of the bed; the nightstand had gone up in a blaze, but thankfully the bed hadn't caught fire ... yet. The edge of the silken sheet hanging over the side started to flicker with sparks. It wouldn't be long before the whole thing went up.

I staggered to the bed and tried to rouse my mother, screaming right into her ear, and when she didn't wake I shook her, urgently trying to get a response. Placing my hand near her nose, I realized I couldn't feel her breathing.

I pulled the blankets away from her and wedged my hands beneath her armpits so I could hoist her up into a sitting position. Her head lolled, and I felt a tidal wave of vomit rising in the back of my scorched throat, but I had to swallow it back down and focus on the task at hand. I had to get her out. Thankfully, there was barely anything to the weight of her, and, by kneeling in front of her, I was able to fling her arms around my shoulders even though I was starting to feel dizzy from the lack of air. That's when I spotted that the arm that was stretched out was blistered and raw.

Gripping so tight to her arms that I was sure I would leave marks in the puckering skin, I heaved her on to my back and staggered out of the bedroom and down the corridor, leaving the crackling flames behind me.

Awkwardly shuffling with all the speed I could manage, I got her down the stairs. Lois was on the telephone. 'Hurry!' she was saying. 'As quick as you can!'

Lois helped me get Mother out the front door and down the steps. We laid her on the ground, moving the hair from her face, fearing the worst.

My mother. Images of her flashed through my mind – storybooks and songs before falling asleep at night, when she was able to look after me and soothe me before it turned the other way round for a time; her arms wrapped around me with her big moon belly that held Nick inside; the way she drank two bottles of red wine the night that

Father left, and I had to hold her hair when she vomited it all back up again.

I needed her to be all right.

There was a slight rise and fall in Mother's chest then – barely perceptible, but there nonetheless. She was alive, for the moment at least.

'She's breathing!' I found myself saying out loud, turning to Lois and seeing her eyes were shining. I could have cried then as she helped me to stand, and I weakly wrapped my arms around her. She held me tightly, and over her shoulder I watched the crackling flames.

The whole building was ablaze. It would be a miracle if everyone had made it out alive.

I looked around at the faces of the household staff, desperately trying to spot Nick among the crowd. Perhaps he'd got out before I reached his room? But I knew, deep down, that he wouldn't have left Mother alone ... No, when the fire started, he must have been somewhere else, and was still there, trapped by the flames.

Then I heard it, the sound of pounding at the window of the reading room. I could see the fire flickering, the smoke billowing, and the tiny fists balled up against the glass.

Nick.

I didn't give it a moment's thought; there wasn't a moment's hesitation. My brother needed me.

I heard a clock somewhere strike midnight.

I went into the flames again.

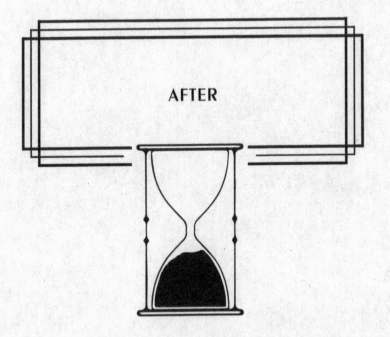

AFTER

48

We underestimate our ability to cope if the terrible something does come to pass.

The doctors said that if I hadn't gone in, Mother and Nick would both have died – Mother from her burns and Nick from smoke inhalation. The doctors said I saved their lives. They didn't know that I'd managed to save my own too. I wept because we all survived, and because I knew that I was changed irrevocably.

The day that Mother was released from the hospital, she had a simple ring on her finger – Geoffrey Garton had asked her to marry him, and we were to move into the family home he kept in the Hamptons, where he promised to keep Mother in the lifestyle she'd become accustomed to.

I started to see Dr Albass once a week. The unhealthy thoughts still lapped at my ankles, even though I was more able to ride the wave of panic when it threatened to envelop me. Seeing Dr Albass gave me the chance to start viewing the thoughts as something separate from me, something that I could cope with, unpleasant as they might be. Having the space to give them air left me feeling more able to manage their ebb and flow.

Wade was proving difficult to trace – he'd also managed to evade arrest – but I had no idea where he might have ended up, seeking sanctuary.

Although some of the initiates had escaped, the police had arrested forty individuals at the Georgian mansion that night. They'd managed to connect Imperium Mortis to five unsolved murders in New York over the last two months, and I had no doubt that many more would come to light. But who had been captured? And who had escaped?

*

A few weeks after the fire, I decided to go say farewell to Pitch House. Geoffrey let me take his car, and as I drove over the hill, where my home should have been rising proud, the building appeared instead as a blackened smudge, a blot on the landscape. My home had been transformed into a smoking ghoul, a shadow of what it used to be. It was burned in its entirety, no wing spared. The windows gaped like toothless mouths, their glass shattered by the heat. The whole east wing had collapsed in on itself. Above it all, the sun shone beatifically.

I brought the car to a halt and stepped outside, instantly overwhelmed by the stench in the air. How could it still singe my nostrils weeks later? The air felt as if it were full of sparks. Our family home, conceived in the mind of my father and made real through the potent combination of his graft, his desire, his ability to imagine ... and all of it brought to ruin through the darkest whims of Death Magic.

All that family history. Gone up in smoke.

I walked a lap around the house. The stables had also been destroyed. The servants' quarters had collapsed. I passed by the wing that used to hold the long gallery and the Collection. The damage was breathtaking. My Collection – every tiny shred of proof of my existence on earth – gone. A strange, bitter laugh bubbled up and out of me.

It was all gone.

The hours of labour on the house itself, the design and imagination that had gone into every single wall and floor, the bed where I slept, the luxurious silken sheets, the grandfather clock with a secret panel inside, the one photograph I had of Lois, my mother's jewellery, the vanity where she did her make-up every morning, dress after dress after dress for every social occasion, my own clothes, the sage-coloured sweater that Lois had liked me in best, my father's books, the shelves that held them, the desk where he wrote, the mounted shotgun, Nick's books on botany, his teddy bears, the things I obsessively collected, the taxidermy rabbit with two heads, the mermaid, the vases from Ancient Greece, the pinned butterflies and everything that had belonged to my older brothers, the items I always thought might eventually become less painful to sort through ...

All of it. All of it was gone.

I owed no debt to Death Magic and swore to myself that I never would again.

MARCH 1921

49

It was a new season after the house had been destroyed, and we had settled into an unfamiliar sort of safety. As spring began to lighten the evenings once again, life seemed brighter too. Still, though, I often thought of Wade, and wondered where in the world he had vanished to, with the extraordinary funds that had once been my inheritance. I would find myself thinking of Violet, of Hugo Leery, of Joy, of Ada, and wondering what their future held, what fate the law would impose upon them.

But my life continued. It had to. And I was so, so thankful for that.

*

I was standing in front of a university admissions panel, awaiting their final question.

'Why law?' the college professor asked.

He had an encouraging smile, which was more than I could say for the two other professors sitting in front of me. To his right was a straight-laced and severe-looking man who had begun taking notes from the moment I walked in the room, and to his left was a mousy little fellow with a tiny moustache that looked like it had been attached with glue; he hadn't asked a single question.

I took a deep breath to steady myself. My palms were sweating, but I knew that I could handle this. I had practised, and I knew what I wanted to say. Geoffrey's words of encouragement echoed in my ears – *Let them know what it is about you, as an individual, that makes you care.*

'First and foremost, the intellectual challenge and problem-solving nature of law is something that I have always had an interest in from a young age. My father strengthened my mind by teaching me the principles of cryptology. The moment of decrypting a particularly fiendish code is one of great satisfaction, and this is what I imagine it must feel like to win a case. Likewise, I believe the skills he taught me prepared me to look at challenges from an interesting angle and be willing to work at them until answers emerge.'

The professor in the middle was nodding his head. It was a straightforward way to begin. They couldn't disagree with the notion that law required me to be a good problem-solver. I cleared my throat. Here was the moment where it could go very well for me or very wrong. It all depended on whether they were willing to consider my arguments.

'Human beings are driven by emotion,' I said. 'I have an interest in the new science of psychology and the way that the human mind functions. There are some schools of thought that suggest there is nothing we do or say that isn't prompted or triggered by an emotion beneath the surface. Crime is one such expression of emotion, and I believe a lawyer's job is to uncover the emotional motivation beneath the layers of behaviour – like pulling back the sheets from a bed in the morning.

'Aristotle said "The law is reason, free from passion", but I disagree. I believe that the fundamental principles of law are based on passion, on the degree to which we can understand that human beings make their choices according to the things that affect them. The role of the lawyer is to uphold the things that we, as a society, have chosen to value, and if we can empathize and listen we are more in a position to support lasting change in people's lives through the application of fairness and justice.'

The professor who had been writing had stopped. His pen was hovering above the page, and he was looking at me with a slight frown. 'An interesting argument,' he said. 'Do you mean to say that people are devoid of responsibility in the face of their emotions?'

My throat went dry. I felt as if he were wilfully misunderstanding me, trying to trip me up. *That's his job*, I remembered. *Just keep calm. Breathe.*

'Absolutely not,' I said. My fingers tingled by my sides, and I fiddled a little with the hem of my jacket. 'All action is a choice, but I believe that the more we can grow to understand an individual, a client in this case, whether that be the defendant or the prosecutor, the closer we can get to the truth at the heart of the issue – motive.'

383

He was scribbling away again, and it seemed that his pen was moving faster than my brain. The professor in the middle was smiling at me still and bobbing his head up and down. Had I managed to make my point succinctly enough? Had I managed to communicate what was in my heart?

When the interview was finished, I shook hands with each of them, and as I was leaving I overheard them muttering about me.

'Well, that was a nuanced perspective.'

'Very mature for his age.'

Yes, I felt as if I had aged a hundred years. That was the impact of facing down death – and a secret society that held it in the highest esteem.

I headed back to the college campus, feeling light. Spring blossoms were decorating the trees, and flowers were emerging from the ground. I walked past a group of students sitting on the grass, uproariously debating the content of the seminar they had just attended, which seemed to be on the subject of mythology. There was a lightness to everything as I moved through the campus, and for the first time I found I could really imagine myself studying, making new friends, crafting a life for myself here.

Lois was waiting for me by the clock in the centre of the quad and rushed up to wrap her arms around me.

'How did it go?' she asked, a little breathless. She had, of course, already had a secure offer to begin studying in the fall.

'As well as I could have hoped,' I said. 'It's hard to tell. I used the psychology argument, like we practised.'

'Yes!' she said, clapping her hands together. 'I'm so glad that you didn't lose your nerve! Honestly, I think it will set you apart from the other candidates.'

'At least I'll always be able to say that I did my best,' I said, placing a kiss on her temple.

I hadn't let fear stop me from attempting the interview, and that felt like an achievement in itself, whether or not they granted me a place on the course.

*

I returned home that day, and Nick greeted me with a smile. 'You have a letter,' he said.

Who would be writing to me? A little shiver ran its way down my spine as Nick rushed off to fetch the letter. It was a small, unassuming white envelope. I opened it up and slipped out a piece of paper and a photograph of a wooded area, painted symbols on the trees.

The Ignis Society has unfinished business. Are you in?

There was only one person who would send a letter like that. Wade. I felt certain that if I were to crack the message he'd left on the trees, I'd find him. And a future where we could finish what we started, eliminating Death Magic once and for all.

While I still lived alongside fear – both the rational and the irrational – I knew that there was nothing that I couldn't handle. I had faced the worst, and I had emerged on the other side, stronger and more resilient. My heart might race, and my muscles might tense, but I always had my breath to still the turbulent waters of my mind.

Whatever happened in the future, I would be able to face it. There was no need to make the decision immediately.

I had plenty of time.

THE END

Acknowledgements

A Dark Inheritance is, as the title would suggest, a very dark story. It's about grief and fear and suffering in many forms … But overwhelmingly, deliberately, the overall message is one of hope. This is a book where the protagonist struggles with anxiety, but the word *hope* appears more times than the word *fear*. My thanks go to the following people, each of whom helped me to hope that this dream of mine, to write and see my words in print, could become a reality …

To my agent, James Wills, for seeing potential in the very early manuscript that would change many, many times before becoming this book. Thank you for your patience, your mentoring, your commitment to this story and for championing me every step of the way.

To my editor Naomi Colthurst, for your boundless enthusiasm and incredible gift for storytelling and problem-solving, and for being able to see the story I was trying to tell and helping me to excavate it. Working with you has taught me so much about writing and I'm so excited for what is coming next!

To the Penguin team, who have put so much care and attention into this book. To Millie, for your creativity and encouragement, which saw me through a particularly tricky stage rewriting this book during lockdown. To Shreeta, for making copy-editing such a smooth process. To Jane, for having such a keen eye for the details. To Sam, for reading with an eye for the authenticity of the American voice of Felix. To Andrea, for designing the cover of my dreams. To everyone involved in the unfolding journey of rights, publicity, marketing and sales – thank you for getting behind *A Dark Inheritance* and getting it in the hands of readers.

To New Writing North, your crucial support via the Northern Writers' Awards at a very early stage in my career made all the difference in this book becoming a reality.

To Lorna Evans, for your generosity with your expertise in psychotherapy in guiding my efforts to present this topic responsibly and with respect, and for teaching me so much about the mind-body connection.

To my colleagues at Waterstones, for all your excitement about this book – thank you for welcoming me to our shop and for teaching me so much.

To Miss Collins, for your words of encouragement when I was ten years old – your belief I could do this one day stayed with me.

To the friends I know I can always count on, thank you for listening to me talk about my writing for years, and for your belief in me when it was needed most – to Amy (why not us?) and Thea, to Rach, to Lindsay. To Danny, for the long, winding conversations about plot and story, and for sticking with me all these years. To Laura, for your friendship and support – you've seen it all on this journey, the highs and the lows. Thank you for walking with me. To Sarah and Curtis for your incredible hospitality, enthusiasm and prayers, and to all of Book Club – Nina, Lucy, Jen and Emily – for all the prayers and encouragement.

To my family – I am fortunate to be part of such a large and amazing family and so grateful to know that there are so many people who are cheering me on in my writing career. I can't wait to finally share this book with you.

To Granny, for being my very first reader every time, for always believing in me, even when I don't believe in myself, and for being there to talk with me every single day. Thank you for supporting me so unconditionally. I'm in awe of the bravery you've shown this year.

To Grandad, for every happy memory we shared in the sunshine, and for being the person we could all depend upon. This book is dedicated to you. I wish I could have put it in your hands.

To Eliza and Stella, for being the best sisters I could have ever wished for. You make my world brighter just by being in it.

To my parents, for raising me in a house full to bursting with books, and for all the ways, big and small, that you've supported me. I am so grateful for your love and understanding. R, thank you for your patience and calm presence, and for writing a story that had my name in it when I was little. Mum, thank you for teaching me to read, for inspiring me with your hard work and incredible resilience, and for sharing a love of stories to last a lifetime with me – it all began with you.

To my husband, Jake. I couldn't have done this without you. Thank you for building this life with me. There's nobody else I'd rather be on this adventure with.

To my daughter, Imogen. When I started writing this book, I couldn't even have imagined you, and now you have changed my world forever and filled it with so much joy.

To God, whose timing has never let me down.